JORDAN'S JOURNEY

WAGNER BRIGADE

BOOK THREE

ASHLEY A QUINN

TCA PUBLISHING LLC

ISBN is 978-1-959943-27-3

One

A bitter wind ripped inside the store as the doors slid open, blasting Jordan MacDowell in the face as he exited. He tucked his chin, trying to edge his ears below the collar of his coat, and hurried across the parking lot to his restored Bronco. It was cold enough to snow, but it wouldn't. Not down here. At his house up the mountain, though? The flurries were already flying when he left to get dinner and groceries.

Reaching his car, he lifted his head as he took his keys from his pocket to unlock the door. Paper flapping in the wind under his windshield wiper caught his attention. He groaned. Not again.

Jordan shoved the key in the lock and twisted it, then opened the door, tossing the grocery bags over the console and onto the passenger seat. He leaned around the door and snatched the note, then climbed into the car. Once he had the engine running and the heater blasting, he unfolded the paper, already knowing it would say something similar to all the others. A line of romantic poetry scrawled in flowing feminine handwriting covered the bottom half of the page. He crumpled the paper in his fist and tossed it onto the passenger floorboard. Just once, he wished he could catch her in the act of leaving one of her missives. If he could get her on video or take a picture, maybe he could get the cops to do something. But no one wanted to touch the daughter of the city council president without proof. It didn't matter that everyone knew she was cuckoo. Everyone was too afraid of her father.

Cursing, Jordan shook his head and put the car in gear. He'd been an idiot to go out with her in the first place. But he'd been thinking with the wrong head, blinded by perky boobs and a firm, round butt. Now he couldn't get rid of her.

Jordan glanced both ways, then turned out of the parking lot and headed for home. A mile from his house, his phone rang. He glanced at it and saw his friend Dean's name. Grimacing, he sped up a bit. He should have taken a different car, one that he could connect his phone to. But he liked the Bronco, and with the snow on the ground up in the hills, the four-wheel drive was nice. His pickup was a four-by-four, too, but it still didn't do great without some weight in the back. He hadn't gotten around to that, even though it was mid-January and he should have by now. At this point, he probably wouldn't bother. He'd been driving the Bronco most of the winter, anyway.

His mailbox came into view, and he swung into the driveway. Snow and gravel crunched under the Bronco's large tires as he drove toward the house. Pulling up under the carport by his back door, he shut the car off and got out. Once he was inside, he set his bags and the now crumpled note on the counter and called Dean back.

"Hey, man. Thanks for calling me back. I know it's getting late," Dean said when he answered.

"It's not that late." Jordan glanced at the clock, then

grimaced. It was a little later than he thought. He hadn't realized how long he'd worked on Mrs. Brown's car this evening. But he'd wanted to get it back to her in the morning. He knew she needed it to go visit her sister in Phoenix, who was in a nursing home there. "I went to town and was on my way back when you called. What's up?"

"Brooke wanted me to ask if you've considered her offer yet."

Jordan sighed and leaned back against the counter. "She sure is persistent." He pursed his lips and stared out the window at the gently falling snowflakes illuminated by the pole light in his yard. Brooke McGinty's offer to be chief mechanic at the new resort she planned to build in Costa Rica was a tempting offer, but he still wasn't sure if he wanted to uproot his life to take the job. "It's not like I don't have time to decide. They're still in the planning stages, right?"

"Yes, but if there's one thing I've learned about that woman in the last few months, it's that she likes to plan ahead. She's already wooed Ezra away from her father and convinced him and his wife that they need to come down and be part of the new resort. She mentioned something about a cultural center. I don't think Ezra stood a chance once his wife got wind of that idea. Apparently, she had a blast setting up the little museum at the Asheville resort and welcomes the chance to do it again. And Brooke heard about Annabeth and Margot's plans to open a clinic down here and wants to invest." Dean sighed. Jordan could envision him scrubbing his hands over his face in exasperation. "All I've heard about for weeks are the plans for the clinic and resort. You need to say yes and move down here so I have someone sane to talk to."

Jordan chuckled. "What about all your other buddies? Surely, they're not all that involved?"

"Ford is, of course. And Max has thrown himself into

helping with the plans. I think that has more to do with Margot and her girls than anything else."

Jordan would agree with that. He remembered how the man acted at Thanksgiving. Margot's twin toddlers adored him, and he'd done little to discourage that.

"Asher's not too bad about it," Dean continued. "And Sam rarely talks to begin with. Edie's just excited to have other women around. She might act tough, but there's a girlie side there she likes to let out from time to time."

An image of the sassy redhead popped into Jordan's brain. He'd like to see that girlie side too. She'd look incredible in a form-fitting dress and heels. Though he had no complaints about the shorts and tank tops she favored. They showed off her curves just fine.

He rolled his eyes. It was thoughts like those that got him into trouble. It was hard to turn them off, though. He loved women and their curves.

"Well, it sounds like she'll have ample opportunity to do that soon."

"Yeah." Dean blew out a breath. "So, what can I tell Brooke?"

"That I'm still thinking."

"I knew you were going to say that."

"Then you should have just told her that and saved yourself the phone call."

Dean chuckled. "But then I wouldn't get to tell you to stop being a dipshit and make up your mind."

It was Jordan's turn to huff a short laugh. "Why does she want me for the job, anyway? I'm sure there are other candidates more qualified."

"Maybe. But you know why, Jordie. If it weren't for the evidence you found—"

"Anyone with half a brain could have seen the cut brake

lines and found that blood," Jordan interrupted. "I didn't do anything special."

"To her, you did." Dean's voice grew quiet, but stayed firm. "To Annabeth too. And to me. You brought a lot of people closure. And you're part of the group now, whether you like it or not. She knows she can trust you."

"She doesn't know me."

"Doesn't matter. She trusts me and I trust you, so there you go. Just say yes and put us all out of our misery."

Jordan chuckled again. "I'll think about it."

Dean sighed. "Fine. So, how's life? You work on any cool cars lately?"

"Not really. My Porsche." He'd bought a Porsche 911 a few months ago. It was in rough shape and he'd been busy restoring it. "Most of the time, it's routine stuff. Oil changes, tires, alternators. Although, the rat's nest I took out of Jake Smith's air filter was interesting. It was full of grass and shredded Playboy magazines that came out of his garage."

"Old Mr. Smith keeps Playboys in his garage?"

"I guess so. Must like to look at them when he tinkers out there." The old man liked to build scale models. They were all over his house. He'd given one to Jordan a few years ago of a 1969 Ford Shelby GT Mustang. It sat on his checkout counter now.

"So, that's it, huh? No interesting letters?"

Jordan frowned, his mood souring. "That's why you really called. It wasn't to ask about Brooke's job offer. It was about my damn stalker."

Dean huffed. "Can you blame me? It's a little creepy that she's sending you love poems. Has she sent any more?"

For a moment, Jordan hesitated. He didn't want Dean to worry—because there really wasn't anything to worry about. But if he didn't tell him and he found out anyway, it would hurt his feelings. They didn't keep secrets.

Pressing his lips together and clenching his teeth, he glanced up. "Yeah. There was one on my car tonight when I left the grocery."

"How many does that make now?"

"Seven."

"Did you keep them like I told you to?"

"Yes, Dad." Jordan rolled his eyes.

"Don't get sassy. I'll fly up there just to beat your ass."

Jordan laughed. "You might be a SEAL, but I can still best you." He'd been studying martial arts since he was eight years old. Dean might be bigger and stronger now, but not that much, and Jordan was quicker.

"Hmm, maybe. But in all seriousness, you need to be careful. Mercy Dixon is a crazy bitch who has her daddy's money and influence at her disposal. She's not untouchable, but damn near it. I still can't believe you got involved with her. She was a nut in high school. What were you thinking?"

"I wasn't. Keeley's punch robbed me of my common sense."

Dean scoffed. "Don't blame her. You drank it, knowing how strong it was."

"In my defense, it's not normally quite that strong. Someone spiked it. But you're right. I have no one to blame but myself." He'd gone to his friends', Keeley and Logan's, party with the full intention of getting a little drunk. He'd had a long, busy, frustrating week and had wanted to blow off some steam. He'd done that. A little too well. When he woke up the next morning, Mercy Dixon had been naked in bed next to him. That was several months ago now, and even though he'd told her at the time it was a mistake and didn't bear repeating, she'd been chasing him ever since.

"You need a girlfriend. Maybe then she'd back off."

Jordan barked a short laugh. "I've tried that. Went out with a couple women. She's scared them both off. The first one told me she didn't want to get in the middle of my relationship with Mercy, and the second just refuses to return my calls."

"You just need to find someone who isn't afraid of her."

An image of Edie's scowling face popped into his head. Now there was a woman who wouldn't be intimidated. Too bad she was in Costa Rica. And that she hated his guts. He didn't quite understand why she did, though. He'd been nice to her—at first. He hadn't exactly been unkind since then. Just teasing. She rose to the occasion so well.

"Well, that's easier said than done. Especially around here."

Dean sighed. "I guess that's true. But hey—think of it this way—it's just more incentive for you to take Brooke's job offer and move down here."

"Her job offer, which doesn't even start for at least a year?"

"Oh, we'll find plenty to keep you occupied. Ford alone will keep you employed full time. He always needs a mechanic for his boats."

"I'm a car mechanic."

Dean scoffed again. "We both know if it has an engine, you can fix it."

Jordan grunted, not wanting to confirm or deny that. It was true, but he didn't want to encourage his friend to continue this line of conversation. He *was* considering Brooke's offer. But it was a lot to think about. A move like that wasn't one to undertake lightly.

"All right, fine. I get it. Shut up, Dean," Dean said. "Just watch your back, okay? She's not backing off, and things could turn violent if she starts to feel like she's losing you."

"I know, and I will. Eventually, she'll get tired of me not giving in or she'll set her sights on some other poor sap and will leave me alone." An idea hit him. "Hey, that's not a bad idea. Maybe I can find someone who doesn't mind her crazy and set them up."

Dean laughed. "You'd probably have an easier time finding that elusive woman who can stand up to her."

Again, Edie's face popped into Jordan's brain. "Yeah. I'll keep my eyes open for both."

Two

Edie Campbell glanced back, waiting on the wave to reach her where she sat on her gently rocking surfboard. As it approached, she laid flat and started paddling, building up speed. The wave reached her and she hopped to her feet, slicing through the water. Droplets sprayed her face as the tail of her braided red hair whipped around as she moved. Exhilaration brought a smile to her face. There wasn't much like surfing. It was as close as a person could get to walking on water.

A dolphin broke the surface in front of her. "Crap!" She turned her board sharply to the right, trying to avoid it. The move popped her into the wave, which pulled the board from under her. She crashed into the water. A searing pain tore through her hand as it made contact with her board. The fin had sliced the side of her palm. Battling through the churning water, she rose to the surface. A quick glance revealed no trace of the dolphin.

Shaking her head, she looked at her hand. Blood ran down her arm. The gash was deep. "Dammit." She needed to get to shore. Edie threw her uninjured arm over her board and kicked her feet, riding another wave to the beach. When she could touch, she walked out.

"You all right?"

Edie looked up at the deep voice and saw her friend Dean Adler standing on the beach in a black wetsuit, a surfboard tucked under his arm. "Yeah," she said. "Nothing a few stitches won't fix. The fin sliced me."

He planted his board in the sand and met her as she came out of the water. "Let me see."

She held up her hand.

"Ouch. You're right. That needs stitches."

Edie grimaced. "Great way to start the weekend, right?"

"Come on. I have a towel in my car we can wrap around that until we can get it sewed up. You're lucky Annabeth's here." He picked up his board and tipped his head toward the parking lot, then set off.

"Why aren't you with her?" His girlfriend, Annabeth Swenson, was a doctor. She'd come down for a short visit since it was a long weekend in the U.S.

"An early morning surf sounded nice. And I need to talk to you."

Edie blinked up at him in surprise. "Oh? About what?"

"Jordan."

Her mood soured even more. Jordan MacDowell rubbed her the wrong way. It was his smile. It was too sexy. Too confident. He knew he was handsome and thought it could get him anything. "What about him?"

"He's having some issues back home. I wondered if you could help." They reached his car, and Dean pulled open the rear passenger door and leaned inside, emerging with a beach towel. "Here. Wrap that around your hand. It's clean. Mostly."

She took the towel and wrapped it around her bleeding

hand as best she could, then held pressure on it. "How can I help your friend back in the States? I'm not Asher. I can't get on the computer and go bing, bang, boop and make things happen."

Dean propped his hands on his hips and stared at her, chewing on the corner of his mouth. Edie got a sinking feeling in her gut.

"What? Why are you looking at me like that?" she asked, scowling. Whatever he had to say, she wasn't going to like.

"He's having issues with a woman."

Edie snorted. "That's a shocker." In the few days Jordan had been in Costa Rica, she'd seen him sidle up to more than one woman at Sam's bar. He'd even disappeared with one for a while. It didn't surprise her that his womanizing ways had finally caught up to him.

"It's not like that. This girl—" He broke off and glanced away. "She's different."

The concern in Dean's voice dispelled some of her amusement at Jordan's predicament. "Different how?"

"Crazy."

"Crazy cuckoo, or crazy dangerous?"

"Are they really that different?"

She tipped her head. "True."

"She's a local woman whose family—her dad, especially—has a lot of money and influence. They only dated a short time before he broke it off, but she won't take the hint that he's not interested anymore."

"What's she doing?"

"Leaving him love letters and scaring off his dates."

Edie scoffed. "That's it?"

Dean rolled his lips in, glancing at the ocean again before settling his jade eyes on her. "I know it doesn't sound like much, but I've just got this feeling." He shook his head. "It's not going to end well. Not if we don't do something."

"We? Again, I'm not Asher, Dean. I don't know what I can do."

He tipped his head toward the truck. "Get in. I'll explain while I drive you to my house."

Edie clenched her teeth. She wanted an answer now, but she knew she needed stitches more. After stowing their boards in the back, she climbed into the passenger seat, buckling up while Dean got in and started the car. He turned around, and they left the parking lot.

She turned in her seat, keeping her hand raised and pressure on the wound. "What is it you think I can do to help your friend?"

Dean pursed his lips and sent her a quick glance. "Don't get mad, okay?"

Her eyebrows drew together. "Just spit it out."

"I want you to go there and pretend to be his girlfriend."

Shock made her eyebrows go the other direction. "You want me to what?"

"Be his girlfriend. He needs someone who won't be intimidated by this woman. Maybe even someone who will warn her to back off."

"So tell him to find someone like that."

"I did. But that could take a while. In the meantime, there's no telling what she could do."

It was on the tip of Edie's tongue to give a hearty, "Hell, no," but something in his tone stopped her. "You're really worried about him, aren't you?"

Dean blew out a breath and ran a quick hand through his hair. "Yeah. I just—I don't know. It's just a feeling."

Edie looked out the window, chewing on one corner of her mouth. She really had no desire to be anything to Jordan MacDowell, but Dean was her friend. And if she was the one who needed help for a friend, he'd say yes in a heartbeat. She turned to him. "If I go, is he going to welcome the help?"

"Probably not at first, but you're persistent. Persuade him." He sent her a wry smile.

Edie rolled her eyes. "Is that a nice way of saying I'm bossy and overbearing?"

Dean chuckled. "No. Well, not entirely. You are bossy. But you're also usually right about things. So, will you do it?"

She sighed. "I guess. But I swear, if he tries to convince me we need to practice certain parts of being a couple, I will castrate him and feed his balls to a rattlesnake."

"Ow." Dean shifted in his seat. "Be sure to tell him that up front."

"Don't worry, I will." She'd make it abundantly clear she was only there to run off his lady friend. Nothing more. She wasn't interested in becoming his next conquest. Even if he was exceedingly pretty to look at.

THREE

A buzz vibrated Jordan's leg for the third time in fifteen minutes. He ignored it, like he had the previous two times. It was his personal cell. Whoever it was could wait until he wasn't covered up to his elbows in grease. Mr. Bainbridge's ancient Buick had rebelled during its tune-up, blowing a seal. It wasn't a difficult fix; just a messy one.

The bell on his front door chimed, signaling someone had entered. He didn't look up. "I'll be with you in a moment," he yelled through the open doorway.

"Don't stop on my account."

Jordan froze at the husky female voice. A delicious shiver went through him. That sounded like Edie. She had one of those sultry voices that would be right at home singing some bluesy love song in a swanky nightclub that catered to the rich. He frowned and forced his mind to shove thoughts of her away. It couldn't be her. "Sorry," he said, tightening the nut that held the engine housing in place. "There. Done." He straightened and turned, freezing again. His eyes went wide. It *was* her. "Edie?"

She grinned and waggled her fingers at him. "Hi." Her blue eyes flashed with amusement.

Jordan made his muscles move and picked up a rag, wiping his hands. "What are you doing here?" His gaze caught on the white bandage on her hand, and a quick, painful thought hit him, stealing his breath. "Dean—is he—?"

She waved her hands. "He's fine. But he is why I'm here." Some of the levity left her face.

"What? I don't understand."

Her mouth flattened. "I heard about your woman problem. I'm here to help."

His—oh, God. He scowled and tossed the rag onto the open tray of his toolbox. "Dean's got a big mouth."

"No. He cares."

"Regardless, I don't need the help. She's sending notes. Accidentally running into me when I go places."

"Scaring off your dates?"

"It's all temporary. Eventually, she'll meet someone else and ruin his life instead of mine. I'm glad Dean cares, but you really didn't need to come all this way. And seriously, what are you going to do, anyway? Beat her up?"

Her lips twitched. "That might be fun, actually. But no." She sucked in a breath, squaring her shoulders. "I'm your new girlfriend."

He knew he looked like a deer caught in someone's headlights, but he couldn't help it. Those were the last words he expected to come out of her mouth. Then his male brain kicked in. His surprised expression morphed into something more calculating, and he sauntered closer.

Edie's eyes narrowed, and she shook a finger at him. "No. I can see what you're thinking. This does not come with any benefits. I am here to get this woman to leave you alone and make sure no one gets hurt. You can keep your hands to yourself."

Jordan pouted, still walking toward her. He stopped closer than what was probably appropriate. She didn't back away, though. He hadn't expected her to. "How am I supposed to convince Mercy you're my girlfriend if I can't touch you?"

"Use your words, Jordie. Make that silver tongue of yours useful."

An immediate smile lifted one side of his mouth. "I can think of several ways I could use it."

Her cheeks colored, matching her flaming hair. She crossed her arms and glared at him, blue eyes flashing.

Jordan chuckled. "No dice? Damn. I think I'd like to get a taste of you."

She rolled her eyes, then dropped her arms and spun away. "I knew this wasn't going to work. I told Dean it was a ridiculous idea. I mean, you're an adult and can take care—"

He grabbed her non-bandaged hand and spun her around, stopping the flow of words. She let out a startled gasp as he pulled her into his chest. Those azure eyes flashed with fire again, and her surprised expression quickly morphed into a glare.

"What are you doing?"

"Proving I can behave." He held her gaze.

She swallowed hard. "You call this behaving?"

"Am I kissing you?" His gaze dropped to her lips. They were pink and plump and full.

"No."

"Touching somewhere inappropriate?" His fingers twitched as he said the words, but he kept his hands firmly where they were on her back.

Her glared turned into a thoughtful frown. "No."

"See? Behaving."

Again, she rolled her eyes, then pushed out of his embrace. Jordan let her go, needing the space himself. Edie did things to him just by being in the same room. Touching her was a bad idea. Yet he wanted to do it again.

"That was hardly behaving."

"It was a demonstration," Jordan countered. "If you're going to play the part of my girlfriend, you need to be comfortable with me touching you, even innocently. No one will ever believe we're involved otherwise." As crazy of an idea as it was for her to play the role of his girlfriend, he had to admit, it was a good one. She was perfect for the job. Gorgeous and smart, she was precisely his type. That she was also fierce, bold, and basically fearless meant she could take on Mercy with ease.

Edie propped her hands on her hips and studied him. "So, are you agreeing to the plan? If so, you're jumping on the bandwagon pretty quickly. Why aren't you trying to convince me to go home?"

Jordan shrugged, mulling over his reasons. Even with all of her qualifications, only one really stuck out. "Dean asked you to help."

"And you just do whatever Dean wants?"

"No. But I trust his judgement on things like this. His idea for me to find a girlfriend with a backbone is a good one. I've been thinking about who might fit that bill locally, but having you here saves me the trouble." Everyone else he had in mind was either taken or would want more out of the deal than what he wanted to offer a pretend girlfriend.

"God forbid you have to use your actual brain and not the one down there." She nodded toward his crotch.

"Ouch." He laid a hand over his heart. "You wound me."

She gave him a mirthless smile. "Hardly. Your ego can take it."

He chuckled again. Of that, he had no doubt. Having her around would be a challenge he readily accepted. She stirred his blood, but she also stirred his mind. "So, how long are you staying?"

She lifted a shoulder, but before she could reply, movement outside caught Jordan's attention. He muttered a curse and stalked toward Edie again.

Four

Edie felt her eyes grow round as she caught sight of the fierce expression on his face. Flutters started in her belly as he closed the distance between them. "Jordan, what are you—"

He grabbed a fistful of her dark coat and pulled, hauling her into his bigger frame. Her breath froze in her lungs as the flutters erupted into flames. She'd always thought the depictions in books of women turning to boneless mush when a guy manhandled them were silly. Not anymore. It was hot.

"Don't push away," he whispered as he tucked his face in the crook of her neck.

She couldn't if she tried.

The bell on the door chimed, and a cold blast of air ghosted over her. Enough of her senses returned for her to notice that while he was acting like a man who wanted to devour her, his rigid posture told a different story. A moment later, she understood why.

"Hello, Mercy." He raised his face from her neck, but didn't back away.

The name registered. This was the woman harassing him. She raised her hands and clutched Jordan's work shirt. Time to remember why she was here. She glanced over her shoulder and smiled at a blonde woman in a white parka and gray leggings. "Hi. Sorry about the show. I've been out of town and couldn't wait until tonight to see him." Edie turned back to Jordan and pecked a kiss on his nose. "I should go and let you get back to work. We're still on for dinner, right?"

He didn't miss a beat. "Yep. Do you want me to cook? I know you've had a long day already."

"Wait." Mercy interrupted them. "Who are you?"

"This is my girlfriend, Edie Campbell." Jordan smiled at Edie. "Honey, this is Mercy Dixon. She's—an old friend."

"Oh, hello." Edie extended a hand to Mercy. "It's nice to meet you."

Mercy stared at her hand with something akin to disgust. Expression flat, she took it, then stuffed her hands into her parka pockets.

"Are you from around here? I don't recognize you, and I know most everyone," Mercy said.

"No. I actually live in Costa Rica. Jordan and I met a few months ago when he came down to visit a friend of his."

"Oh." Her expression brightened.

Edie realized she might have made a mistake. Now Mercy thought she'd be leaving, which would open the door for her again. She hadn't wanted to lie and then later get tripped up.

"Edie's thinking about moving here, though. Aren't you, babe?" He draped an arm around her shoulders.

"Yep." She went with his prompt, knowing she needed to do some damage control. "That's what my visit now is all about. We're trialing the whole living together thing." She gave him a sweet smile, hoping she wasn't laying it on too thick. They wanted to look believable. Not sappy.

"I didn't think you were seeing anyone. You went out with that one woman—Justine, was it? And there was a Nicole, too, right? But that was months ago, wasn't it?"

Jordan waved a hand. "Those were just drinks between friends."

Mercy raised an eyebrow, looking skeptical. "Really? I didn't know you knew either of them. From before, I mean."

"Oh, yeah. We met through some mutual friends years ago. Nicole and I just caught up, but Justine was feeling a little down, so I took her out to cheer her up."

Edie gave him a subtle pinch on the side. She could tell he was making things up on the fly. Mercy didn't need too many details. It would be harder to keep their lies straight. Plus, she could go verify some of this with those women.

He squeezed her shoulders ever so slightly. "In any case, Edie's the only woman for me. So, what brings you in? Is it time for an oil change in your BMW?" he asked.

"My Lexus. I don't drive the BMW in the winter very much, you know that."

"Oh? I haven't paid that much attention."

Edie resisted the urge to roll her eyes and call him a liar. She would bet her surfboard he knew every car every person in this town drove and how much they drove it.

Mercy bristled. "Well, anyway, it's time for the Lexus to be serviced."

"Okay." Jordan stepped away from Edie to go behind the counter.

A bereft feeling settled over Edie's shoulders, replacing his arm. She frowned slightly. What was that about?

"Let's see." He woke up the computer and clicked on the screen. "I can do a week from Thursday at eleven."

"You don't have anything sooner?" Mercy sidled up to the counter and leaned on it.

Edie's mouth dropped open as she watched the woman tug down the zipper on her jacket and press her chest against the counter's edge, making her boobs pour over the top of her low-cut lavender top. Some women had a lot of nerve.

To his credit, Jordan didn't spare her cleavage a glance.

"Sorry. Thursday is the earliest. This cold snap we've had hasn't been kind to people's cars."

Mercy's mouth pulled down. "Fine. I'll take it."

His head bobbed once, and he typed her name into the computer. "Do you want a reminder card?"

"No. I'll put it on my calendar." She already had her phone out and was entering the information.

"Okay. I'll see you next Thursday, then."

Finished adding it to her calendar, Mercy slipped the phone back into her large black purse. She tossed him a seductive smile with her pouty red lips. "I can't wait."

Yuck. Edie's expression stayed clear, even as she mentally grimaced in disgust. The woman was trying too hard.

With a quick wave of her fingers, Mercy turned. She paused long enough to glare at Edie, then flounced out the door. When the chime died, Edie looked at Jordan. "She's a real piece of work."

He snorted. "Yep."

"Why on earth did you encourage her?"

"Because I'm a man, and she's not exactly ugly."

Edie's brows rose at his admission. "Not physically. But personality-wise?"

He nodded. "I get that. Now. And I'm paying for it." He came around the counter to stand in front of her. "Thank you for playing along."

"That's why I'm here." She stepped around him. "I'll let you get back to work. We can talk more about this plan at dinner tonight." She headed for the door, ready to get away from greasy, grimy, sexy Jordan.

"Wait."

So close. She glanced back.

"Where are you staying?"

Her saccharine smile returned. "I already told you. Congratulations. You now have a live-in girlfriend."

FIVE

J ordan eyed his house with trepidation as he drove up the driveway. He wasn't sure what to expect when he went inside. And Edie would be inside; he was sure of that. He hadn't given her a key, but she would find a way in. Would he face an amicable Edie, and they'd have a good discussion on their plan and how they would execute it? Or would she be surly and defensive, demanding he follow along like a whipped mule? He hoped the former, but probably a blend of the two was the best he would get.

Deciding to park inside tonight, the garage door rolled up as he pressed the button. He drove in, past Edie's rented red SUV sitting in the driveway, and shut off his car. Getting out, he went in the house. A delicious aroma assaulted him the moment he stepped through the doorway. Edie stood in the kitchen at the stove. She glanced over her shoulder at him.

"Hi." She offered him a quick smile.

"Hey. That smells delicious. What is it?" He shed his coat and hung it up, then walked toward her, stopping on the far side of the long island that separated the kitchen from the living room.

"Just a quick stir fry. Do you want to shower before we eat? You have a few minutes, if so."

Surprised at how congenial she was being, it took him a moment to process her words. "Um, yeah. Thanks."

She sent him another quick smile.

Jordan walked through the living room and up the metal staircase. He cast a glance at her over the balcony railing as he headed for his bedroom. A frown marred his face. What was she up to? Why was she being so nice?

Hurrying through his shower, he donned a pair of black athletic pants and a dark green t-shirt with his garage's logo on it, then went downstairs. Edie had two plates on the counter and was heaping vegetables and chicken on top of rice. Jordan walked to the silverware drawer and grabbed two forks.

"Do you want something to drink with your food?" he asked.

"Water's fine."

He filled two glasses from the dispenser in the fridge and carried them to the island. She set the plates next to them, and they sat down.

"This looks good. Thank you."

Edie picked up her fork and speared a piece of chicken and a bell pepper. "You're welcome. You need more rice, by the way. I used the last of it."

"I'll add it to the list. For future reference, there's a tablet in the drawer next to the fridge where I keep a running grocery list. Put whatever you want on it."

She nodded, scooping up another bite of food.

"So, how did you get in? I'm not surprised or upset. Just curious."

She grinned. "For a man with some fancy toys, the lock on the back door of your garage is pathetic."

Jordan scrunched his nose. "That bad, huh?"

"Ten seconds. I picked the lock in ten seconds. You don't even have an alarm system. What the hell?"

He shrugged. "I live in the mountains, away from most of the riffraff in town. I never felt the need."

"I have an alarm, and I live even further off the beaten track than you."

"You're a woman, and you live alone. It's smart."

She let out a snort. "Why do men assume I need special protection just because I have boobs and a hoohah?"

Jordan choked on the piece of chicken in his mouth. He coughed and reached for his water while she kept talking, ignoring his plight.

"I have the alarm because it's prudent. It gives me—or anyone with one—a few extra moments to prepare. Or it scares off whoever broke in. Just because I can defend myself doesn't mean I want to." She shook her head and stabbed a chunk of carrot. "I don't know why guys think they have to be all macho and prove they can fight. Just put in an alarm. It's safer." She frowned at him. "Are you all right?"

He cleared his throat again and wiped at the tears on his cheeks from his coughing fit. He was sure his face was red. "Fine. Chicken went down wrong. You, um, make a good point."

"Of course I do. I'll research alarm companies tomorrow. We'll find a good one that won't bankrupt you."

"Sounds good." Even if he wanted to argue with her and tell her he didn't want one, he wouldn't. She did make a valid point. And with what was happening with Mercy, it was probably a good idea. The last thing he needed was her sneaking in while he wasn't home. "So, about this dating plan..."

"You're wondering what it's going to look like?"

He nodded.

"We don't want to make a big deal out of it. That'll look too forced. I say you go about your daily life. We can go out to dinner a few times and be seen. Maybe you can show me some of the sights around here, just like you would any woman who was moving in with you from out of state."

That all sounded fine. "Okay. But what about us?"

She frowned. "What do you mean?"

"We don't know each other. People are going to ask me questions about you. What do I tell them?"

"The truth. Lying will just trip us up. And we have no reason to lie about who I am or how we met. We just need to embellish things a little. Instead of telling people you drive me crazy, I'll tell them how handsome I think you are." She tipped her head and bared her teeth in a smile.

"Gee, stroke my ego, why don't you?"

She laughed. "You know what I mean."

"Yeah. Okay. So, do we just hope your mere presence makes Mercy back off? I've dated two women since her. Neither lasted more than a single date."

"Did you sleep with either of them?"

Jordan bristled in his seat. "I'm not a man-whore."

She grinned again. "Is that a yes?"

"No. And no. I never slept with either of them. Mercy's the last woman I had sex with. And it was one night." He glanced at his plate, pushing his food around with his fork. "One night I now completely regret." He looked up, deciding to be honest. "I like sex, Edie. And I love women. I won't apologize for that. It's never come back to bite me before. I've always been careful. There have been a few one-night stands through the years, but they're always with women I've met before. I don't hook up with random women. And I see them again, just not sexually. It's more of a, we're at the same bar again and acknowledge each other type of thing."

She snorted and rolled her eyes. "Sure."

"Seriously. I don't pick up tourists in Tucson, or

anywhere else, for that matter. Most of the women I sleep with I date."

"What about that one in Costa Rica at Sam's bar? The one in the hot pink minidress?"

His brows dipped in thought, then his expression brightened. "Lola? We went down to the beach. She was hot." His eyes widened as he thought about how that sounded, and he held out a hand. "Not like that. Well, she was, but that's not what I meant. She was warm. Overheated. I offered to walk her down to the beach so she could get some air. She was a bit tipsy. Once she cooled off, I helped her call her sister, who picked her up. I went back to Dean's after that."

Edie blinked twice. "Oh."

"I'm not a cad, Edie. I don't know where you got that impression."

Lines furrowed the area between her eyebrows, and she scooped up another forkful of her dinner. She stayed silent.

Jordan clenched his teeth, not knowing what else to say to improve her opinion of him, so he let it drop. "If you want, you can come to work with me. I could use someone to man the desk. I had a receptionist, but she quit just before I went down to Costa Rica, and I haven't been able to find a replacement." Trudy had been amazing, but he understood that she needed to find a job she could do from home so she could take care of her ailing mother. He'd given her a generous severance for all the years she'd put in with him and wished her well.

She glanced up. "It's been over two months since you were down there. How have you not found anyone?"

"One, I haven't tried too hard. I've been busy. There were a couple of people who applied, but they weren't a good fit for one reason or another." Ideally, he needed someone who knew cars and could help get the best information from the customers as well as make recommendations when they just needed something simple, like tires or wiper blades. He'd had two women apply, and neither of them knew much about cars. The lone man to apply, though he had car knowledge, couldn't work many hours because he was going to school to become a mechanic. He'd told that kid to come back when he finished school and they'd talk about him coming on full time to work on vehicles.

"Okay. I guess I could do that. And I could help you find a replacement, I suppose."

"That would be great. I'll pay you, too, while you're here." He frowned as a thought occurred to him. "Who's managing your surf shop while you're gone?"

"Dean. And probably Max. My assistant manager is still there too. Don't worry. I left it in good hands."

"Oh. Well, good. I wouldn't want your business to suffer because you're here helping me."

She waved a hand. "We have a system worked out that when one of us is on a protection case, the others cover our businesses. Max and Sam covered Ford's charter business while he was on the water with Brooke. Dean mostly works for Sam, but he floats around where he's needed." She lifted a shoulder. "It works."

"Explain this operation to me. I didn't ask too many questions when I was down there. I know Brooke ended up with Ford because of someone they both know. It sounds like this happens regularly, though. That your little group takes on bodyguard jobs."

"Nothing's official. Ford just knows people. And the people he knows sometimes know people who need help. Like Brooke. A few months before she was there, the brother-in-law of one of Ford's colleagues from the Navy was having issues with a co-worker. He asked Ford to help, and Ford flew to Seattle and talked to the brother-in-law. With some technical help from Asher, they figured out the co-worker was trying to sabotage the company they worked for and steal the patents for a machine to sell to a competitor."

"Wow."

"Yeah. We do a lot locally. You'd be surprised by the number of people who need our expertise. Ford never asks for payment, though. None of us do. A lot of the locals—especially in the rural areas—can't afford it. But they bring us things. Mostly food. Which is fine. I'll take homemade *sopa mariscos* over money any day."

"What's that?"

"It's like a seafood stew."

"Sounds good."

"It's delicious. You'll have to try it the next time you're down."

"Only if you show me where to get the best."

She looked down at her plate. "Um, sure."

"So, tell me more about yourself."

She glanced up with a frown. "Why?"

Jordan chuckled. "I should at least know where my girlfriend is from, don't you think? And if she has any siblings? Who her parents are?"

"Oh. Um, I guess that's true. I'm from Oregon. Near Coos Bay. I have a younger sister, Esther. She still lives up there and teaches kindergarten. Our parents are there too. My mom's a teacher—middle school language arts. My dad's a maintenance technician at a factory."

"What are their names?"

"Rose and John."

"How did you end up in Costa Rica? I mean, you sound like you love your family." He could hear it in her voice.

"I do. But—" She stopped and pressed her lips together, then continued. "When I left the Army, I wasn't in a good place. I didn't want to bring that home to my family. Ford offered me a place to stay. To heal."

"And did you?" His voice was quiet.

"Well enough, I suppose. I don't wake up screaming every night now."

Jordan's heart thumped at her admission. He could only imagine the things she'd seen and been through. "That's good. I'm sorry you ever did."

She shrugged. "It is what it is."

"Why did you join the Army?"

"College money. My G.I. Bill paid for my degree in linguistics."

Jordan's eyebrows shot up. "You have a degree in linguistics?"

She nodded.

"And you own a surf shop? Why aren't you working for the CIA or some other federal agency?"

"Because I don't want to. I wanted to work as a translator on the ground with the Army. Which I did. And then everything went to shit. Can we talk about something else, please?"

"Sure." He didn't want to push her. He'd learned more about her in that short conversation than he did in the few days he was in Costa Rica. "What do you like to do besides surf?"

She let out a long breath. "Um, read. Play cards with the guys. Fish and hike."

"No movie nights with a bowl of popcorn?"

She smiled. "Only with my sister. Essy loves Christmas movies. What about you? I've told you about my life."

"I'm an only child. My mom lives in Tucson, but we're not terribly close. She doesn't have the greatest taste in men, so I don't go over there much. We mostly keep in touch through calls and texts."

"What about your dad? Is he living?"

"As far as I know. He went to jail for fraud for ten years when I was eleven. When he got out, I heard from him once.

He hired a private investigator to track me down, then showed up where I worked, wanting to reconnect." His voice grew hard at the memory.

She frowned. "You turned him away?"

"Considering he stole my social security number when I was a kid, then asked me for a loan to secure an apartment the first time he saw me as an adult, yeah, I did. I told him his parole officer should be able to help him find a job. And he wasn't homeless. He was staying at a halfway house until he could afford a place to rent. He was just looking for an easy way out of there."

"That's a shame he has to be like that. I can't imagine not having my dad in my life."

"You're lucky. My parents both leave something to be desired."

"I'm sorry."

"Don't be. I turned out all right."

"You did." She glanced around. "You've done well for yourself. And you've stayed out of trouble."

He grinned. "Mostly, yes. My silver tongue works on more than just women."

She chuckled. "I bet. What about hobbies? Or do you tinker with cars in your free time too?"

"I do. But like you, I also like the outdoors. I hike and camp a lot. Not so much into reading, though I do. I like baseball, so I watch the Diamondbacks play on TV."

She rolled her eyes. "You sound like Max and Sam. They love baseball. Dean does too."

"You don't?"

"It's all right. I'd rather watch Essy's movies, though." She scooped up the last of her food and ate it. Jordan followed suit. She pushed away from the island and got up. "Do you have the notes Mercy left you?"

He frowned at the abrupt change in subject. Apparently,

she was done with the personal stuff. "Yeah. They're upstairs in my office."

"I'd like to see them."

He opened the dishwasher and set his plate and fork inside. "I'll go get them."

Six

Edie breathed a sigh of relief when Jordan walked away to get the notes. The picture of the man in her head was not jiving with the one she'd just had dinner with. Sure, he was still charming and affable beyond belief, but there was another side to him she hadn't expected. One with strong morals and a keen intelligence. Though, honestly, the intelligence shouldn't have surprised her. He owned a successful business at the age of twenty-nine, and she'd seen him at work with Wendy's car. He knew what he was doing.

Gathering up the dishes from dinner, Edie scraped the leftover stir fry into a container and put it in the fridge. She found a pair of gloves under the sink and put them on to keep her bandage dry. They were too big, but they still did the job. Adding dish soap to a sponge, she set about washing the pans.

"You didn't have to wash those. I could have cleaned up."

She glanced over her shoulder at the sound of Jordan's voice. "It's fine. I don't mind. But thank you." She swished the sponge around, then rinsed the skillet. "Did you find the notes?"

"Yeah."

She quickly washed the rice pot, then set it next to the skillet on the towel she'd spread out. Rinsing out the sponge, she removed the gloves and crossed to the notes he laid on the island.

"Sorry they're a little wrinkled. After the first couple, well, they just made me angry. I crumpled a few and tossed them onto the floorboard of my truck."

The pages crinkled as she leafed through them. "It's fine."

"I don't know where they're all from. Or maybe she wrote them." He shrugged. "I don't know."

"She didn't write them. This one's Shelley. From *Love's Philosophy*." She flipped to another page. "And this one is Charlotte Brontë."

"How do you know that?"

Edie smiled at his incredulous tone. "My mom's a language arts teacher, remember? She loves poetry. I grew up on this stuff."

"So what does it all mean? I mean, I get that they're love poems, but is there some other meaning behind them?"

"Hmm, maybe." She skimmed through the lines; something about them said something to her. "What order did you get these in?"

"Um, let me see." He held out a hand. Edie passed him the papers. He shuffled them around, then handed them back. "The first one is on top."

Edie read them again, and a pattern emerged. "She's getting more aggressive. The first couple are just her expressing her love for you. They all do, really. But the last couple—" She looked up into his gray eyes. "She's basically saying she'll do anything to catch and keep your attention. Dean was right. She could be dangerous." Suddenly, his certainty that there was more to this situation made sense. She was glad she'd come.

"Wonderful." Jordan ran his hands down his face. "So, now what?"

"We continue with our plan. I'll start working for you. We'll fake date and make it known we're together. But we stay vigilant, in case she tries something."

"I'm not so sure about this now, Edie. I don't want to put you in danger."

"I can handle myself. I'm more worried about you. She might try some stronger tactics to get you to be hers."

"I can take care of myself too. Just because I wasn't military doesn't mean I don't have skills."

She flattened her lips. "I didn't mean to imply you're helpless. I know you're not." Her eyes roved over the muscles straining the chest and sleeves of his t-shirt. When she met his eyes again, a smirk sat on his full lips. She chose to ignore it. "But you haven't been trained to study your surroundings. It's like second-nature to me. I'm constantly scanning my environment for threats."

He stepped closer, something hot springing to life in his eyes. "Even now?"

Oh, especially now. She swallowed. "Yes."

The smirk came back. "Good to know."

Edie thrust the notes against his chest. "Glad we've cleared that up."

He grinned and covered her hand. She yanked it away, leaving the papers behind, then stepped back. "I hope you don't mind, but I'm going to go read for a bit and go to bed. It's been a long day." She curled her fingers into a ball, lightly pressing against the healing cut on her hand, using the pain to try to erase the feeling of his muscles beneath her hand and his calloused fingers over hers.

His smirk softened into a smile. "Of course not. Come on. I'll show you to the guest room."

"I already found it." After she let herself in, she'd walked through the house and dumped her bags in the only other room besides his that had a bed.

"Oh. Okay. Um, I leave for work around seven-thirty. The garage opens at eight."

She nodded once. "Sounds good. I'll see you in the morning."

"Okay. Goodnight, Edie."

"Goodnight." Without another word, she fled.

SEVEN

"I've got you down. Thank you for calling." Edie waited for the customer on the other end to say goodbye, then hung up. No sooner did she put the phone down than it rang again. She stared at it for a second, eyes round. She didn't know how Jordan got anything done all day. It had been two days since she started working here. If the phone wasn't ringing, people were coming and going, picking up and dropping off cars. It never ended. Blowing out an exasperated sigh, she picked up the phone again. "MacDowell's Garage. This is Edie. How may I help you?"

"Oh, um, hi. I need to make an appointment." A woman's soft, surprised voice came over the line.

"Okay. What are you looking to have done?" Edie cradled the phone on her shoulder and clicked on the appointment screen.

"My car's making a knocking noise. It's done it before. Jordan put a new sensor in and it quit for a while, but it's doing it again. Is he there?"

"Yes. He's working on a vehicle. How does Friday morning sound?" Jordan had varying degrees of severity for his bookings. His standard service appointments were booked out for a couple of weeks, but he had a few slots still open this week for more major problems.

"What time?"

"If you can drop it off when we open, or the night before, he can work on it that day."

"I can drop it off in the morning. Jordan usually gives me a ride to work."

Edie frowned. That was the first she'd heard of him doing something like that. "I'll have to check with him. What's your name?"

"Chelsea Bridges."

"Can I put you on hold?"

"Sure."

"Okay. It'll be just a moment." Edie pushed the button on the phone to hold the call, then set the receiver down. Rounding the desk, she pushed through the glass door to the garage. "Jordan."

He rolled out from beneath a pickup. "Yeah?"

"There's a Chelsea Bridges on the phone. She says her car is knocking again. I want to book her in Friday morning, and she said you usually give her a ride into work when she drops off her car."

"Oh. Yeah, that's fine. She works at the vet clinic down the road a few minutes, so it's not far. I do that for several people. If they mention it, just say yes."

Her opinion of him shifted again. "Okay." Backing through the door, she went back to the phone.

"Hi, Chelsea. Sorry about that. I'm new, so I don't know all the ins and outs of Jordan's business yet. He said that's fine. Do you want me to book you in for Friday?"

"Yes, please."

Edie took down Chelsea's information and confirmed the

appointment. Wishing the woman a good day, she hung up and reached for her water.

The chime on the door sounded. Edie took a quick sip and set the bottle down. "Hello." She smiled at the woman who walked in. "How may I help you?"

"I'm picking up my car. Andrea Harris?"

Edie scanned the wall of clear hanging folders, looking for the woman's name. Quickly finding it, she lifted it off its hook and removed the paperwork and keys from the folder. "Let's see. That'll be three-oh-six fifty-two, please."

Andrea handed her a credit card. Edie took it and swiped it through the reader.

"You're new. You weren't here Monday when I dropped the car off."

Edie glanced up, nodding. "I started Tuesday."

"I bet Jordan's glad to have the help. He's always swamped."

"Yeah. I'm only temporary, though. Just until we can find someone permanent."

"Oh? That's nice of you to fill in. You must be good friends."

A corner of Edie's mouth lifted as she tore off the receipt. "You could say that. He's my boyfriend." She hadn't been shy about telling people who she was. They wanted word to get out that he was taken. "Could you sign that, please?" She pushed the strip of paper and a pen across the counter.

The woman took the pen. "I didn't know Jordan was dating anyone. He's always so busy. I didn't think he had time to date."

Edie studied the woman. She sure was nosy. "Well, when it's right, you just know, and you make time."

"I guess that's true." Andrea signed her name.

Edie passed her the keys from the pouch. "There you go. It should be parked outside."

"Thank you." She took her keys and headed for the door. Her head turned toward the garage as she walked, slowing as she looked through the glass.

Edie followed her gaze and saw Jordan leaning over the pickup engine he'd just been under. His charcoal work pants were taut over his butt. She couldn't blame the woman for lingering. He had a tush as chiseled as his jaw.

The phone rang again. Edie reached for it, watching as Andrea Harris finally left. She had an inkling now why the woman was so nosy. She was probably hoping to catch his eye too.

Edie shook her head as she answered the phone. Jordan really did need a girlfriend. A real one. Or even a wife. Maybe it would hold all the women at bay.

Eight

Jordan shut off the garage lights and walked into the reception area. Edie smiled from behind the desk.

"Are you finally done?"

"Yes." He glanced at the clock. It was five-fifteen. Only fifteen minutes past closing time. That was a record for him. Since Trudy quit, he'd been spending hours every evening, and on the weekends, playing catch-up. "You want to go out to dinner? It was busy in here today. I don't know about you, but I don't feel like cooking."

Her smile widened, and she shut the computer down. "I like that plan. Go wash up. I'll finish in here."

"Okay. I'll just be a minute." He walked past her to the back and the employee restroom. He scrubbed his hands with the degreasing soap he kept in the dispenser, then returned to the breakroom. Opening his locker, he unbuttoned his work shirt and shrugged it off his shoulders.

"All right. I emptied the trash and—" Edie's words cut off.

Jordan glanced back to see what was wrong. She stood in the doorway, staring at him with wide blue eyes.

"What are you doing?"

"Changing out of my greasy shirt." He pulled a clean t-shirt off the top shelf of his locker and thrust his arms into it. "I figured I should look at least a little presentable when I take my girl out to dinner." He sent her a cocky grin.

She rolled her eyes and walked into the room, going to the locker next to his to get her coat. "I have a feeling you could show up in something utterly outrageous and no one would notice anything but your face."

He put a hand to his cheek and frowned. "What's wrong with my face? Did I miss some grease?" He'd checked in the mirror when he washed his hands, but it had looked clean.

She laughed. "I meant that you're pretty. People will be too busy staring at your face to notice your clothes."

"Oh." He chuckled. "I think I'll be outshined tonight, though."

Edie blushed. "Not in a million years."

Jordan frowned, studying her. Did she not think she was beautiful? "No. You outshine the sun, Edie."

"You don't need to flatter me, Jordan. I'm not actually your girlfriend. It won't get you anywhere."

He slammed his locker door, then spun her around to crowd her against the black metal. It pissed him off that she still wanted to see him as a man-whore, but more so that she didn't see the beauty in herself. "It's not flattery when it's true."

She stared up at him, surprise in her wide blue eyes.

"And you don't need to be my girlfriend for me to pay you a compliment. Does no one ever tell you how beautiful you are? They should. You have hair like the hottest flame and skin like alabaster. And your eyes—they're so blue and deep I could drown in them. No one will be looking at me at dinner. They'll all be wondering who the gorgeous redhead is."

"Oh," she breathed, still staring at him, wide-eyed.

Heat unfurled in Jordan's belly the longer he held her

gaze. He'd noticed Edie the moment he'd walked into the terminal at the airport in Golfito. Her fiery red hair set her apart from the other people milling about. Then she turned those laser-focused blue eyes on him and speared him straight in the heart. She was the most beautiful creature he'd ever seen.

He lifted a hand and pushed a tendril of hair that had come loose from her braid away from her face. Her smooth skin was like silk beneath his calloused fingers.

"Jordan..." Her whisper held both a plea and a warning.

He chose to listen to the plea and lowered his head. Holding her gaze, he made sure she knew his intentions, not closing his eyes until he was within a hairsbreadth of her lips. The first touch of his mouth to hers sent an arc of fire through him, melding their lips together. With a sharp inhale, he pressed harder, deepening the kiss. Her hands came up and curled in the front of his shirt, and she kissed him back.

Not wanting to get too carried away, he held onto his sanity somehow and gentled the kiss. When he pulled back and looked at her, she still had her eyes closed. They fluttered open, desire turning the bright blue pools to the color of a turgid sea. He clenched his jaw and stiffened his spine so he didn't kiss her again. He didn't want to scare her off. Her role in his life might have started off as a ruse, but now he wanted to change that and make it a reality. He could see a future with her. She was as skittish as a cornered cat, though. He didn't want her to lash out, so he stepped back. "Where do you want to eat?"

She blinked twice, her expression morphing from stunned to shocked, then to the cool mask she so often kept in place. "Don't do that again. And wherever. You know what's good around here, not me."

He ignored her first sentence, knowing he couldn't

promise anything. "There's a small diner just down the road that has good burgers. How does that sound?"

"Fine." She turned and reached into her locker for her coat.

Jordan opened his again and took out his jacket, shrugging into it.

"We need to stop at a store on the way home. I brought the grocery list with me. We're out of some things."

He nodded. The locker door clanked as he shut it. "I'm glad you remembered. I noticed that too, but I forgot to grab it."

She grabbed her purse and closed her locker. Jordan led the way out the door, locking up behind them.

NINE

What the hell just happened? Edie followed Jordan out of the building and got into his Bronco. Her lips still tingled from their kiss, and a hum coursed through her body.

Why did I let him do that?

It wasn't like he hadn't given her ample warning. He'd held her gaze, his eyes telegraphing his intentions. She could have pushed him away. That would have been the end of it. But her stupid brain had short-circuited and kept her rooted to the spot. It wanted to know what it felt like to kiss him. Well, now it knew. She knew.

She turned her head, looking out the window, and closed her eyes briefly. She was such an idiot. Now she only wanted a repeat. Getting involved with Jordan MacDowell was not part of the plan. She knew she should have said no when Dean asked her to do this. Jordan was too tempting. Too sexy. Too —everything. And he was a complication. She was content with her life. Happy. And she feared what throwing a wrench into it would do to her emotional stability. She really didn't want the dreams to come back. She'd worked hard to banish them. To deal with the past and put it behind her. Opening the door on such wild emotions could unleash others, even if they weren't related.

She just had to resist him. That was all there was to it. She couldn't risk falling back into the hole she'd climbed out of. It wasn't rational, she knew. How could intense desire and need reopen all her emotional wounds from war? But the fear was there. Maybe the door on those memories and feelings wasn't as tightly closed as she'd thought.

Jordan pulled into a small parking lot next to a painted brick building. Edie got out and followed him inside. Warmth and the scent of French fries hit her the moment she stepped through the door. The familiarity soothed some of her frayed emotions. They sat down at a booth, and Edie plucked a menu from the holder, hiding behind it. She wasn't ready to look him in the eye yet.

"Well, hello. Who's your friend, Jordan?"

Edie looked up from her menu to see an older woman wearing a black server's apron and a pencil stuck into her gray bun, smiling at them. She held a notepad and another pencil.

"Evening, Lori. This is my girlfriend, Edie."

The woman's dark eyes lit up. "Girlfriend?" She turned to Edie. "You must be something special. I think the last time he brought a date in here was his senior year of high school."

Jordan chuckled. "It hasn't been that long."

"It has too. You take them all into Tucson. You don't bring them home."

"Well, he brought me home," Edie said. "Quite literally. I've moved in." She liked this woman. She wasn't swayed by Jordan's charm.

Lori's eyes grew round, and she put a hand on her chest. "I never thought I'd see the day." She looked at Jordan. "Jordan MacDowell's in love."

The look of pure terror on his face made Edie roll her lips

in to stifle the laugh that wanted to break free. It only lasted a moment before his charming smile took over.

"What can I say? When you know, you know." He turned up the wattage on his grin and directed it at Edie. Fire burned in his eyes.

Her blood heated in answer. She cleared her throat and looked at Lori. "He promised me the best burger I've ever had. Is that true?"

"It is." She put her pencil to her notepad. "What do you want on it and how do you want it cooked?"

Edie and Jordan put in their orders, then Lori hurried away to get their drinks. When she was out of earshot, Edie folded her hands on the table and pierced him with a look. "Did you bring me here to spread the word about our relationship?"

"No, actually. I just wanted a burger. I didn't think about how people would react."

Edie glanced to where Lori disappeared into the kitchen. "She seems to know you well."

"She ought to. I've been coming here since I was a teenager. Before that, even. My mom would bring me here sometimes when she had the money for us to eat out. Lori's worked here as long as I can remember."

She tipped her head, studying him. "You love this town, don't you?"

He lifted a shoulder. "It's home. I grew up here. I can't really imagine living anywhere else. I mean, I would if I had to, but I've never wanted to. Even when my mom decided to move into Tucson right after I graduated high school, I couldn't bring myself to go, even though it would have been easier to continue living with her. I found a cheap apartment, ate ramen and peanut butter a lot, and worked nights until I got all the training I needed to get a good job."

Edie looked out the window, thinking about her own

hometown. At one point, she felt that way too. When she'd joined the Army, she knew it would take her away, but deep down, she always thought she'd go back. Now she wasn't sure. She missed her family, but Costa Rica was nice, and she was happy there.

"Okay. Two root beers."

Glass thudded on the table. Edie turned and smiled at Lori as she set down the second frosty mug.

"Your food should be out in about ten minutes. Can I get you anything else?"

Edie shook her head.

"We're good. Thank you, Lori," Jordan said.

The older woman smiled. "Sure thing. Flag me down if you need something." She spun on her heel and walked away.

"So, did you have any luck putting together an ad for me for a new receptionist?" Jordan picked up his mug.

Edie snorted. "No. If the phone wasn't ringing, someone was coming through the door. I'll try tomorrow, but I might have to work on it at home. How did you ever get anything done without help?"

"I worked a lot of evenings, once the front door was locked and I was 'officially' closed." He air-quoted with one finger. "Weekends too."

"Wow. That takes some commitment."

"It's my business. If it fails, I have no income. Plus, I can't let my customers down. Many of them depend on their vehicles for work and don't have other means of transportation."

There was that good guy coming out again. She liked it better when he was being flirty. It was easier to ignore his charm. She changed the subject, and they spent the next few minutes talking about the town. When Lori returned with their food, she'd learned they had a great pizza place, a bowling alley where teenagers liked to hang out on Friday nights, and a small public library that was big into holidays.

Once they wolfed down their food—Edie was much hungrier than she'd thought—Jordan paid the bill and they left.

"Can we add root beer to that list?" Jordan asked as they got into the car.

Edie chuckled. "Hit the spot, did it?"

"Yeah. I haven't had it in a while. I wouldn't mind making some root beer floats one night."

Her mouth watered. She hadn't had a root beer float in ages. "Sounds good." She made a mental note to grab both root beer and vanilla ice cream.

He steered the Bronco through the town streets to the small grocery store. Inside, Edie grabbed a cart.

"You lead," she said. "I don't know where anything is."

He took off down the first aisle. "Do you have the list?"

She reached into her small purse and pulled it out, handing it to him. He glanced over it, then walked faster. Edie trailed behind him, adding one or two things she wanted.

"We need to figure out how we're going to split the grocery bill while I'm here."

He waved a hand. "Don't worry about it."

"You are not paying for all my food, Jordie."

He plucked a bag of granola off the shelf and gave her a look over his shoulder. "That wasn't what I meant, Edith."

She narrowed her eyes at the use of her given name. She shouldn't be surprised he employed it, though. Not when she called him Jordie. "What did you mean, then?"

"I figured we'd probably end up taking turns, and that it would all more or less equal out."

"Oh." That made sense.

He dropped the bag in the cart. "Yeah. Oh." Turning, he walked down the aisle, away from her.

She blew out a breath, ruffling her bangs. *Way to put your foot in your mouth, Edie.* Pushing the cart forward, she rounded the end of the aisle and entered the next one.

A jolt of jealousy speared her as she saw Jordan smiling at a brunette woman with legs for days. Her dark hair was pulled up into a messy bun, highlighting her long neck and high cheekbones. She looked like a fashion model.

Edie rolled the cart closer. Jordan spotted her. The look he sent her was not one she expected. It practically screamed, "Thank you for rescuing me."

"Hey, babe. This is Alyssa. Alyssa, this is my girlfriend, Edie Campbell."

Edie smiled at the woman whose pretty smile had disappeared behind her shocked expression. "Hello. I'm just meeting all of Jordan's friends today. You're the third or fourth one."

"Oh, well, he always was rather popular. Him and his friend, Dean. Have you met him?" A slight smugness crossed her face.

"Actually, I've known Dean for a couple of years. He's how Jordan and I met."

Disappointment flashed in the woman's eyes. "Oh."

Giving the tall woman a saccharine smile, Edie maneuvered the cart around them. "I'm going to go grab the produce we need, Jordie." She was ready to go home, completely done meeting the pretty women who flocked to him. "It was nice to meet you, Alyssa."

"You too." Alyssa gave her a tight smile.

Edie's lips barely twitched. But what she heard as she walked away made a smile spread over her face.

"We?"

It was just one word from Alyssa, but it held a wealth of jealousy, and made Edie feel like the beautiful woman Jordan thought she was.

TEN

The hair rose on the back of Jordan's neck, telling him he was no longer alone. He finished his kata, then shifted, turning to look at the door. Edie stood at the edge of his practice mat.

"Sorry," she said. "I didn't mean to interrupt. I didn't know you were already awake."

It was Saturday, but that didn't make a difference to him. He was an early riser, preferring to get a workout and some martial arts practice in before he did anything else.

"You're fine. I told you to use the room whenever you wanted."

She set her water bottle down on the bench against the wall. "True. That still doesn't mean I want to interrupt you, though." She propped her hands on her hips and studied him. "How long have you been doing that?"

"Taekwondo?"

She nodded.

"Since I was a kid. I'd watch tournaments on TV and imitate the competitors. I got more serious about it though in high school. I was flirting with the wrong side of the law. We got a new neighbor who was a cop, and he offered to train me, but I had to keep my nose clean." Jordan held his arms wide. "And now here I am."

She hummed an acknowledgement. "Fancy a sparring session?"

One of his eyebrows shot up. "You want to spar with me?"

Edie nodded again.

"Babe, I've got eight inches and fifty or sixty pounds on you."

A slow smile spread over her face. "Don't tell me you're afraid you'll get your butt whipped by a girl."

Jordan chuckled. "No."

She cracked her knuckles and stepped forward. "Then let's do this."

He stared at her, not blinking. "You're serious."

"Yes, I'm serious. I could go for a good sparring session. I do this with Asher all the time."

Jordan pictured the tech analyst who was built like an elite runner. Which, honestly, he was. The man ran marathons for fun. His muscles were built for speed and endurance. Jordan's were built for manhandling large, heavy car parts.

"Edie, I don't want to hurt you. And what about your hand?" He motioned to the still bandaged cut across her palm.

She glanced at it briefly. "It's fine. I'll take the stitches out in a few days. It's not like I'll hit you with my palm. And you won't. I'm quick and tougher than I look." She rolled her shoulders as she moved toward the center of the mat.

He put his hands on his hips and continued to stare at her.

"Oh, come on, Jordie. We'll set some ground rules if it makes you feel better." She laid out a few guidelines.

Jordan sighed. He could tell she wasn't going to let this go. "Fine. But don't say I didn't warn you."

That slow grin of hers came back, and she crouched.

A zing went through Jordan's veins, tempering his

concerns. He hadn't had a good spar since Dean was here last. He matched her stance.

One moment, he was staring into her amused blue eyes, and the next, he was staring up at the ceiling. Edie's laugh filled the room.

Jordan groaned. "What the hell?" He lifted his head and looked at her. "No fair. I wasn't ready."

"Sure you weren't. Get up and try again. I haven't even broken a sweat." She bounced on the balls of her feet.

Huffing a laugh, Jordan got up. "Okay." He wagged a finger at her. "You won't take me by surprise again."

"You sure?" She exploded into action.

Jordan threw up his arms and countered her moves. She whirled away and brought a foot up. He knocked it down, then again as she used the other foot. He reached out, using his longer arms, and bound hers to her torso.

"Give up?"

"No." She broke his hold and grabbed his fingers, twisting his arm up behind his back.

He grunted, then rolled, bringing them down to the mat, straddling her. "Come on, Edie. Just tap out. You can't win."

"That's what you think."

Somehow, she slithered a leg out and rolled, hooking it over his shoulder to reverse their positions. For several minutes, they rolled across the mat, climbing to their feet to spar, then ending up back on the mat.

When she laid him flat once more, Jordan waved his arms. "Enough. I'm done."

She sat back, grinning. Sweat dripped down her face and dampened her hair, turning the bright flames into banked embers. "You're giving in?"

He nodded. "You forget; I did a whole workout before you showed up."

She rose to her feet. "Excuses, excuses. Admit it. I beat

you."

Jordan found a quick burst of energy. He sprang to his feet and lunged, wrapping his arms around her waist and pulling her down. Sprawling over her, he used his weight to keep her down, pinning her hands above her head. "You didn't win. It was a draw."

She laughed. "No. You called mercy. I won. Let me up."

"No. Admit it's a draw."

"No."

"Admit it, or we're staying right here." Though that probably wasn't the best idea. Flat on top of her, this was the closest they'd been since their match began. He could feel every curve of her body under his.

"We both know I can get out of this." Despite her words, her body stayed relaxed.

"Then why don't you?"

Something flashed in her eyes. The low hum that vibrated through Jordan's veins erupted into a pulse of need.

He jumped up and turned away, hiding the half-aroused state of his body. "What do you say we go for a hike today? You said you wanted to explore the area." He crossed the room and picked up his water bottle and took a drink.

"Sure. Let me shower and change."

He nodded, glancing at her. That calm, cool mask of hers was in place, but her rigid body language told him she wasn't as unaffected by their encounter as she wanted him to believe. "We can leave in about thirty minutes, if that works?"

"That's plenty of time."

He picked up her water bottle and tossed it to her, wanting to keep her at a distance. It would take very little prompting for him to grab her and kiss the daylights out of her.

"Thanks." With a wave of the bottle, she spun on her heel and left.

Eleven

The Bronco's tires hummed as Jordan drove down the road to the trailhead in Saguaro National Park. They'd decided to hike the desert trails in deference to the snowpack in the mountains. Edie was fine with that. She didn't care for the snow.

He pulled into a layby and parked. She climbed out and met him in front of the truck.

"Stick to the trail or wander?" he asked.

"Wander. We have a compass and GPS. And we'll see more stuff off the trail."

He nodded once. "Let's go."

Taking an initial reading of their location, they set off. Edie inhaled the clean, crisp air and smiled softly. This was the way hiking was supposed to be. Dry weather, not too hot, clean air. Costa Rica only had one of those things—the clean air. Otherwise, it was a damp, sticky, tropical sauna. She didn't hike there; she just surfed. But here? She could do this every day when the weather was like this.

They walked in silence, content to take in their surroundings. Edie let her mind wander. So far, her time in Arizona had been easy. Busy, but easy. Jordan's little friend hadn't reared her head again after she came in to make an appointment. It was surprising, and Edie didn't know what to make of it. Either it would be way easier than any of them thought to get her to back off, or she was planning something.

Edie would bet on the latter. She'd seen the calculating look in the woman's eyes. She wasn't going to just give up. Which was fine. She welcomed the challenge.

A rabbit shot out from under some scrub brush, dashing away. Edie jumped.

"You okay?" Jordan paused to look at her.

"I'm fine. It just startled me. So what other kind of wildlife can we expect to see?"

"Mostly just small mammals at this time of year down here. The lizards are hibernating."

"Are there any larger mammals?"

"Javelinas. They get deer higher up. Sometimes, I see them at home. We have bears and mountain lions too, so watch yourself if you go wandering around outside."

Edie's face pulled. "Okay. I was hoping to get away from things with teeth. We have jaguars, though they usually stick to the forest. One of the many reasons I don't go hiking in the woods there."

Jordan chuckled. "And you seem like such a nature girl."

"I like the ocean."

"There are things with teeth there. Probably more so than what you'd see on land around here."

"I grew up with sharks, though. I've been playing in the ocean since I was little. I also know not to surf under certain conditions. There aren't conditions to avoid predators on land."

"That's not necessarily true. Certain animals are more

active at certain times of the day. And at certain times of the year. Like, I wouldn't want to go hiking in the mountains unprepared in the spring. Bears are coming out of hibernation, and mama bears have cubs."

She tipped her head. "True. I think I'd still rather take my chances in the ocean."

They walked several dozen yards before she spoke again. "You know, I've seen pictures of these cacti, but in person—" She paused and shook her head, staring up at the giant saguaro cactus they'd come across. "This thing is unreal." It had to be every bit of thirty feet tall.

"This isn't even the tallest one. They can reach fifty feet. It's too bad it's not spring. They flower. It's gorgeous."

Taking out her phone, she took a picture of it. "Mother Earth is fascinating."

They resumed their walk. Jordan pointed out several species of cacti and other vegetation. Edie took more pictures, fascinated by the desert landscape. She was a coastie. Minus her time in the Army, she'd always lived by the sea. This was all foreign to her.

A couple of hours into their walk, a squawk drew their attention. Edie paused to take a drink and watched the buzzards circling overhead. They'd found something to snack on. She resumed her pace as she swallowed and promptly tripped on a rock. The cap to her water bottle went flying out of her hand and off into the scrub. "Dammit."

"Problems?" Jordan looked over.

"I dropped the cap to my water."

He walked her way. Edie scanned the ground. "I think it rolled into the brush." She pointed and moved closer. Crouching, she peered into the scraggly scrub. Not seeing any snakes or scorpions, she reached in to move the thin branches aside. Her hand brushed a piece of pink fabric. She pushed it aside and froze. "Jordan."

"Did you find it?"

"No. Look." She shifted so he could see into the bush. "Is that what I think it is?"

On the ground, under the fabric, were the scattered bones of a human arm.

TWELVE

"Hell." Jordan straightened, pressing his lips together. He took off his pack and retrieved the GPS tracker. Noting the location, he took out his phone. "I don't have any reception. Do you?"

She stood up and found her phone. "No."

"Let's hike back to the trailhead and call the police. I noted the coordinates." For good measure, he took a picture of the readout. His mind whirled with where the bones could have come from; none of them good.

After tying a piece of gauze from the first aid kit to the bush, they set off at a quick clip back to the layby that served as a parking lot for the trail. Doing more jogging than walking, they made the trek in nearly half the time. Jordan opened the back of the Bronco and took out two more water bottles, passing one to Edie. Water trickled over his chin and down his neck, but he didn't care. Even with the cool temps, they'd still run a couple of miles.

Thirst quenched, he checked his phone again for a signal. Three bars shined in the corner. He dialed 911 and waited. When the dispatcher answered, he gave her a quick rundown on what they'd found, and she dispatched a unit to their location.

"You know, I was just thinking how cushy this assignment was." Edie leaned on the side of the Bronco next to him, sipping on her water. "Guess I jinxed us."

"Oh, it was you? Good to know." A corner of his mouth lifted.

"Yep." She sighed. "So, who do you think it is? Has anyone been reported missing lately?"

"Not that I know of. It might be a migrant."

Edie frowned. "That's just sad."

He agreed.

A ranger was the first to show up. He and Edie briefed the man, finishing as the first police car arrived.

Jordan smiled as he saw the man who emerged from the cruiser. "Mike." He walked over, leaving Edie at the truck, and held out a hand. "I'm glad it's you." Mike Deyo had been a few years ahead of Jordan in school. They'd become friends in the last ten years, bonding over martial arts and cars.

Mike Deyo shook Jordan's hand. "What's going on? Dispatch said something about body parts in the desert."

Jordan nodded. "Edie and I went for a hike. She dropped the cap to her water, and when we went looking for it, we found bones from someone's hand and arm in the scrub."

"Just an arm?"

"Yeah. I'm thinking scavengers probably pulled it in there."

Mike sighed. "Great. I better call the state and see if they have a cadaver dog. The rest of those remains could be anywhere."

"We might want some ATVs too. It's several miles in." Jordan hooked a thumb over his shoulder.

"I'll call the station," the ranger said, having overheard. "Have them bring ours."

"Perfect. Thanks." Mike offered the man a polite smile, then he turned to Jordan again. "So, who's the woman?" He tipped his chin in Edie's direction.

Mentally, Jordan crossed his fingers. He didn't like lying to friends, but for the sake of continuity—and his sanity—they needed to keep up appearances and keep their story straight. "My girlfriend, Edie Campbell."

Mike's eyebrows shot up. "Girlfriend? How long has that been going on?"

"Since Costa Rica."

"Wait. Is she the chick you told me about? The one who took one look at you and decided she hated your guts? How'd you pull this off?"

"My charming smile." He grinned, then chuckled. "I don't know. We've been talking. Mostly me pestering her with random memes and thoughts." That part was true. He'd see something online that would make him think of her, and he wouldn't hesitate to text it to her. At first, she told him to stop bugging her, but then she started to reply with memes of her own. Honestly, he'd just wanted to be friends. She was important to Dean, so he wanted to get to know her—to get to know all of his friends down there. She was the toughest nut to crack, though. "I invited her up to go on a date and see if we could make something of this. She's been here a week. I can't imagine her going home." That part was true too. He didn't want her to leave. If he got his way, she wouldn't.

"Hey, that's great." Mike smiled. "I'm happy for you. You guys will have to come over for dinner. I'm sure Carmen would love to meet her."

"I'll say something to Edie, thanks."

"Say something to me about what?"

Jordan turned and smiled. "Dinner at Mike's. Honey, this is Mike Deyo. He's a friend. I was telling him about you, and he invited us over for dinner with his wife."

"Oh. Gotcha." She held out a hand and smiled at Mike. "It's nice to meet you."

"Likewise," Mike said, shaking her hand. "Sorry about the circumstances."

"Me too. But I'm coming to see that I should always expect the unexpected with Jordan."

Mike laughed. "That's the truth."

"Hey. I'm not a trouble magnet."

"No, but you do have a way of making things happen," Mike said.

He could see that. He hadn't scared Edie off yet. In fact, he thought she was softening toward him a bit.

The second ranger arrived a few minutes later, towing a trailer with two ATVs.

"Are we coming with you?" Jordan asked Mike.

"Yeah. I need you to show me where you found the bones. GPS will only put us in the vicinity."

"We tied some gauze to the bush," Edie said. "Hopefully, it didn't blow away." She climbed on the back of the ranger's ATV. "There were some vultures flying around too."

"Okay." Mike hopped on the second one and motioned for Jordan to get on behind him. They set off, the sound of the ATVs breaking the peaceful quiet of the desert. The ride to the GPS coordinates took less than ten minutes.

As Mike cut the engine, Jordan hopped off, scanning the landscape for a piece of flapping gauze. The vultures still circled overhead. They were in the right place.

"There," Edie said.

He glanced at her, then followed the line of her finger as she pointed.

Mike held up a hand, motioning for them to stay back, then approached the scrub, crouching in front of it.

"There's some pink fabric, and the bones are underneath," Edie said.

Leaning in, Mike paused. "I see it. It's definitely a hand and arm." He stood up. "You guys didn't see anything else on your hike? No other bones?"

"Not human," Jordan said. "I saw a deer skull and a few ribs. That was it, though." All of those bones had been old and weathered. "Do you want us to poke around?"

"No. I'm going to rope this off, then take you guys back to your car. We need to have a crime scene unit come out and comb the area." He turned to the ranger. "Do you have scene tape in your kit?"

The man nodded and opened the compartment under the seat of his ATV. He pulled out a roll of yellow police tape. Together, the two of them cordoned off the area. Jordan hung back with Edie.

"This is crazy," she muttered. "And not how I pictured our day would go."

"Me, either." He blew out a breath and scrubbed a hand over his face. The day wasn't over yet, either.

Thirteen

Jordan yawned and blinked hard, trying to concentrate on the wires he was reconnecting. This was his last car for the day. Thank God. He planned to eat dinner, chill out with Edie for an hour or two, then go to sleep. He was still tired from the weekend. They'd gone home after Mike released them from the scene, only to have to go back and give formal statements. Sunday, he spent the day doing the garage's books and cleaning the shop.

He heard the bell on the shop door chime and glanced over to see who was here to pick up their car. If it was Miss Pacey, she'd have to wait. He wasn't done yet.

But it wasn't. It was Mike. His friend turned his head to look at Jordan, then motioned for him to come inside. Grabbing a rag, Jordan entered the shop, curious. "Hey. What's up? You have news on the remains we found?"

"Actually, yes. Can you tell me where you were roughly eight weeks ago?"

Jordan's spine stiffened. "What? Why? Who is it you found?"

"Just answer the question, Jordan."

"He was in Costa Rica with me, most likely. Or Arkansas," Edie interjected. She came out from behind the counter to stand beside Jordan. "What's this about?"

Mike stared at them for a beat. "We found more remains. A leg and part of a torso. It's a woman. There were still clothes on the body. The M.E. found a piece of paper in her pocket. It had your number on it."

"My number?" Jordan pointed to his chest. "On a dead woman?"

Mike nodded.

"Do you have an ID on her?" Edie asked.

"No. We're still working on that. There was a little flesh left, which led the medical examiner to estimate she's been dead about eight weeks. He's running DNA. We're still looking for the rest of her. It looks like coyotes got a hold of her."

Jordan's stomach churned. That was not a pleasant picture. "I don't know who it could be. I haven't given my number out in a while. Not since I met Edie. The last person was Justine Lammers. Before that, I went out with a woman named Nicole Steiner. I haven't talked to either of them since our one and only date."

"Why didn't you see either of them again?"

"Mercy."

"Mercy? What? Were they pity dates?" Mike's frown mirrored his confusion.

"No. Mercy Dixon. She scared them both off. When I called Nicole to set up another date, she told me she didn't want to get in the middle of my relationship with Mercy. It didn't matter that I denied having a relationship with her. She didn't want the drama. A couple weeks later, I went out with Justine. I thought things went well, but she never returned my calls. I figured Mercy got to her too."

"Okay. I'll look into their whereabouts. And I'll talk to Mercy. Is there anyone else you can think of?"

Jordan shook his head. "Those are the two most recent. Anyone else, I don't know why they'd be carrying around my number. Was it my cell phone number? Or for the garage?"

"Your personal cell. Can you send me some verification of your trip if I need it?"

A quick skitter of unease slid down Jordan's spine. "Should I call a lawyer?"

"You can. But I don't plan to ask you any more questions right now. If I do, though, I would say yes, definitely."

"This is insane, Mike. I didn't hurt anyone."

"I know that, but I still have a job to do. And we don't know that she was murdered. Maybe she took a hike and got hurt, then couldn't get to help. We're still in the early stages of this. I'm just finding all the puzzle pieces right now."

Jordan blew out a breath. "Yeah, okay."

"I'll let you know what I find out. If you hear from either of those women, call me." Mike turned, heading for the door.

"I will."

With a quick nod, Mike left.

Edie crossed her arms and stared after him. "I don't like this."

"You heard him. She could have died from an accident. And I know I didn't do it if she was murdered."

"Right, but with the love notes you've been getting, and now a body in the desert with your phone number on her?" She shook her head and dropped her arms. "I'm calling Asher." She walked back to the desk.

"Asher? Why?"

"To give him a heads up. Maybe he can hack a camera or something and see who entered the park back then. Get an ID."

Jordan raised an eyebrow. "He's not God, Edie. Evidence doesn't just magically appear for him." He didn't even know if there were cameras at the park. Near the visitor's center, sure. But elsewhere? He doubted it. "Even if he can get into the stored footage, there's nothing that says he'll be able to identify the right person. Thousands of people visit that park every week."

"I know that." She gave him a fierce frown as she picked up her phone. "But I've seen him do crazier things. If anyone can find out who that woman is, it's Asher Horn."

FOURTEEN

Edie stared at the poems Jordan had received, trying to pick out clues. Asher had asked her to send pictures of them, which she did. But while she had them all out, she wanted to look at them again. Asher had seen the same pattern she had; the escalation of this woman's obsession. It wasn't hard to imagine where this would leave if they didn't stop her. It may have already reached that point.

She sighed and rubbed her eyes. It had already been a long day.

Her phone rang. She picked it up and saw a FaceTime call from Ezra coming in, making some of her fatigue melt away. With a smile, she answered. "Hey. Oh! Hi, baby." She waved at the infant sitting on Ezra's lap. His daughter, Gretchen, was four months old. The baby cooed and continued to chew on the plastic ring clutched in her tiny hands. "Gosh, she's gotten so big."

"It's because she eats all the time." He smiled, glancing at the girl.

"Well, that's what she's supposed to do."

"I guess. So, how are you doing? Ford told me about your

little trip. Have you killed Jordan yet?" His blue eyes carried a mischievous twinkle.

Edie sighed. "No. There have been times I've wanted to. But no, he's still kicking."

Ezra chuckled. "Good. Fill me in on what's going on. Is there anything I can do to help?"

"From North Carolina? No. There's not a whole lot anyone can do right now. Jordan's received several unsigned love poems. He thinks they're from a woman named Mercy Dixon. I called Asher, and he's digging into her life. He's also looking into a couple of women Jordan dated briefly. We found some skeletonized remains when we went hiking Saturday. The authorities think it's a woman, and they found a piece of paper in her pocket with Jordan's cell number on it."

Ezra let out a low whistle. "Whoa. Freaky."

"Yeah. They don't know who she is yet."

Gretchen let out a squall and waved her plastic ring. Ezra bounced her on his knee. "Do they have an idea?"

"I'm not sure. And even if they do, she'll be hard to identify. They've only found her torso and one arm."

His eyes widened. "She was dismembered?"

"No. Well, probably not. The police think scavengers got a hold of her body. The arm and hand bones I found were under some scrub brush."

"Oh. That makes sense." He bit the corner of his mouth and glanced to the side.

Edie frowned. "Hey, are you okay?"

"Huh?" He looked at her. "Oh. Yeah. Just—preoccupied."

"With what?"

"Life. Did Ford tell you Brooke wants us to move down to Costa Rica?"

"I heard that rumor, yes." Honestly, she wasn't surprised. Brooke and Ezra had a bond that went beyond employer and employee. He'd saved her life. He was good at that. "Do you not want to move?"

He sighed. "It's not that. I just—" He paused and shrugged. "I want to be settled, is all. I thought we were here. I'd like to stop moving. Have more babies and watch them grow up, you know?"

"What does Amy think?"

"She's gung-ho for this new project. And I don't blame her. It sounds exciting."

"Maybe you should talk to her about how you feel." She did not want to offer him any advice other than that. As much as she cared about Ezra and would love to have him down there close by, he needed to hash things out with his wife.

"Yeah. I plan to. I guess I just wanted to hear what another woman thought of a move like that."

Edie rolled her lips in, taking a breath through her nose. *Oh boy.* "I think it depends on the woman. And that you need to talk to your wife."

He huffed. "Fine."

She chuckled. "You act like you're afraid of her."

"I am. She's only gotten more fierce since Gretchen was born. But I'm probably overthinking this. It just seems like a big move, you know? Taking our family to another country."

Edie shrugged. "Maybe. You've never shied away from risk before, though."

"Yeah, but there weren't kids involved then."

"I think you'll all be fine. Humans are built to adapt. But talk to her. She might have some of the same fears you do. It might help if neither of you feel like you're alone in that."

He tipped his head. "I never thought of it like that."

"Where is Amy, anyway?"

"At a fundraising event. She'll be home in a couple of hours. Until then, it's just me and the munchkin." His voice softened, as did his expression when he looked at his daughter.

He bounced the girl again and blew a raspberry on her cheek, making her giggle.

Edie grinned. They were adorable.

A knock on her bedroom door sounded. She turned. "Come in."

The door swung in, and Jordan loomed large in the doorway. "Hey. I popped some popcorn. You wanna watch a movie?"

"Sure." She could use the distraction. She wasn't getting anywhere staring at the poems. "Give me a minute?" She tipped her head to the phone in her hand.

Jordan frowned, seeing the man on the screen. He waved. "Hello."

"Hi," Ezra said. "Come closer."

Edie closed her eyes for a quick moment. She knew that tone. Ezra was about to go big brother on her. She sighed.

Jordan walked in, hovering near the back of her chair.

"Jordan, this is Ezra. Ezra, Jordan."

A look of recognition replaced Jordan's curious frown. "Ah. I've heard your name mentioned. It's nice to meet you."

"You too. I was telling Edie that if you guys need anything to let me know. I can be there in a few hours."

"Don't be so quick to shirk your boring dad-life," Edie said.

A sardonic smile tilted his lips. "I used to wish for more boring days. Who knew I'd miss being a Night Stalker?"

Edie chuckled. "I did. But what you have now—it's worth the more sedate pace."

Ezra looked at Gretchen. "Yeah. Yeah, it is." His smile widened. "Okay. I'm going to go now so you can watch your movie. This one needs a bath and a bottle and to get to bed." He stood the baby up on his knee. "Wave bye to Aunt Edie." He lifted the baby's fist and waved it. Gretchen squealed and stomped her tiny feet.

Edie laughed. "Bye, sweet girl." She waved.

"All right. Call me if you need help." Ezra gave her a stern look.

"I will. Go put her to bed."

"Yep. Goodnight."

"'Night." She touched the screen and ended the call.

"Aunt Edie?"

She looked back at Jordan, who stared at her with one eyebrow raised.

"I didn't realize you had that kind of relationship with him."

"It's complicated."

"How? Who is he? I mean, I know he's a military pilot you all know, but there's more there." He frowned. "Did you two used to date?"

"No. We—served together." She stood up, forcing him to back away or get hit by the chair. "I don't want to talk about it."

Jordan held up his hands. "Okay. What movie do you want to watch?"

Grateful he let it go, she shrugged. "Something fun. We have enough drama going on already."

"Sounds good." He turned and led the way out.

Edie followed, brushing a hand through her hair. A quick flash of twisted metal and flames went through her head. She slammed the door on those thoughts. They could stay where she'd locked them away.

After grabbing the popcorn and some drinks from the kitchen, they settled onto the couch. Jordan picked up the remote and turned on a streaming app.

"Tell me if something looks interesting." He started scrolling.

Edie only partially paid attention, nodding absently when he stopped on a dramatic comedy. The movie started, but she struggled to watch. She was too busy trying to reinforce the walls of the prison she'd built around her memories.

"Hey." Jordan's hand covered hers. "Are you okay?"

She looked at him. "Of course. Why wouldn't I be?"

He studied her; those gray eyes stripping away layers and making her feel like a bug under a microscope. She held his gaze, though, refusing to let him see any weakness.

"I don't know. But you're not fine. You haven't watched any of the movie."

"Yes, I have."

"Okay. What happened in the last few minutes?"

Edie glanced at the screen. It was frozen on two characters talking in what looked like a museum. "They had a conversation."

"About what?"

She pressed her lips together. "I'm fine, Jordie."

"Don't."

"Don't what?"

"Don't throw up your walls and shut me out. If you don't want to talk about it, that's fine. But don't lie to me."

Edie clenched her jaw and swallowed. Damn the man. He wasn't supposed to be understanding and kind. She could deal with him better when he was his usual charming, happy-go-lucky self. "Fine. I have stuff on my mind. I'll deal with it. It's no big deal."

"That's another lie. You don't let things get to you, I've noticed. Not like this. I still think you should talk about it, but I get wanting to keep secrets. There are just some things that are too painful to discuss."

She frowned, hearing something in his tone. "What is it in your past that makes you feel that way?"

He drew in a deep breath. "I'll talk if you will."

Her jaw worked. Dammit. He would go and turn that around on her. "Never mind. I'm not that curious."

"Edie."

"No. I'm sorry, Jordan. I can't talk about it."

"Maybe that's why you should."

The low, caring tone of his voice threatened to tear down the walls she'd just shored up. Part of her wanted to tell him everything. She'd never felt the urge to do that before. With anyone.

Fearful of her own feelings, she stood up. "You know, I'm pretty tired. I think I'll go to bed. Goodnight."

"You can't run from how you feel forever, Edie. Eventually, it'll catch up. Don't get so tired you can't fight back."

When did he get so wise? She shook off the thought. It didn't matter. She looked at him. "There's nothing to fight. It's all chained up."

"Chains rust and break."

Edie sighed. "Not mine. Goodnight." She hurried away before he could say more. Or before she could admit he was right.

FIFTEEN

The smile of welcome on Edie's face died when she saw who walked through the door. "Hello, Mercy." She'd forgotten until now that the woman had an appointment to get her car serviced today.

Lips tight, Mercy walked forward. "Hello. Still here, I see."

Edie fought to keep her expression polite. "Yes. I don't really have plans to go anywhere." And not just because she wasn't getting anywhere on her search for a replacement receptionist. Someone needed to fight off the women Jordan attracted.

Mercy hummed and laid her keys on the desk. "Will this take long? I have a lunch date with a friend at noon."

Taking the keys, Edie shrugged. "He's a little behind. You might want to call your friend and tell them you could be late."

Mercy's mouth tightened even more. "I'll just go talk to Jordan. I'm sure he'll understand." She moved toward the door set into the wall of windows.

"You can't go in there."

The woman stopped and turned angry blue eyes on Edie. "Why not?"

"It's a liability thing. There are numerous ways you could get hurt out there." Edie offered her a sweet smile. "I'm sure you understand."

A muscle twitched in Mercy's jaw. "He's never had an issue with it before."

"Yes, well, he's usually too busy to notice such things. But I'm here now, and my number one goal is to make Jordan's business run efficiently. Taking time out to talk to you will just add to his backup. Why don't you have a seat? Would you like some coffee while you wait?" She would kill this woman with kindness. It was kind of fun to watch her get angrier the longer Edie went without giving her the response she wanted.

"I'm fine, thank you." Mercy walked over to the bank of chairs near the window and perched on one.

Edie logged her car into the system, then put the work order and the keys into a hanging pouch and put it with the others. Mercy's car was next, since it wasn't a drop-off, but Jordan was finishing a repair on one that was.

The phone rang, and she answered it, adding an appointment to the calendar for next week. When she hung up, her gaze naturally traveled the room. Mercy stared at her. Edie did her best to ignore the woman. She could think whatever she wanted. No doubt, she was imagining ways to get Edie out of Jordan's life.

"I've never known Jordan to date someone so... athletic." Mercy said the word like she'd called Edie ugly.

"Oh? I guess he's decided he wants someone willing to go with him on his adventures into the outdoors."

Mercy scoffed. "Jordan doesn't like the outdoors that much. He'd rather work on a car."

Mentally, Edie rolled her eyes. Mercy didn't know Jordan at all. She only knew the man she wanted to know, who was based on some ideal she'd made up in her mind. "Yes, well, I can do that too."

"I don't doubt it." Mercy held up a hand, checking her perfect nails. "Some women are just built for physical labor."

Edie wanted to laugh. She'd much rather work on a car or do any other kind of "physical labor" than sit around on her butt painting her nails and worrying about her hair. She knew that if the zombie apocalypse hit, she'd survive. Mercy, though, would be one of the first to get eaten.

"All I can say is, all that muscle must make you good in bed. I can't imagine what else he sees in you."

Edie clenched her teeth. "I'm not rude, like some people." She pinned Mercy with a stare.

The other woman tipped her nose up but didn't say anything else. Thankfully, the phone rang again, cutting off their conversation.

As she hung up, Jordan came through the door to drop off the paperwork for the job he just completed and to grab the next work order. He spotted Mercy, nodded at her in greeting, then looked at Edie. "Can you order us some lunch? I'll change the oil in Mercy's car, then we can eat."

"Sure." She pulled a pad of sticky notes closer. "What do you want?"

"Sandwiches are fine. Or a wrap. Ham or chicken. You know what I like."

She nodded. "Do you want chips and a drink?"

"Just chips. And a cookie."

She jotted that down.

"You really should eat better, Jordan," Mercy said. "Why don't you come to lunch with me?"

"Won't your friend mind?" Edie said.

Mercy glared at her. "No." She looked at Jordan. "Let me buy you a steak. We're going to Milago's. I'm sure you've worked up an appetite."

"I'm good, Mercy. But thank you." He lifted the clear pouch with the work order for her car. "I'll have your vehicle done in about thirty minutes. Did you need anything besides an oil change and fluid top-up?"

Mouth turned down, she shook her head.

"Okay. I'll be back soon." With that, he ducked out of the room.

Edie opened the food delivery app on her phone and found the local sub shop Jordan liked. She spent the next few minutes putting in their order and was grateful that the garage phone stayed silent.

Unwilling to sit at the counter and act busy while Mercy sat there glaring daggers at her, Edie went into the breakroom and grabbed the broom. She'd tidy up a bit. There was always sand to sweep up, she'd noticed. It was a lot like home, actually. She kept expecting to walk out the door and see the ocean. All she saw here, though, was more sand and some cacti.

The next half hour passed in a slow march as Edie tried to find things to keep herself busy. The phone was uncharacteristically silent. She almost went out into the garage and asked Jordan if she could help him, but stopped herself. She didn't want Mercy to come back and try to claim Edie sabotaged her car. The woman was probably petty enough to do that.

When their food arrived, she welcomed the distraction. Smiling at and thanking the driver, she took the bag into the breakroom and arranged the food on plates. She heard the inner door open, then Jordan's voice telling Mercy her car was ready.

Setting the plates on the counter, she went back to the desk. "Go wash up and eat. I'll check her out."

"You're sure?"

Edie nodded.

He smiled, then pecked her on the cheek. "Thanks, babe. I'm starving." Turning, he walked away.

Edie looked at Mercy and smiled. "Let's get you on your way, shall we? So you don't miss your lunch date."

Mercy stayed stoic as Edie checked her out. She took her keys with a glare and stomped out of the office.

"Bye." Edie waved at her, but doubted Mercy saw or heard her. The door was already swinging shut. Chuckling, she went into the breakroom. Jordan sat at the little table, inhaling his sandwich. She picked up her plate and sat across from him.

"Thanks for ordering lunch."

"You're welcome." She unwrapped her sandwich and took a bite.

"Mercy didn't look very happy."

Edie chuckled. "She tried to insult me, but I wouldn't rise to the bait. Then she had to watch you kiss me and call me babe. Maybe it'll make her angry enough she'll leave you another love note and we can catch her in the act."

"That would be great. One less thing to worry about. I don't suppose Mike called with an update, did he?"

"No."

Jordan grimaced. "Damn. I'd really like to know who that was we found."

So would Edie. Asher hadn't had any luck in finding out, either. He was still running down info on the names she gave him.

"I don't know how they ever catch and convict people. Justice runs at a snail's pace."

"You got that right."

"Let's talk about something more pleasant. What do you want to do this weekend?" He crunched on a chip.

"We don't have to do anything."

He arched an eyebrow. "We're supposed to be making people aware of our relationship. Can't do that if we're just sitting at home."

She pressed her lips together. "Fine."

"How about Sabino Canyon? There are waterfalls there. We could go into Tucson for dinner afterward."

"I guess that would be okay."

He chuckled. "Don't sound so excited."

Edie huffed and raised a chip to her mouth. "Sorry. I'm not used to one, having a boyfriend, and two, to planning things. Not anymore, anyway. I work. I surf. Occasionally, I have dinner with the guys. Most nights, I hole up in my little cottage with a book."

"I usually work on my project car. My Porsche is starting to feel neglected."

She sat a little straighter. "You have a Porsche?"

He nodded. "An old one. Nineteen seventy-six Carrera."

"That's one of the original nine-elevens. Not the newer ones with the fancy stuff."

His eyebrows shot up. "You know Porsches?"

"My dad and grandpa both love cars. I grew up around all that."

"It makes more sense now why you're so good at the front desk. I'll show it to you tonight, if you want. It's in my shop at home."

"Sure." It had been a while since she'd gotten her hands greasy on a car. It might be a nice change of pace. She'd enjoyed working with Jordan the last couple of weeks.

The phone rang, and she got up to answer it. Walking into the reception area, something in the garage caught her eye. Smoke drifted through the air.

"Jordan!" Not waiting for him, she ran through the door, looking for the source. It seeped in under the large bay doors.

"What's wrong? Oh, shit." He whirled, grabbing the fire extinguisher from the wall.

Edie waited until he had it ready, then pressed the button to roll up the door. A small pile burned near the door.

"What is that?" he asked.

"I don't know. Put it out so we can look."

He pointed the nozzle at the flames and squeezed the trigger. White foam shot out, smothering the fire.

Edie picked up a crowbar and crouched next to the smoldering pile. She poked through it. "It looks like pictures."

"Of what?" He sank to his haunches next to her.

She nudged a ruined picture aside, revealing a face on another. She looked at Jordan. "You."

Sixteen

Jordan swiped a hand down his face and stared at the smoldering pile of paper while they waited on the police. Why would someone burn pictures of him and leave them for him to find? It didn't make any sense. Mercy's notes had been love poems.

His gaze strayed to Edie. Unless they were meant as a warning for him. That she wasn't happy about his new relationship.

Well, too bad. Even if it wasn't real, he liked Edie. Sure, she drove him crazy some days, but she was funny and smart. Witty. Gorgeous. Not for the first time, he wondered if it would be worth it to persuade her to turn this into something real.

An unmarked police car turned into the lot. Jordan glanced up, frowning when he recognized the driver. Mike parked nearby and got out.

"What are you doing here? Why didn't dispatch just send a uniformed officer to take the report?"

Mike walked closer, his gaze on the charred pile on the ground. "I heard it come in and recognized the address. I know you're technically in town, but with what's going on, I wondered if it might be related, so I told them I'd take the call. What happened?"

"We were eating lunch, and I got up to answer the phone," Edie said. "I saw the smoke coming in under the door. Jordan put it out with the fire extinguisher." She pointed to the red canister sitting by the building.

"Did either of you touch anything?"

"I used a crowbar to see what it was." Edie crossed her arms. "Once I saw the picture of Jordan, I stopped and we called you."

"Good." Mike walked closer to the burned pile and took a folding ruler and a small camera from his jacket pocket. He laid the ruler on the ground next to the pile and snapped a couple of pictures, then, using a pen, he rifled through the paper. A few times, he paused to take more pictures.

Jordan stared over his shoulder, feeling sick as he saw more of what was there. Most of those pictures were recent, but in a few, he could tell they were taken over the summer because of the way he was dressed. Whoever had taken them had been watching him for a long time.

Mike got up and walked to his car, opening the trunk. He came back a few moments later with a paper sack and a small broom and dustpan. With careful, efficient movements, he swept the burned pictures into the pan and dumped them into the paper sack. Folding it closed, he sealed it with a label and wrote on it. "Okay. I need statements from you both. Hang on a second." He walked back to his car and put the bag in the trunk, then came back with a clipboard. "Let's go inside."

Jordan turned and led the way, heading for the breakroom. They settled around the table, and Mike passed them each a sheet of paper. "Fill out the info at the top, then write exactly what happened in your own words."

Silence reigned in the room for several minutes while he and Edie wrote. Jordan filled his page, then read through it, making sure he didn't miss anything. Once he was sure it sounded okay, he signed the bottom, then slid it across the table to Mike. Edie did the same a minute later.

Mike skimmed them, nodding as he finished. "Can you show me your security footage? Maybe it caught something."

Jordan grimaced. "Doubtful. All my cameras are inside, except one, which is pointed straight out from the door to encompass most of the parking lot. It doesn't get much of the front of the building. The cameras in the garage bays point at the bays."

"Well, let's look anyway."

The bell over the front door chimed.

Edie glanced out front. "You two go look at the footage. I'll see who's out there."

"You're sure?" Jordan asked.

"Yes." She got up and left.

Jordan led Mike into the office, then sat down behind his desk and logged into the computer. He found the folder that stored the security camera footage and opened it. "There you go." He got up and gestured for Mike to take his place.

Sitting down, Mike scrolled. Jordan stood behind him and watched. The only car that came into view was Mercy's as she left.

"Who's that?" Mike pointed at the screen.

"Mercy. She brought her car in for routine service. She left just before we spotted the fire."

"Really?" A thoughtful look crossed his face.

Jordan could tell what he was thinking. He'd had a similar thought. That maybe Mercy had moved on from scaring away the women in Jordan's life and turned her intimidation tactics on him.

"What time did you spot the fire? Do you remember?"

"Not exactly." A thought occurred to him. "But the phone rang. That's why Edie spotted the fire when she did. She got up to answer the phone. There will be a record of the time."

"Perfect." Mike jotted down the timestamp on the video, then got up. "Let's go look at the phone."

They went out front, where Edie was talking to the customer that came in. Jordan nodded to Jim Franks.

"Jim. How are you?"

"Can't complain. Especially not when I get to talk to this pretty lady. Where did you find her?"

"Edie's my girlfriend. She's helping out until I can find someone permanent."

"I think you should just hire her full time. Best welcome I've ever had here." He smiled at Edie again.

Jordan fought to keep the eye roll in check. Divorced and on the far side of middle-aged, Jim Franks was forever flirting with younger women.

"I'm glad I could make your experience with us a good one," Edie said. She offered the man a polite smile. "Why don't you have a seat? Jordan will get to your vehicle as soon as he can."

Jim tipped his head in acknowledgement. "Sounds good." He ambled away and sank into a chair.

Edie turned to them, her polite smile turning exasperated. "I'm really glad your uniform is a t-shirt and not a polo," she said, keeping her voice low. "He'd probably have tried to look down my shirt." She made a face. "Bleck. Anyway, what's up?"

"We need to look at the recent call history. Get a time-stamp on that phone call that brought you out here," Jordan said.

"Oh." She stepped to the side and gestured to the phone. "Have at it."

Jordan moved forward and hit the buttons that would bring up the call history. He showed Mike the call.

"Okay." Mike wrote it down.

Jordan did the math in his head. Mercy left a couple of minutes before Edie noticed the smoke. "Is it possible, Mike? Did she set the fire?"

"Maybe. In any case, I need to talk to her. If she didn't, she might have seen something."

"She said she was headed to lunch with a friend. Milago's, right?" Edie looked at Jordan.

He nodded.

"Okey-doke. I'll go track her down." He didn't make a move to leave, though. Instead, he stared at Jordan.

"What?"

"Any idea who might want to leave burning pictures of you outside your place of business? Other than Mercy, I mean? Because I feel like there's more going on. Call it detective's intuition."

Jordan's gaze flicked to Edie. She pressed her lips together and nodded.

Mike frowned. "What's going on? What do you two know?"

Jordan glanced past him at Jim. The man stared at his phone, but didn't scroll, obviously trying to listen in. "Let's talk in the back."

The three of them traipsed into the breakroom, and Jordan closed the door until it was open just a sliver.

Mike crossed his arms and arched an eyebrow, silently waiting.

Jordan sucked in a breath. "Edie and I aren't actually dating."

"What?" Mike's frown deepened. "What does that have to do with—"

"I'll explain." Jordan held up a hand.

"Please do."

"So, you know about how Mercy scared off my dates."

Mike nodded once.

"Around the same time, I started receiving notes. Love poems. They'd show up under the wipers on my car. I had one slipped under my front door at home. Since it was around the time I last talked to Nicole Steiner and Justine Lammers, I figured it was Mercy."

"Why didn't you report this? And what does she have to do with it?" He nodded to Edie.

"Actually, I tried to report it. I called the station, and the officer I talked to basically gave me the brush off. I wasn't too concerned, then, though. Mercy seems harmless; you know that. I figured she'd eventually get tired of chasing after me and set her sights on some other poor soul. Except she hasn't. I told Dean about it, which is why Edie's here. They're friends, and she and I met in Costa Rica just before the notes started. He made what I thought was a joke about me needing a girlfriend. The next thing I knew, Edie was at my door."

He stopped and rubbed his temple. "The idea was to show Mercy I was with someone. Someone she couldn't scare off."

"Well, obviously, it's not working."

"No."

Mike sighed. "Okay. I guess I need to talk to Mercy for other reasons now. Do you have these notes still?"

"They're at home."

"Bring them to me after work. Is there anything else you're hiding from me?"

"No. That was it, I swear." Jordan held up his hands.

"Good. If you get any more letters or anything else happens, you call me immediately." He stared hard at Jordan, then Edie, clearly not pleased.

"We will," Jordan said.

With another long look, Mike walked around them and left.

"Well, that went well," Edie said, staring after him.

Jordan huffed a short laugh that turned into a groan as the door chimed with Mike's exit. "Yeah." What a mess.

SEVENTEEN

E die shut herself in her bedroom and called Asher. She didn't know what was taking so long for him to track down those women. Considering what happened today, she wanted an update. Things were escalating. They needed more information.

He picked up on the second ring. "Hey. How's Tucson?"

"Escalating. What have you found out about Justine Lammers and Nicole Steiner? It's been almost a week. How do you not have anything?" She knew she sounded demanding and harsh, but she couldn't help it. The fire had her rattled.

"Whoa. What crawled up your butt?"

"Sorry." She huffed and sat down on the bed. "I'm a little on edge. Someone set fire to a bunch of pictures of Jordan right outside his shop in town. Our plan to scare off his stalker isn't working."

Asher sucked in a quick breath. "Well, crap."

Edie could picture him running a hand through his hair.

"I haven't called because there isn't much to report. As far as I can tell, Nicole Steiner is going about her daily life like normal. I've tracked her on some public cameras, and nothing looks suspicious. Justine Lammers, I haven't seen at all. She works from home, so that's not surprising. If she does grocery delivery, she'd have little reason to leave."

"You haven't seen her anywhere? Not even a coffeeshop or a restaurant?" It felt strange that Justine wouldn't appear anywhere. Edie could understand that if it had only been a week or so, but it had been two months.

"Not one near a public safety camera, no."

"Hmm... Are you able to pull up her credit card history?"

He groaned. "I don't like doing that. Credit card companies are getting better and better about thwarting unauthorized users. I'd rather not get caught."

Edie's mouth twisted. "Fine. I just think it's weird you haven't spotted her anywhere. Maybe I should drive over there and take a peek at her house."

"What do you mean by 'take a peek?' If you mean break in, don't."

"Relax. I wasn't planning on that. But I might knock on her door. Pretend to be selling something. Or I might just sit outside her house and watch for activity."

"Do you want me to ask Dean to come up? He's better at surveillance."

"He is, but no. If too many people come into Jordan's life, it might make whoever this is suspicious."

"You don't think it's Mercy anymore?"

"I'm not sure what to think. I know what Jordan's said, and I know how she's acted in my presence. Beyond that, I don't have any evidence that she's the one behind this. There are so many women who could be doing this. He draws them like flies to a picnic without even trying. It could literally be someone he barely knows. I think we need to keep all the possibilities open."

"I agree. From what I've been able to uncover, I don't think it's Nicole Steiner. Her routines are just too regular.

He's getting these notes at all different times on different days of the week, yes?"

"Yeah."

"She works a steady nine-to-five job. It's not her."

Edie sighed. "Okay. So how do we figure out who it is, then?"

"We just have to wait. I know that's not what you want to hear, but it's the truth. Are the police involved now?"

"Yes. Jordan left a little while ago to take the notes to the detective. He's the same guy investigating the body we found in the desert." They'd come home from work and Jordan had grabbed the notes and headed back to town. Edie stayed behind to call Asher and make dinner.

"Maybe they'll get some prints or DNA off of them."

"Maybe." She wasn't hopeful, though. "This is turning into more than I bargained for. I thought I'd be coming up here to act all lovey-dovey to convince some crazy bitch to leave him alone, then quietly fade away once she gave up. It's more serious than that. I'm worried she'll hurt him."

"I'm more worried she'll hurt you."

There was that, yes. "I'm being careful."

"I'm sure you are. Just don't underestimate this woman or get complacent. Stalkers can be capable of some scary stuff, even if they seem like the most unassuming person."

That was definitely not Mercy Dixon. But it did fit some of the other women she'd met. It was all a big mess.

After enquiring about how the others were doing and chatting for a few more minutes, Edie hung up. She traipsed back to the kitchen to finish dinner, mind still whirling with the possibilities. She didn't know what to think.

Eighteen

Jordan walked into the police station carrying the file folder of letters and asked to speak to Mike. The officer working the front desk had him sign in, then gave him a visitor's badge and showed him back.

Mike looked up as Jordan and the officer approached. "Hey. Thanks for coming in."

Jordan nodded and took a seat on the other side of the desk. The officer who escorted him left. "Not a problem. I want to find out who's behind this. I'm sick of the games she's playing." He handed Mike the folder.

"Is this all of them?"

"Yeah."

Mike opened the folder.

"They're in order of when I got them. Edie noticed a pattern. They've gotten progressively darker."

Mike's brow furrowed as he read through them. "Yeah, I would agree." He closed the folder. "Why did you wait so long to come to me?"

Jordan lifted a shoulder. "They're just notes. Sure, it's

weird, but there's nothing menacing about them. It's more annoying than anything else. Like I said earlier, I figured it was Mercy, and she couldn't take a hint."

"I don't think it's her."

"What?" Jordan sat forward. "Why not?"

"The business down the street from you has cameras. She pulled onto the street about a minute after she walked out your front door. Not enough time for her to pull the materials from her car, place them, set the fire, and then leave. She didn't do it."

"Did those cameras catch who did?"

Mike's mouth pursed. "No. You sit too far down in a hole. You need more cameras outside. That one you have only shows a slice of your parking lot."

"Dammit." Jordan slumped back and frowned.

"The lab is working on the burned material I scooped up. I'll get this to them too. Maybe we'll get lucky and they'll find the same prints on both. Then it's a slam dunk."

"So long as the prints are on file."

"True. But it's still a place to start. I'll figure it out. You can tell your fake girlfriend she can go home."

Jordan's frown deepened. He didn't want to do that. Having Edie around was nice. He still hadn't thought of a way to convince her to go on a date with him for real.

"Jordan?"

Blinking, Jordan looked at his friend. A knowing smile sat on Mike's face.

"You like her, don't you?"

"Maybe. But don't tell her that. She'll run."

Mike held up his hands. "Your secret is safe with me. I hope she does stay. You seem happy with her. Just make sure you two leave the detecting to me, yeah?"

Jordan pressed his lips together. "I promise to try."

Mike frowned, then sighed. "She's right. You're trouble."

A quick grin flashed over Jordan's face. "So is she."

"Wonderful." Mike shooed him away. "Go home. I'll let you know when I get results back."

"Sounds good. Thanks, Mike." Jordan stood.

"Oh, one more thing. Carmen wants to know if you guys want to have dinner Saturday night."

"Sure. Let me double check with Edie, but I don't think that will be a problem." He would get her there one way or another. He wanted her to get to know his friends. "Can I text you tonight or tomorrow?"

"Yep."

"Okay. I'll see you later." With a nod, Jordan left.

After turning in his visitor's badge and signing out, he climbed into his truck and headed for home. The road hummed under his tires, but it couldn't drown out the whine the engine took on when he got into the hills and the grade changed.

Letting off the gas, he used the paddle shifters and changed to a lower gear. It helped but didn't eliminate it. He groaned. "Oh, come on. You're practically brand new." Cursing modern car manufacturing, he coaxed the truck up the road. This was why he preferred older vehicles. They were just built differently. Modern cars had too many parts.

The truck kept slowing. No matter how hard he pressed the accelerator, it wouldn't go any faster. His transmission was gone. Jordan coaxed it to the side of the road and shut off the engine, setting the parking brake. Grabbing a flashlight from under the seat, he popped the hood and got out. He shined the light on the engine, looking for anything amiss. From the top, nothing looked wrong. Laying down on the ground, he tipped his head and pointed the light at the truck's underbelly. A wetness coated the undercarriage.

Jordan reached a hand in and swiped his fingers through it, then sniffed it. "Damn." It was sweet and had a reddish tint. He was leaking transmission fluid.

Standing up, he opened the driver's door and reached for his phone in the console to call Edie to come get him. He'd call his buddy Everett, who ran a towing service, and have him tow the truck to the garage in the morning.

He found Edie's name in his contacts and called her. It rang several times before she picked up.

"Hey. You on your way home? Dinner's ready."

He smiled at the picture she painted. It was nice having someone to come home to. "Not quite. My truck broke down. Can you come get me?"

A beat of silence passed. "Isn't it new?"

"Newish. It's leaking transmission fluid and won't accelerate. A hose probably popped off, or I hit a rock and poked a hole in the line. I'm about a mile from the house. Just drive toward town. You can't miss me."

"Okay. I'll be down in a few minutes."

"Thanks." He hung up. Leaning against the door frame, he texted Everett, asking him to come pick up the truck in the morning. Thirty seconds later, his friend responded, agreeing.

A burst of light caught his attention from the corner of his eye. Jordan lifted his head and turned to see a light blue mid-size SUV turning onto the road at the base of the hill. He stepped out away from the truck, ready to greet the driver and tell them everything was fine. A frown creased his forehead, though, as he realized the vehicle wasn't slowing. Around here, if people saw someone on the side of the road, they stopped. But this car wasn't. If anything, it was coming faster.

He stepped back, closing the door and edging toward the rear of his truck. The car's engine revved. Jordan kept going, skirting the tailgate. He wasn't sure what this guy was up to, but he wanted to be well clear of his car. He had no desire to get squished.

The car veered right, coming directly at him. Jordan dove for the scrub, rolling as he landed. The car entered the dirt on the passenger side of his truck and went around it, back onto the road.

Sitting up, he watched as the car screeched to a halt. It idled for a moment, then backed up. Jordan sank lower, not wanting to be seen. The driver shifted the car into park, then opened their door. The interior light didn't come on, so Jordan couldn't see who it was.

Headlights rounded the bend a hundred yards further up the road. The driver of the car that almost hit him slammed the door and put the car in gear, doing a quick three-point turn and racing back down the hill.

Jordan waited to make sure it kept going. The other car neared, slowing down. It was Edie. She pulled up beside his truck, and he stood from his hiding spot. He walked toward her as she got out.

"Jordan?"

"Over here."

She turned, peering through the darkness. He turned on the flashlight so she could see him.

"What are you doing over there?"

"Did you see that car that just turned around?"

"Yeah. I figured they stopped to see if you needed help."

"They didn't. They tried to run me over." He still couldn't believe it.

"What?"

"Yep." He reached her.

She stared at him with wide eyes, then blinked, turning to look at his truck, then back to him. "What are the odds you broke down on accident?"

Jordan's lips flattened. "Not good. I think I might get

Everett to come tonight now to tow my car, instead of in the morning."

"I would. You need to call Detective Deyo too."

He rubbed his forehead and sighed. "Yeah." Mike was going to love this.

NINETEEN

Edie followed the tow truck to town, a fierce frown on her face. Why would someone try to run over Jordan? Was it his stalker? If so, why did she escalate so quickly? It didn't make any sense. A couple of weeks ago, she was sending love poems. Today, she lit pictures of him on fire and tried to kill him? Why? What changed?

She didn't have any answers, but this case just became much more serious. After Jordan looked at his truck and talked to Mike, they were going to have a serious conversation about his safety.

They pulled into the garage parking lot. Edie waited for Jordan to hop out so he could help Everett back his truck into a bay, then parked. Mike, who'd brought up the rear of their convoy, parked beside her. Loud beeps filled the air as she got out of her car. Everett leaned out the driver's side window, watching the orientation of Jordan's truck as he backed it into the garage. Eventually, Jordan let out a quick shout and crossed his arms like an X to halt him. Edie and Mike hung back while the two men unhooked the pickup.

Chains clanked as Jordan stowed them on the tow truck. "That should do it, Everett. Thanks."

"You're welcome. I hope you figure out what's wrong." Everett touched his temple, then tipped his fingers at him and climbed into his truck. The engine rumbled as he put it in gear and drove away.

Mike walked forward. "You ready to look at this thing?"

"Yes."

"Okay. I'm taking video of everything as you work. And you need to wear gloves."

Jordan nodded and turned, taking a couple steps to the workbench on the back wall. He grabbed a handful of black latex gloves and passed them out. Edie wasn't sure she'd need them, but she put them on anyway.

"We ready?" Jordan asked.

Mike turned on his digital camera. "Yep."

Jordan activated the lift and raised his truck until he could walk underneath it. Mike joined him, and Edie crowded around the edge, peering in. Mike raised a second camera and took several still photos before Jordan touched anything.

"What do you see so far?" Mike asked.

"Nothing except a bunch of transmission fluid residue that shouldn't be there."

"Can you tell where it came from?" Edie asked.

Jordan tipped his head and tilted the light. "Maybe. It looks like the majority of it ran down right here." He gestured to a spot with the light. Reaching up, he touched the hose and ran his hand along it. About six inches up, he paused.

"What?" Mike leaned closer.

"I feel the break. I can't see it though. It's on the side. I need to take it apart."

"Do it."

Jordan grabbed some tools and got to work. Mike continued to record, documenting every step.

Once the hose was out, Edie peered down at the hose Jordan held. A one-centimeter gash marred the surface. "That's a clean cut." She pointed.

"Yeah. A rock didn't do that." Jordan looked at Mike. "Someone sabotaged my truck."

"But where? You drove it into town and it worked fine, didn't it?" Mike frowned, stopping the video.

"It did. I didn't notice the sluggishness until I was on my way home. A cut like this, it would have drained fairly quickly. Someone probably did it while I was at the station."

Mike let out a low whistle. "Someone's bold. We have cameras."

"And I parked not far from the entrance."

"How about we go look at the footage, then?" Edie pulled off her gloves with a snap. She wanted to see who was on that recording. Although, she probably shouldn't. She had a ridiculous urge to track the woman down and beat her up.

Mike hesitated.

"Come on, Mike," Jordan said. "I might recognize the person."

"Fine. But give me that." He held out his hand for the hose.

Jordan passed it to him.

"Let's go." Mike spun on his heel and walked outside. Edie and Jordan followed, waiting for him to put the hose in an evidence bag, and then tailed him out of the parking lot to the sheriff's department.

Edie eyed the building as she pulled up, looking for the security cameras. Finding a parking spot that would have the best coverage, she parked. They went inside, where Mike signed them in, then he led them to a room full of people working at desks, snagging one of them with a tip of his head and a, "Follow me, Foster."

The young man glanced up, frowned, then pushed his

chair back and followed them into a room full of computer screens.

"How can I help you, detective?" The young man nudged his glasses up his nose.

"I need you to pull up the security footage from out front from a couple of hours ago."

The young man sat down and logged in. Edie crossed her arms and watched his fingers fly over the keyboard. A monitor to his right flickered to life and footage from the front of the building played on a split screen.

"This is live, but if we back it up..." His voice trailed off as the video on the screen rewound. "Tell me when."

The footage rewound for several seconds before Jordan spoke up. "There. That's my truck."

"Go slow from the time he arrived." Mike leaned in.

Edie stepped closer. Foster backed the video up to the point Jordan pulled in, then let it play. Because of where he parked, only one camera caught sight of his truck. The driver's side and the front right corner were in full view. It took several minutes before anything happened. Brake lights glowed on the road behind the pickup. A few moments later, a shadow appeared near the tailgate. It crept into the light pool from the streetlamp, highlighting a figure in a dark jacket and jeans.

"Does that look like a woman?" Edie tipped her head as she studied the figure.

"Maybe." Mike leaned a little closer. "It's hard to tell with that bulky coat. The hips look right to be female. Whoever it is, knows the camera is there."

Edie chewed on the inside of her lip, silently agreeing. The person had their hood up and kept their face pointed down. They skirted along the passenger side of the truck, then disappeared from view near the front right fender.

"That must be when they sabotaged my truck. It probably

is a woman. That person is on the small side. They'd be able to easily shimmy under the front and slice the line."

Mike glanced at him. "The question is, did they know what they were slicing? Or were they just hoping to disable you? Maybe the intent was to follow you and offer help."

"Then why didn't they stop? Why try to hit me?"

"Maybe she had time to think," Edie said. "As she followed you, I mean. Maybe she had time to think about why you were at the police station. About you and me dating. It could be something in her head snapped. I think it will be interesting to see what happens next. Whether the attacks continue or whether she goes back to her previous pattern of sending love notes. And what those notes say if she does."

"Agreed." Mike straightened. "Okay, Foster, make me a copy of that and send it to my email." He looked at Jordan and Edie and tipped his head toward the door.

Edie trailed the men out of the room.

"So, what do we do now?" Jordan asked when they stopped down the hall.

"You two go home and lock yourselves in." Mike gave them a pointed look. "I'm going to call my wife and tell her I'll be home late, then I'm going to see if any of the businesses across the street caught the vehicle on video that our perpetrator rode in."

"And if they didn't?" Jordan raised an eyebrow.

"Then we'll cross that bridge when we get to it. Go home." Mike's expression turned stern.

Jordan's eyebrows drew together and his mouth parted. Edie grabbed his hand and tugged, halting whatever he was about to say. He looked at her.

"Come on. Let's go home and eat. There's nothing more we can do tonight." She turned to Mike. "Thank you for your help. We'll let you get to work. I hope you don't have to stay too late."

"Thank you." Mike offered them a slight smile. "Have a good night." He lifted a hand in farewell, then turned and strode away.

Edie tugged on Jordan's hand and led him toward the door.

"Okay, why didn't you argue with him about going home? I want to know what he finds out. I know you do too."

"I do. But we'll be in the way. And he's your friend, so he'll keep you in the loop. You can talk to him in the morning." It was a valid reason for why they should leave, but it wasn't her only one. She was uneasy about leaving the house for too long. There was still no security system in place at Jordan's. She was hoping the woman decided enough was enough for tonight, but when someone went off the deep end, there was no guarantee how they would act.

Jordan blew out a breath. "Fine. Let's go home."

TWENTY

"Whoa." Edie tossed her hands up to block Jordan's kick. They were sparring again, and he was on a different level from the last time. She backed up, blocking several more moves, then ducked under his arm to get out of the corner. "Did you decide you didn't like being beat by a girl?"

"No." He came at her again.

She was ready this time. Snagging his arm, she pulled them together, then swept his feet out from under him. He rolled, though, and pinned her to the floor.

Breathing hard, she let her arms flop to the side. "Damn. What's gotten into you?"

Jordan rose and held out a hand to help her up. "Sorry. Did I hurt you?"

"No." She let him pull her to her feet. "You just seem more—focused, I guess. Are you okay?"

He ran a hand through his damp hair and shrugged. "Well enough, I suppose. I'm just anxious. I know it's only been two days, but Mike needs to hurry up and give me an update. If I'd been going through an intersection when my transmission died, and another car was coming, things could have been much worse than me needing to replace some parts on my truck. I'm tired of waiting for answers, and I wish I could do something—anything—to move things along." He stalked over to the bench by the wall and picked up his water to take a drink.

Edie agreed. But the justice system only moved as fast as it did. Sometimes, waiting was part of the game. She tipped her head as the idea she'd been mulling over since she last talked to Asher ran through her mind again. "You know, there is something we could do."

"What?"

"So, I can't shake the feeling that the woman we found in the desert and your stalker are connected. Mike was pretty sure it wasn't Nicole Steiner, but he hasn't said whether he's been able to get ahold of Justine. How about we take a trip into Tucson and see if we can track her down?"

He took another drink, eyeing her over the rim of the bottle. "Only one problem with that. I don't know where she lives."

Edie grinned. "Asher can tell us."

With a chuckle, he rolled his eyes. "I don't know how he puts up with you guys. You're constantly demanding he dig up stuff."

"He loves it. Honestly, I think he'd be bored to tears if he wasn't hacking into some database." She held up a hand. "Sorry, he doesn't like that term. Let's just go with digging."

Jordan chuckled again. "What did he used to do before he moved down there?"

"CIA analyst."

"Seriously?" Jordan's eyebrows shot up.

Edie nodded.

"Why did he leave?"

"He got burned out."

"Well, I'm glad he's on our side."

"Me too." Edie picked up her water. "Come on. Let's go change. I'll shoot him a text. It shouldn't take him long to find that information."

Ten minutes later, he proved her right. As she stepped out of the shower, her phone dinged from the counter. She glanced at it and saw his reply. After dressing and winding her wet hair into a braid, she headed downstairs. Jordan leaned against the counter, sipping coffee from a travel mug.

He turned when he heard her coming. "Hey. Ready?"

"Yep. As soon as I get some of that." She pointed at his mug.

He opened the cabinet in front of him and took out another travel cup.

She took it and poured the last of the coffee in it. "Okay, let's go."

"What's the address?" Jordan asked as they headed for the garage.

Edie took out her phone and read it to him.

He nodded. "I know where that is. Let's take the Bronco."

She wouldn't argue. If there was one thing she hated, it was navigating an unfamiliar place.

The road hummed beneath the tires as they headed down the mountain and toward Tucson. Edie sipped her coffee and watched the scenery pass. It was a pretty morning. A few wispy clouds decorated the bright blue sky. The sun bounced off the desert floor, giving the world a golden glow. There was a bite to the air, but she'd noticed it didn't seem quite as cold as when she first arrived. Spring was on its way.

They kept their conversation light until they reached Justine's neighborhood. He turned tense, and Edie's attention was on their surroundings. She saw a shopping mall and asked him to pull in.

"Why?" He changed lanes so he could turn.

"I want to drive."

"What? What's wrong with my driving?"

"Nothing, but I've been trained to do surveillance. You haven't, and you'll muck things up."

He rolled his eyes, but made the turn into the lot. "Sure, okay. I'm not dumb, Edie. I think I can handle driving past her house."

"There's more to it than that." She unbuckled and reached for her door handle as he came to a halt. They switched places, and she turned them around. Two turns later, they were on Justine's street.

"I don't see why you want to drive. I would think you'd want to be a passenger so you could observe better." He stared out the window as he spoke.

"I can observe just fine like this." She drove at a steady pace down the street.

"Hey, that's her house. Why aren't you slowing down?" He pointed to a beige single-story house, turning his head to look as they passed it.

"And that's why I'm driving. If we slow down, it makes us look suspicious."

"Okay, but how can you tell anything going by that fast? There was no car in the driveway, but she has a garage. Or she could be at work."

"Slowing down as we pass won't tell us anymore than that. We need to sit and watch the place." She went around the block, then pulled to the curb a few houses down from Justine's and parked.

"So, we just sit here now?" He glanced at her, then turned to look at the house.

"For a little bit, yes."

"Don't tell me you plan to go knock? What will you say if she answers? Hell, what will I say? 'Hi, Justine. Remember me? The guy you blew off? I'm here to introduce you to my new girlfriend.'" He rolled his eyes.

Edie chuckled. "*You* will stay in the car. I'll pretend to be someone thinking about moving into the neighborhood." She nodded toward the house across the street with a for sale sign in the yard. "As a single woman, you can never be too careful. She'll empathize with that."

He tipped his head. "Okay, that's a decent plan."

"I told you I knew what I was doing."

"Where did you learn all this? Did Dean teach you? It feels like something he would do as a P.I."

"I've gone on a couple stakeouts with him in Costa Rica, yes. The basic surveillance, though, the Army taught me." She'd done her fair share of light recon. Everyone did. When she was deployed, anytime they left the base, everyone put their head on a swivel.

"What else did the Army teach you?"

"Oh, many, many things, Jordie." And not all of it was good.

The door she'd reinforced on her emotions earlier in the week rattled. She turned away from it and pretended not to hear it. "You know, I think I'll go employ another thing the Army taught me." Sometimes, there was more information to be had by talking to people. She opened her door.

"What?" Jordan grabbed her arm. "Wait. Are you going to knock?"

"Not exactly." She had a plan in mind, but didn't feel like detailing it to him. He'd find out soon enough when she did it. "I'm going to check out the house and talk to the neighbors."

"Why?"

"Because they often know things about us we don't think they do. If she's varied her routine, the neighbors have probably noticed." She pulled her wrist free. "I'll be back. Stay here." Before he could say more, she slid out of the car and shut the door.

That bite to the air cut through her fleece jacket. She pulled the zipper a little higher and stuffed her hands in her pockets. She missed the warmth of home. Winter was not her thing. Not even an Arizona winter.

Edie scanned the street, looking for homes that looked occupied and which of those had the best view of Justine's house. She picked the home across the street and to the left. A blue minivan sat in the driveway, and she could see movement through the front windows. Before she went there, though, she went up to Justine's door. The mailbox was stuffed full, and the house had an air of disuse about it. She lifted a hand and pretended to knock. She wasn't ready to talk to Justine yet, but she wanted anyone who happened to glance out to see her trying to contact the woman.

After waiting a minute, she crossed the street to the house with the minivan and pushed the doorbell. A moment later, the white door cracked open and a woman not much older than herself answered. Edie could hear kids yelling and laughing inside.

"Hi." Edie put on a bright, cheerful smile. "I'm looking for my friend, Justine Lammers. She lives across the street." She turned slightly, nodding toward the house. "We were supposed to meet for lunch, but she didn't answer the door. Do you know if she's home?"

"I haven't seen her." A thoughtful frown covered the woman's face. "Actually, I haven't seen her in a while. Not her or her car."

"That's unusual?"

"Yes. She goes out for dinner several nights a week to get takeout and usually comes back about the same time I get home from work, so I see her pull in sometimes. She goes out on the weekends a lot too. The kids and I spend a lot of time in the front room, and we see her car pull out. She hasn't done that lately now that I think about it."

"Do you remember the last time you saw her?"

"Oh, gosh. It's been a couple months. Is everything okay with her?"

Edie didn't answer. "If you see her, will you tell her Jane stopped by and that I'm sorry I missed her? We must have gotten our wires crossed." She offered the woman another smile.

"I sure will. I hope you get ahold of her."

"I'm going to try her again. Maybe she was just in the bathroom."

"Could be. Okay. Have a nice day."

"You too." Edie stepped off the porch and crossed the road. This time, when she went up to Justine's door, she made contact. But there was still no answer. Having an excuse with the neighbors about why she was on the property, she wandered around the side of the house. There was no fence, so she walked up to the back door and knocked there too. "Justine?" Peering through the window, she saw a shelf full of dead plants on the opposite wall. No one had been inside in quite some time.

Edie went back out front and returned to the Bronco. A disturbing thought was now circling through her mind.

"Well? Anything?" Jordan asked as she got in.

She closed her door. "I'm not sure." She stared out the windshield at Justine's house. "The lady across the street hasn't seen her and confirmed that her routine is different. When I looked in one of the rear windows, I saw a bunch of dead plants." She turned her gaze on Jordan, a pit in her stomach. "I think the body in the desert might be Justine Lammers."

TWENTY-ONE

Thoughts swirled through Jordan's head. He drummed his fingers on the dash and stared at Justine's house. He didn't want to believe she was dead. And especially not because of him.

A car rolled past them, slowing, and turned into Justine's driveway.

"Who's that?" Edie leaned forward.

"I don't know. It's not her, though." A man was driving. He stopped in the drive and got out, going to the front door and pounding on it.

"He doesn't look very happy," Edie remarked.

"No, he doesn't." Jordan reached for his door handle. "Let's go find out why."

Edie put a hand on his arm. "You stay here. I'll go."

"Edie—"

"You need to keep your distance. Mike and I know you didn't hurt her, but if it comes back that the person we found was her, and she was murdered, you're still technically a suspect because of what she had in her pocket."

His lips flattened, but he sat back and nodded. "Fine. But if he gets pushy, I'm coming over there."

"I'll be fine."

"Don't care. Go." He couldn't—wouldn't—sit here and watch some guy berate her or get in her face. It didn't matter that he knew Edie could defend herself. Jordan's macho male side wouldn't let him.

She got out and crossed the street, raising a hand and calling out to the guy. Jordan slid into the driver's seat and rolled down the window, straining to hear. Muffled voices reached him, but the guy's angry face had him on edge. So did Edie's posture. The man had left the porch and was on his way across the grass to talk to her. The relaxed air she'd started with was gone. Her shoulders were back and straight, and she'd spread her feet slightly. She was prepped for a fight.

Jordan got out of the truck and jogged closer.

"—owes me for three months if she doesn't pay on the first." The man stuck a finger in Edie's face.

"Hey!" Jordan reached them. "I'll kindly ask you to get your finger out of my girlfriend's face. What's your problem?"

"Jordie..." Edie hissed.

He ignored her and kept his focus on the man who had taken a step back.

"I was just telling her that if she talked to her friend to tell her she owes me rent money. I'm filing an eviction notice if she doesn't pay up by the first."

"You're Justine's landlord?"

"Yes."

"How far behind is she?"

"Two months. If she doesn't pay on the first, it'll be three. I've called several times and left messages. I've even sent letters, giving her notice of the penalty fees and my next steps. I wanted to give her a chance in person. She's a nice girl." The man's gaze darted to the side. "But she didn't answer the door."

Jordan's brow furrowed. The guy gave off a sleazy vibe. He would bet the man's "chance" he intended to give her didn't involve money. "Do you have a key to get inside?"

"No. She changed all the locks."

I wonder why. Jordan bit back a snort. "Okay, well, I'm sure she has her reasons for not answering if she's home. If we talk to her, we'll be sure to tell her to settle up with you." His words were clearly dismissive.

The man took the hint and backed toward his car. "You do that. And tell her I'm kicking her out if she doesn't pay up. And even if she does, I'm not renewing her lease in May. Damn woman's nothing but trouble." He turned and stalked to his car.

Jordan stood with Edie and watched him pull out of the driveway and leave with a squeal of his tires.

"Wow, he's a piece of work." Jordan glanced at Edie. She glared at him, her hands propped on her hips. "What?"

"I told you to stay in the car."

He rolled his eyes and turned around to go back to the Bronco. "He got in your face. I told you I wouldn't stay put if he got pushy."

"I can take care of myself, Jordie."

He looked at her over his shoulder as he reached for the driver's door, a bit miffed at her attitude. "I'm aware, Edith. Get in the truck."

She stomped around to the passenger side and got in. "I don't know who you think you are, but I don't need a protector. You're not my boyfriend. And even if you were, I can still take care of myself."

"What I think I am is your friend." Jordan turned in his seat, draping his left arm over the steering wheel. "And I defend my friends. Even if they don't need it."

"We're not friends."

"Really? Because it sure feels like that's what we've become over the last couple of weeks." He faced forward and cranked the engine. "My bad." He put the car in gear. "You know, relying on people isn't a bad thing, Edie. Going it alone is a terrible way to live. People need other people."

"I'm fine. I have friends."

"Sure you do. How many of them know the real you? The person under the brave mask you wear that hides the pain you've locked away?"

She crossed her arms and stared out the window.

"You can't hide her forever, Edie. One day, she's going to demand to be let out, and it won't be pretty if you don't deal with her."

"I'm fine."

Jordan let out a soft snort and shook his head. Stubborn, mule-headed woman... He sat back, steering them out of the neighborhood in silence. She was done talking, he could tell. But he'd said his piece. He could only hope she'd mull it over and actually listen.

Twenty-Two

Jordan glanced at Edie as they walked up to Mike and Carmen's front door later that night. She still wasn't really talking to him. Once they got home, she'd retreated to her room. He'd gone down to his shop and worked on the Porsche's engine, so he wasn't tempted to knock on her door and coax her into opening up. She would when she was ready. He hoped. It was a good sign that she'd still agreed to dinner tonight. Mike knew the truth about their relationship. There was no need for pretense, and she could have declined.

He knocked on the door. A moment later, it opened to reveal Carmen Deyo's petite form and smiling face.

"Hello! Come in!" She motioned them inside, then shut the door behind them. "Let me take your jackets."

Jordan shrugged out of his coat and handed it to her. Edie pulled off her fleece jacket and did the same.

"Hey, guys." Mike came around the corner from the kitchen. "Dinner's almost ready. Why don't we have a seat?" He gestured toward the L-shaped gray couch in the living room.

"You guys go on ahead," Carmen said. "I need to finish up a few things."

"Oh, do you want help?" Edie took a step toward her.

"No, no." Carmen shooed her toward the living room. "Go sit. I'm fine. Thank you, though."

"Of course." Edie smiled and headed for the couch behind Mike.

Jordan felt himself relax a bit. Maybe she'd start speaking to him in more than one-word sentences before they left.

He perched on one end of the couch. Not surprisingly, she sat on the other, leaving the entire middle seat between them.

Mike sat in the adjacent chair. As soon as he was settled, he looked at them both and raised an eyebrow. "Did you two have a fight?"

"No." Edie crossed her legs, her expression blank.

Mike blinked and looked at Jordan for confirmation.

"No. Just a difference of opinion. Everything is fine."

"Difference of opinion on what?"

"Life," Edie answered. "Did you know Justine Lammers is missing?" She sat forward, changing the subject.

Mike blinked again at the abrupt shift, then frowned. "What? She hasn't returned my calls, but no one has reported her missing."

"That's because she works from home and doesn't have any family nearby."

Mike's frown turned darker. "How do you know that?"

Jordan bit back a groan. She was going to get them in trouble.

Edie rolled her lips in. "I have—resources."

"What sort of resources?"

"Good ones. We also talked to her landlord today."

"Edie—" Jordan closed his eyes and sighed.

Leaning forward, Mike propped his elbows on his knees and studied them. "Start at the beginning, please."

Edie glanced at Jordan, a small amount of hesitation on her face now.

He shook his head. "Uh-uh. You opened this can of worms. You can explain."

Her expression soured. "Fine." She glared at him, then looked at Mike. "Jordie was a little ouchie this morning, so I suggested we get out of the house. We took a drive into Tucson and did some surveillance at Justine's. According to her neighbor across the street, she hasn't seen her in a couple of months. As we were getting ready to leave, a man showed up. He didn't look happy, so I pretended to be her friend. I didn't even get my whole spiel about why I was there out of my mouth before he was sticking his finger in my face and telling me Justine needed to pay him."

"Apparently," Jordan cut in, "she hasn't paid her rent in two months. She'll be late for the third month and face eviction if she doesn't pay him by Thursday."

"Her mailbox was completely full too. I think you need to seriously consider the possibility that the body we found is Justine Lammers," Edie said.

"I already have. I've just been trying to get enough evidence to get a warrant for her house."

"I'd say you have it now," Jordan said. "Go talk to her landlord and have him give you a statement. Her neighbor too."

Mike glanced away, a thoughtful look drawing a crease on his forehead. He turned to Edie. "You're trouble." A lopsided smile softened his words. "But please, let me handle this?"

She held her hands up. "I'm more than willing to let you do the legwork. I'll only get involved if I think Jordan's life is in danger."

"So, why did you go today, then?" Mike tipped his head.

"Because we needed answers, and the justice system moves at a snail's pace. No offense."

"None taken. I'm well aware that there's a lot of red tape in my job."

"Dinner's ready." Carmen walked up with a bright smile.

"Oh, great. Thanks, honey." Mike stood.

Carmen led them into the kitchen. "This is buffet-style because I'm lazy and don't want to dirty up a bunch of serving dishes and carry it all to the table." She chuckled. "Grab a plate and help yourselves."

"I will take your cooking any way I can get it." Jordan picked up a plate but motioned for Edie to go first.

"Right?" Mike said. "It's one of the many reasons I married her."

Once their plates were full, they wandered over to the dining table near the sliding glass doors and sat down.

"So, Edie. Mike hasn't told me too much about you." Carmen looked at her with a smile. "Just that you're a friend of Dean's and are here helping Jordan with some lady troubles. Where are you from?"

"Oregon, originally. Now I live in Costa Rica with Dean." Edie paused. "Well, not *with* with him. Nearby. There's a group of us there who are all former military."

"You were in the military? What branch?"

"Army."

"What did you do?" Mike asked.

"I worked primarily as a translator."

"Really?"

Jordan could see the interest pique in Mike's eyes. He held his breath. Edie didn't like to talk about her time in the service, and Mike was about to ask questions.

"What made you leave? Did you not enjoy it?"

"No, I did. But things happen, you know?" She looked down at her plate and concentrated on stabbing a piece of chicken with her fork.

Mike's gaze caught Jordan's. Jordan gave a nearly imperceptible shake of his head, warning his friend to change the subject.

"How many languages do you speak?" Carmen's gaze flicked to Jordan, then to Edie. Jordan could tell she'd picked up on Edie's tension.

"Several. Primarily, I translated Arabic for the Army, but I also speak Spanish, German, French, Russian, and a smattering of Japanese."

"Seriously?" Jordan couldn't stop the word before it popped free. He knew she spoke Spanish, but not all the others.

She looked at him. "The European languages are all Latin-based, so their root words are similar. It's not that difficult to pick them up once you learn one. German was the hardest. Arabic took longer just because it's so completely different. And Japanese. Don't even get me started on that one. There's no real alphabet. It's all based on sounds. And many words have their own symbols. You just have to learn them. I'm still working on it."

"Do you have plans to go to Japan?" Mike asked.

"No. I just like languages, and it fills my days, learning a new language."

"What will you try after you learn Japanese?" Carmen asked.

"Maybe Indian. I'm not sure. We'll see what mood I'm in once I master Japanese." Edie smiled. "I might be ready for something simpler, which would be Portuguese or Romanian."

Jordan shook his head. "And here I thought being fluent in Spanish and knowing some French was good."

She laughed. "It is. I'm just a freak of nature."

"Nonsense." Carmen waved her fork. "You're just intelligent, and that happens to be the area where it manifests. For other people, it's in math or science."

"I guess that's true." Edie smiled at her. "Thank you."

The topic changed, then, as Carmen asked Edie about her family. Jordan learned a little more about what Edie was like as a child. Not surprisingly, she'd been a firebrand, much like she was now. Dinner conversation flowed easily, and soon, they were adjourning back to the living room.

"Have you talked to Mercy?" Edie asked Mike as they sat down.

"Only briefly. I went to Milago's after I left the garage the other day to ask her if she saw anyone in the parking lot or nearby when she left. I didn't want to question her about her relationship with you until after I saw the notes that were left. I haven't contacted her yet about those, but I will. Although, if the incident Thursday night is connected to the notes, I don't think it was her. She doesn't own a car like the one you described. I checked. It's possible she could have borrowed it from someone, but I don't know who."

"I've been thinking about the vehicle too," Jordan said. "About who it could belong to. Several of my customers drive cars like that, but so do a lot of other people. It's a popular SUV."

"It is." Mike's head bobbed once. "Just be careful. It's probably a good thing she's here." He gestured to Edie. "Even if she does play to your reckless side."

Jordan grinned, glancing at Edie. A smirk sat on her lips. "Adventure is the spice of life," he said.

Mike shook his head. "Only if it doesn't land you in jail."

TWENTY-THREE

Warmth seeped into Edie's hands from the tea mug she held as she stared out the kitchen window. Restlessness gripped her. She couldn't make her mind settle down so she could sleep—hence the tea. The day's events—mostly her argument with Jordan and Mike's questions at dinner—swirled through her head. They kept knocking on the door to the emotions she'd locked up so tightly. She was half afraid she'd have a nightmare if she slept. The door was rattling hard in its frame.

Huffing a sigh, she pushed away from the counter. Standing down here wouldn't help her relax. She doubted lying in bed in a dark room would, either, but she had to try. Hopefully, the warm tea would help. What she really wanted was to surf. It required all of her focus and helped her subconscious mind process things.

The sliding door off the living room opened as she crossed to the stairs. Jordan stepped inside. He'd been out in his shop, working on his car.

"Hey." He spotted her and smiled.

"Hi. I'm going to bed." She kept walking, not ready to talk

to him alone. The ride home had been all right; they'd had conversation about their evening with the Deyos to fill the silence. But now? She'd rather not get into her behavior toward him. Maybe in the morning she could apologize for being rude. Though she still didn't intend to talk about her past.

"Edie, wait."

She paused with one foot on the bottom step. "I'm tired, Jordan."

"Me too, but we need to talk. I think we'll both sleep better."

She let out a soft snort. "No." But she turned around. "My head is a jumbled mess, and I just want to go to sleep."

He walked closer. "You need to talk to unjumble it."

"I need to surf."

He stuffed his hands in his pockets. "How about some sparring instead?"

"At this hour?"

"Why not? My mind is racing too. The exercise might help us both."

She glanced toward the second-story, thinking. Either way, she figured she faced a fight to fall asleep. But maybe the exercise would shorten that fight just a little. "Fine. Let me change." She didn't wait for an answer, just dashed up the stairs. In her room, she donned a sports bra and some workout shorts, then headed downstairs. She found Jordan already in his home gym, stretching with his back to her.

Her step faltered. He'd removed his shirt, and the muscles of his back bunched and shifted as he moved. A deep-seated need uncoiled in her belly. She clenched her teeth and tried to push it away. Getting involved with him was a bad idea. She didn't need to add heartbreak to the emotions she'd shoved into the vault in her mind.

He glanced over his shoulder. "You ready?"

She nodded, not trusting her voice. Moving forward, she paused to do some light stretching, keeping her eyes downcast. It wouldn't help relax her muscles to stare at his naked chest. Why couldn't he have left his shirt on?

Once they were both done stretching, they squared off. For twenty minutes, they feinted, parried, and rolled around the mat. Edie lashed out with a foot, and he caught it, throwing her off balance; she tried to spin and catch herself, but the toe of her planted foot caught and she crashed to the floor. All the air rushed from her lungs. Rolling onto her back, she tried to make her diaphragm work.

"Are you okay?" Jordan kneeled next to her.

She nodded, still unable to breathe. Finally, the spasm eased, and she sucked in a breath. She sat up. "I think I'm done now." Fatigue was starting to settle in.

"Yeah. We should hit the shower and go to bed."

Instantly, Edie's mind went to an image of them showering together. She could picture water sluicing over his skin, wetting his hair to run down his neck. Briefly, she closed her eyes, swallowing hard. When she opened them, he stared at her, heat blazing in his eyes. She wasn't the only one to have those thoughts. The need she'd been fighting since she walked into the room blazed hotter.

Jordan stood up and offered her a hand. She took it, letting him help her to her feet.

Tingles raced up her arm and sent a shiver down her spine. *Oh, bad idea.*

She screamed at herself to let go of his hand, but her traitorous body wouldn't cooperate. Instead, it swayed closer to him. Her other hand came up to rest on his damp chest.

A muscle shifted in Jordan's jaw. He brought his free hand up to cover hers and dipped his head.

Edie's feet grew roots, a direct defiance to the part of her standing guard in front of the door to her emotions, desperately trying to hold it closed.

That door flew open at the first touch of his lips to hers. He curled the arm holding her hand, bringing her into his body. Edie tugged her fingers free and slid both hands up around his neck. The sensible part of her brain tried to get up and shut the door, but what flooded out of the vault was too strong. She was no longer in control.

TWENTY-FOUR

One moment Edie was standing, the next, Jordan wrapped his arms around her hips and lifted. She locked her ankles behind his waist, not breaking their kiss as he walked out of the gym, carrying her. They didn't need words to agree on where this kiss was going.

Out in the main room, he broke their kiss so he could watch where he was walking. The wanton woman Edie had fought to hold back refused to let her reasonable side out to play. She peppered his jaw and neck with kisses as he strode toward the stairs, then up to his bedroom on the second floor. When he laid her on his bed, she clutched his hair, holding him close, then latched onto his mouth again.

He groaned and pushed away. "Are you sure about this? I mean, we're not—"

"Shut up and kiss me." Her ability to stop herself was gone. It would take a superhuman effort to overrule this side of herself. She'd been fighting her attraction to him from the moment they met. The needy side of her brain was done and had taken control.

Jordan stared into her eyes for a long moment. Then, like

her, his control snapped. The man who kissed her this time didn't hold back. He plunged into the dark recesses of her mouth and skimmed his hands over her body, stirring her blood as he teased her. Edie wanted to remove the barriers between them, but she couldn't make herself break away to do so. He'd put her under his spell.

In the end, it didn't matter. He removed the barriers for her. With a quick tug, her sports bra whisked over her head, separating them for only an instant. Then his mouth was back on hers and his calloused palms caressed the soft flesh of her breasts. Edie moaned at the feeling. The rough texture of his hands rubbed all the right places.

His mouth left hers to trail hot kisses down her neck. When he peppered her chest with soft pecks, she panted with need. The wet heat of his mouth on the tips of her breasts sent desire pulsing in her core. She clutched a handful of his hair and moaned again. Sleeping with Jordan might not be wise, and it would probably lead to emotional pain, but damn. It might be worth it.

Her shorts and underwear were next, flying down her legs and over the side of the bed. He moved to cover her again, but she sat up, putting a hand on his chest. "Uh-uh. Get naked."

"But I was having fun making you moan."

"You can do that better naked." She wanted to touch too, and his shorts were in the way.

Grinning, he got up and shucked his pants and boxer-briefs. Edie's mouth watered at her first glimpse of what he'd been hiding. She wanted to do more than touch that. After she licked it, she wanted to ride it like her surfboard.

He opened the nightstand and grabbed a condom, tossing it onto the pillow by her head, then crawled onto the bed. The predatory look in his eyes sent a delicious shiver through her. Her core pulsed again. Maybe licking it could wait for the next time. Going straight for the ride seemed like a better plan.

But he wasn't done torturing her. Before she could roll and grab the condom, he pinned her to the mattress and attacked her torso with his mouth. Wedging a thigh between hers, he skimmed a hand over her abdomen and down to cup her core. His fingers skated over the sensitive flesh. She let her legs fall open, and about lost it when he dipped the tip of one finger into her channel.

"Jordie, please."

"Please, what, Edith? Please do this?" He swirled his fingers through the wetness coating her and teased the little nub of nerves that begged for his touch. "Or please do this?" Moving south, he slid one finger all the way inside her.

She let out a breathy moan. "Oh. That." Her hips lifted.

He toyed with her, adding another finger, then another, finding that spot that sent shockwaves through her brain. She flew apart with a shout. Riding the wave, she heard the crinkle of the condom wrapper as the pieces of her mind fluttered back down around her. A moment later, something wider and hotter probed her entrance.

The wanton vixen in her mind came back to life. Edie tipped her head back, closing her eyes, and wrapped her wobbly legs around his waist. "Yes!" she hissed.

"Are you sure you're ready?"

She looked at him, seeing a rakish grin on his face. "Jordan, so help me if you don't put that where it belongs in the next few seconds, I will put you flat on your back and do it myself."

He chuckled and rolled his hips, pushing the tip of his shaft inside. A white-hot flush erupted throughout Edie's body, starting in her head to swiftly move down to her feet and then reverberate back up. Her muscles froze with antic-ipation.

Oh, this was definitely going to be worth the heartache later.

He inched in a little more.

She huffed and squirmed.

It was his turn to moan. "Hold still. I'm trying to make this last."

"No." She squirmed again.

He thrust inside, making them both let out a quick shout of pleasure. After a brief pause to regain some control, he did what she'd been wanting him to do all along. His hips moved in a quick rhythm, building the need he'd doused with his hand only moments before. She met him thrust for thrust.

His cadence faltered, and he growled in her ear. He pushed up on one arm, then reached between them with the other, adding his fingers to the mix.

She went over the edge with a howl. As her body clamped down on his, he let out a grunt, then a harsh moan, and pulsed deep within her.

Panting, Edie's legs fell back to the bed. Jordan collapsed on top of her, breathing hard. He tucked his face into the crook of her neck and dropped soft kisses on it. Edie floated back to earth, his caresses gentling her landing. The skeptical and pessimistic side of her brain stayed quiet. So did her earlier thoughts. They weren't back in the vault, but they were lying low for now.

"Who knew I just needed some good sex to make my mind shut up?" she muttered.

Jordan lifted his head. He cocked one eyebrow, and a smile flirted with his mouth. "Good sex? I'd say it was more than good."

She smacked at his shoulder with a chuckle. "Your ego is big enough. Good is all you get."

"Oh, really? I guess that means I need to try again." He brushed a hand down her side.

Edie laughed again and snagged his fingers. Fatigue pulled at her muscles. She was all for another round, but after she had some sleep. As great as it was, she didn't have the energy for another round. "Later. After sleep."

He pouted, but rolled to the side. "Fine. But you're staying here." Fire lit his eyes. "I want to wake you up with great sex. Not good. Great."

The need he'd ignited earlier settled into a glowing fire in her belly. She could live with that.

Twenty-Five

A sound brought Jordan out of a deep sleep. His eyelids fluttered, and he started to drift off once more, when he heard it again. Coming more fully awake, he realized it was Edie crying out in her sleep.

"No!"

Jordan sat up.

"Ryan..." Anguish laced her voice. "No..." she whispered.

"Edie?" He didn't know who Ryan was, but it sounded like something bad had happened to him. Jordan touched her shoulder.

Her fist shot out, clipping him in the jaw. He fell back with a grunt, but only for a moment. Rising to his knees, he reached over and grabbed both of her arms, pinning them to the bed. "Edie, honey, wake up. You're dreaming." He gave her a gentle shake.

She growled and pulled against his hold.

"Edie." He shook her harder.

"Ezra! Ezra, help!"

Crap. She was dreaming about her service days. He needed to wake her up. "Edith!"

Her eyes popped open, and she froze. For a moment, she stared at him with a blank look, then her face crumpled and she burst into tears. Jordan gathered her into his arms.

Well, he tried. As soon as her cheek touched his chest, she pushed away and jumped out of bed.

He leaned over and turned on the bedside lamp. "Edie?"

She huddled at the edge of the bed, arms wrapped over her naked chest. Her glorious copper hair was in disarray around her tear-stained face.

"I'm sorry," she whispered, then turned and ran.

Jordan stared after her for a long moment. What the hell just happened? His sleepy brain whirled, trying to wrap itself around the last few seconds. When it did, he scrambled out of bed and ran after her. "Edie?"

He paused to listen and heard her footsteps at the bottom of the stairs. Turning right, he followed. "Edie?"

She didn't stop. In the dim light filtering through the windows from the pole lights outside, he saw her shadow cross the living room. She whipped a blanket off the couch, then headed for the back door. Alarm rang through him. What was she doing? "Edie. Honey, stop."

But she didn't listen. The sliding door slid open, hitting the other side with a bang. Jordan cursed and glanced around, looking for something to cover up with. The small throws he kept on the couch wouldn't cut it for his large frame.

He turned and ran toward the closet off the garage, where he grabbed a pair of coveralls. Hopping on one foot, he hastily donned them, zipping them just to his waist and tying the sleeves around his hips before grabbing a jacket. He stuffed his feet into a pair of boots and ran into the garage. Snagging a flashlight from his workbench, he went outside and ran around the house into the backyard. Edie stalked toward the desert in nothing but the soft fleece throw she'd taken from the couch. Worry punched him in the gut. He picked up his pace.

"Edith!"

She glanced back momentarily, then kept going.

"Edie, stop. Before you get hurt. Please."

But she kept walking. Running over the dusty, rocky ground, he finally reached her. "Edie." He got in front of her, blocking her path.

"Move, Jordan." Her voice was rough and tears tracked down her face.

"No. You can't walk into the desert. Especially naked and with no shoes."

"I don't care."

"I do. Let's go back inside."

"I can't. I need to move." She took a step around him. "Get out of my way."

He hesitated only a second before he scooped her into his arms.

She shrieked. "Put me down!"

Jordan held on tight as she bucked in his arms. "No." Turning, he headed for the house.

"Jordan, please. I need—" Her plea dissolved into a body-wracking sob. She shook in his arms and the sound of her cries filled the still desert night. A lump formed in Jordan's throat, and he felt the press of tears in his eyes. It was like a knife to the gut to see her in so much pain.

He retraced her steps and went in through the sliding door. Figuring he might have better luck if he didn't corner her in a room with only one exit, he headed for the couch. He sat down, but didn't let her go.

She batted at the blanket, trying to get her hands free. Jordan didn't stop her, but he didn't put her down. "Talk to me. Please, Edie."

Still sobbing, she tucked her face into his neck. He closed

his eyes and held her close, stroking her back through the blanket and placing gentle kisses on her head. When her sobs quieted to sniffles and soft hiccups, he pulled away slightly and brushed damp tendrils of hair away from her face. "Talk to me," he said softly.

She stared up at him. In the dim light, he could just see the glitter of her eyes. They still swam with tears.

"I'm sorry," she whispered.

"Don't be. Just talk to me."

"I can't."

"You need to. Just so you can let it out."

"There's nothing to let out. I'm fine."

"Bullshit." Anger gave the word a bite. "You just walked into the desert at night, wearing nothing but a blanket, no shoes, and in January. You're far from fine."

She looked away, and he saw the muscles in her jaw work. She stayed silent.

He sighed, still angry that she was denying that she needed to work through whatever was going on in her head, but also feeling a little defeated that she didn't want to talk to him.

"We crashed."

Her quiet voice broke the silence. His heart skipped, and he held his breath, not wanting to discourage her from speaking.

"I was a translator attached to a base in Afghanistan. I wasn't supposed to be on the mission; the Special Forces interpreter was, but he came down with food poisoning. The base commander asked me to fill in, since my unit commander was going. The mission wasn't supposed to be dangerous. Not any more so than a normal trek across the desert. But we got hit with a grenade launcher about halfway to our destination. It took out the tail rotor. Ezra did the best he could to bring us down easy, but with the stabilization gone, we hit hard." She swiped at her face.

"Ryan Seivert, my commander, died on impact from a boulder that came through the fuselage when we hit; it crushed him. Ezra broke his leg. I broke my arm. Banged my head." She lifted her left arm slightly. "The worst part was we couldn't get out and run away. I could, but that meant leaving Ezra behind. I couldn't do that. We had weapons, but his injury made him a sitting duck. And, honestly, it was just as dangerous, if not more so, for me to trek through the mountains to get back to base. They were full of insurgents." She took a slow breath and sniffed.

"We spent the night huddled in the front of the chopper, trying to stay warm, and took turns keeping watch. It was a battle to stay awake. Near daybreak, the insurgents found us."

Jordan sucked in a quick breath.

"Luckily, we were in a Blackhawk. The armored exterior afforded us some extra protection. We had plenty of ammunition too. The main guns didn't work because of the crash, but our rifles did. After a couple of hours, the insurgents backed off. Before they could come back with reinforcements, Ford showed up." She paused and shook her head. "That's when things really went to hell in a handbasket."

She stopped. Her fingers fluttered over his collarbone as she fiddled with the collar of his jacket. Jordan wished he could see her face.

"I thought we were in the clear. We were on our way to Ford's Humvee, but we didn't make it before the insurgents returned," she continued. "The shooting started when I was just yards away. I made it into the vehicle, but Ford and Ezra were still outside. I glanced back as I got in; just in time to see a bullet hit Ford in the side. He dropped to his knees. Ezra grabbed Ford's gun and fired back. He grabbed Ford by the collar with his other hand and hobbled the last twenty feet to the Humvee. Ford's team pulled them both inside while I fired out the window. We beat a hasty retreat once they were in."

"Damn."

"Yeah. The worst part was we couldn't get to Ryan's body. A SEAL team went back a couple of days later and retrieved him. I overheard one of the guys say that the insurgents shot him up and did... other... things... to him." She stopped to pull in a shaky breath, then blew it out slowly. Lifting her head, she made eye contact. "That's what I was dreaming about. Being shot at. What they did to him. What they would have done to me if Ford hadn't come after us."

Jordan clutched her tighter, glad she was safe in his arms. He didn't want to think about what could have happened if she'd spent another day in that wreckage.

"I thought I'd dealt with all this. I talked to someone after it happened. I did all the mental exercises that were supposed to help. And they did. But it also helped to wall off those thoughts. I went home briefly, but I couldn't handle being around my family. The emotions were too intense. I loved them too much, and they loved me. I wanted to talk to them, but couldn't. It hurt too much. So I joined Ford in Costa Rica, hoping I could heal more with time. I guess I just walled everything off, including any intense emotion, not just the ones from that day." She let out a soft huff. "Meeting you broke the lock on the vault door. Tonight, you smashed the door to pieces."

"I'm sorry."

"No. It's okay. I knew when I said yes it might cause me problems. I just didn't think I'd react the way I did. The nightmare I expected. Even the urge to run. I just figured I'd do that with clothes on."

He chuckled. "To be fair, you might have stopped for clothing if I hadn't come after you."

She smiled. "Maybe." Her expression sobered. "All I could think of, though, was how I had to get out. I had to get away. But there's no running from my own thoughts. Not when the things I'd put in place to hold them at bay are gone now. It left me reeling."

"And how about now? Are you still reeling?"

"A little. The fog of fear that made me run is gone. I'm still upset, but I can be rational about things now."

"Do you want me to leave you alone? I really only went after you because I wanted to keep you safe. I mean, sure, I wanted you to talk to me, but I chased you into the desert so you didn't get hurt."

"No." She messed with his collar again. "I think I want you to stay with me. Partly because I'm afraid I'll have another nightmare and try to get lost in the desert again." One side of her mouth lifted.

He smiled. "No more desert."

"Definitely not. Mostly, though, I'm done fighting. Having that vault gone is actually kind of freeing. I didn't realize how much of myself I'd put back there."

Jordan pressed a kiss to her forehead, then shifted forward. "Come on." He stood with her in his arms. "Let's go back to bed. I promise not to let you run away again."

TWENTY-SIX

The morning sun peeked over the mountains as Edie sipped her coffee while staring out the sliding glass doors. She'd awakened twenty minutes ago, the vestiges of another bad dream tormenting her. It hadn't been as bad as the first dream that sent her running, but it was enough to pull her from her slumber. When she saw the time, she decided to just get up. There wasn't much point in going back to sleep.

She'd debated waking Jordan and getting that great sex he promised her. But he'd had as much of a sleepless night as she had, so she let him rest. There would be time for that later.

Her blood heated. There would definitely be some of that later. She guaranteed it. Even if she had to pin him to the floor, she'd get a repeat of last night. She might have told him it was just good, but that had been a way for her to corral the tide of emotions. If she'd admitted just how amazing it was, those feelings she'd been so afraid of might have risen up from the floor of her mind. They'd done it anyway when her guard was down.

She crossed an arm over her middle and rested her elbow

on top, sipping her coffee. The desert glowed gold in the early morning light. She couldn't feel the sun's warmth, but it still filled her. A smile curved her mouth upward. She felt like a new woman. Why had she kept all that bottled up for so long?

Edie rolled her eyes at herself. Because it was easier than dealing with it. She didn't like to cry. Never had. She'd always been the tough sister. Esther was the one who wore her emotions on her sleeve. Edie preferred to let everyone guess how she felt.

She couldn't do that with Jordan. He wouldn't let her. He was like a damn gnat. One built like a cockroach. It didn't matter how many times she swatted him away or stomped on him, he still lived and kept coming back. It used to irritate her, but now she was glad he hadn't stopped messaging her and pestering her to talk about her feelings. Even though she knew she'd likely have more nightmares in the coming weeks as she adjusted to having those memories back out in the open, she was now open to feeling all the good things life had to offer too. Many of those things had to do with him.

Commotion upstairs made her turn away from the door. The bedroom door opened, and Jordan's quick footsteps moved toward the stairs. "Edie?" A hint of panic tinged his voice.

She debated for a split second staying silent to tease him, but he'd been so genuinely worried about her last night, she didn't want to do that to him. "I'm here."

He hurried down the stairs, looking at her over the rail. She could see the relief on his face.

"When I woke up, and you were gone, I thought you'd taken off again. Are you okay?"

Edie had to blink twice before her brain processed his question. He'd donned his boxer-briefs before getting up and nothing else. "What? Oh. Yes. I'm fine. There's coffee if you want some." She lifted her mug and gestured toward the kitchen.

"Maybe in a bit." Heat licked his eyes. "I promised you something this morning. I was supposed to wake you up with it, but you cheated and left before I could."

Edie's core clenched and heat pooled low in her belly. "You looked like you needed the rest."

"What I need is you."

Oh, if that didn't make a girl swoon, what would? She bit her lip and took a step toward him.

Her phone rang.

Cursing, she fished it out of her pocket and glanced at the screen. "It's Asher." Knowing it might be important, she answered. "Hello?"

"Hey, sorry if I woke you. Though you don't sound like I did."

"I've been up for a little bit. Why are you calling at this hour, though?"

"I found Justine's phone and car. They're not at her house."

Edie blinked, then looked at Jordan with wide eyes.

He walked closer, staring at her phone. "Where are they?"

"Oh, hey, Jordan." Asher cleared his throat. "I feel like I'm interrupting something. I'll be quick. They're in a junkyard on the south side of Tucson." He named the business.

"Damn. Someone really does want to frame me. I get auto parts from there sometimes. It's not the only place, though, so that's some good news."

A tiny silver-lining, yes, Edie thought. "How did you find them?" she asked Asher.

"I got into her phone and turned it on, then pinged it. Once I had the location, I got a buddy to check out the coordinates with a surveillance satellite. Her car's tucked into a back corner of the lot. I'm assuming her phone is in it. As of yesterday afternoon, they were still there."

Edie sighed. There went their morning plans. And they had another problem. "How are we supposed to explain how we know where her car and phone are to the detective?"

"You can tell him the truth. He can write it up as a tip from a concerned citizen. And no, before you ask, I didn't task a satellite away from its normal path. I just asked my buddy to look at the coordinates the next time it flew over the area."

"I'm not sure what's less comforting. That it's normal for a spy satellite to fly over the area or that you have access to it. I mean, I get that you're a former spy, but you left that life. That should be an employee-only kind of thing." Jordan's mouth flattened, and he shook his head, glancing at Edie.

She shrugged. Asher wasn't your typical person.

"I don't," Asher said. "My friend does. And I was never a spy. I was an analyst." His tone told Edie he was miffed that someone would call him a spy. She bit back a smile. He was so protective over his little niche talent.

"Sorry," Jordan muttered.

"Anyway, I hope it helps. I'll let you go so you can get back to... whatever it was you were doing."

"Thanks, Asher." Edie looked at Jordan, excitement lighting her eyes. A slow smile bloomed on his face.

"Yep. Call if you need anything else." He hung up.

Jordan spun on his heel. "I'm calling Mike."

Edie followed him upstairs, so she could change her clothes. It only took her a couple of minutes to don some jeans and a sweater. When she walked past Jordan's room, he was on the phone. He saw her and rolled his eyes.

"Yeah, Mike. I'll explain it all there, I promise." He paused. "Okay, bye." He hung up and sighed.

Edie chuckled. "I take it he didn't like being woke up?"

"Nope. Especially when I refused to tell him why we were

meeting. He'll have questions only you can answer." He stood and walked toward her, stopping just inches away. "You know… I haven't said good morning."

A slow smile spread over her face. "You haven't, no."

Bending down, he sealed his lips to hers in a slow, gentle kiss. Warmth spread through Edie's limbs. When they parted, she touched his face and smiled. "Good morning."

He gave her another quick peck. "Good morning, beautiful." He took her hand. "Come on. Let's go see if we can get some answers."

They went downstairs, putting on shoes and coats, then got in his Bronco. As he backed out of the garage, paper flapping under the windshield wiper on her rental caught Edie's attention. "Jordan." She pointed.

He braked and followed the line of her finger, then groaned. "Dammit." He put the car in park.

Edie got out and retrieved the paper, not looking at it until she got back in the Bronco. There, she unfolded it. This poem was an angry one. She glanced at Jordan. "We touched a nerve. She's pissed. And it's aimed at me. This was on my car."

"Probably because it was outside."

"Maybe. But she could have left it in your mailbox. This was on my car. Mine."

Jordan put the car in gear again. "Well, whoever it's aimed at, it looks like we've got another reason to talk to Mike this morning."

TWENTY-SEVEN

Jordan turned at the sound of an approaching car. He and Edie stood outside the gate of Rex's Auto Parts and Wrecking, waiting for Mike and Rex to arrive.

Mike turned into the parking lot, coming to a halt a few feet away. He shut off the engine and got out. "Okay, why am I here?"

Before Jordan could answer, a second vehicle pulled into the lot. It was Rex in his pickup. The man waved and pulled up beside Mike's SUV.

Mike glanced over, his frown intensifying. "What is going on?"

Rex hopped out of his truck, his bald head gleaming in the sunshine. Laugh lines crinkled the corners of his eyes as he smiled at them. "Howdy. I hope you can make this quick, Jordan. The missus will be mad if I'm late to church."

"Hopefully, it will be."

"Hopefully what will be?" Mike propped his hands on his hips. "Will someone please explain why you hauled me out of bed on a Sunday?"

"Do you remember asking me how I got information?" Edie asked.

Mike's frown turned curious. "Yeah."

"Well, I got more. Justine Lammers' phone and car are inside." She pointed at the locked gate.

Eyebrows rising, Mike cursed. "Okay, you have to give me more than 'I know people' this time. How do you know that?"

"One of my friends in Costa Rica is a former CIA analyst. He still has contacts in the government and got some intel on Justine's phone and car. That led him here. He says her car is parked in the back corner." She cast a quick glance at Rex.

The older man's eyebrows arched, then just as quickly dove down over his nose. "Who's Justine Lammers? And why does it matter that I have her car inside?"

"She's missing," Mike said.

"Oh, hell. Okay." Rex ambled forward, pulling a key ring from his pocket.

"You and I need to talk about these friends of yours," Mike said, walking past them toward Rex.

"You can talk all you want, Mike." Jordan followed him, Edie at his side. "She's protective. And they're secretive."

"I gathered that. But if they're going to butt into my investigation, then I need to talk to them."

"No, you don't," Edie said. "You can call this an anonymous tip. Because I guarantee if Asher hadn't called to tell me, he'd have reported it to you via some untraceable email."

Mike huffed and glared, but walked into the junkyard as Rex opened the gate.

"Where's it supposed to be?" Rex glanced back.

Edie told him what Asher told them. Rex nodded and led them through the maze. A minute later, he stopped and pointed. "That it?"

"I'll be damned." Mike swiped a hand down his face.

"Yeah. Rex, call your wife. You might be late to church." He turned to Edie and Jordan. "You two, go wait in your car."

Jordan propped his hands on his hips and frowned. "Mike—"

"No. I'm ninety-nine percent certain that body you found is Justine. The fact that a tip on her vehicle is coming from someone you know, and that the car is parked at a place I'm pretty sure you frequent, I can't have you anywhere near it when we search it. Just you being on the property is bad enough. The D.A. is going to be salivating at his desk with all of this, ready to push print on your arrest warrant as soon as I get a positive ID on that body. Go sit in your damn car."

Jordan ground his molars together, not liking the picture Mike painted. Or being ordered around. "Fine. But don't leave without talking to us. The car isn't the only reason we called. It was just the first."

Mike lifted an eyebrow in question, but nodded. "I won't. Now, go." He shooed them away.

Edie tugged on Jordan's hand. Reluctantly, he followed her back to the Bronco.

"This is dumb," he said, climbing inside. "I want to know what he finds. If it implicates me, I should know that, don't you think?"

"I think we need to find you an attorney."

Jordan growled. He didn't want an attorney. He just wanted this to end. Leaning back, he let his head rest against the seat. "We need a new game plan."

"What do you mean?"

"Pretending to be a couple isn't working. We aren't any closer to finding out who's behind the notes. Or if it's tied to the body we found and Justine's disappearance. I'm betting the remains belong to her. And that she was murdered. How else did her car and phone end up in Rex's lot?"

"I don't know. I also don't know what we can do differently. We've been very public with our ruse, including letting people know we're basically living together. I'm not sure what more we can do."

A crazy, unfathomable idea occurred to him. He looked at Edie, studying her. Would she go for it?

"What?" She frowned at him. "What's that look?"

"I have an idea, but I don't think you'll like it." Especially not now that their relationship had taken a turn for the real. They were no longer fake-dating.

She rolled her eyes. "Just spit it out. The worst I can say is no, right?"

"True. Okay." He took a deep breath. No turning back. "Marry me."

Twenty-Eight

E die knew her eyes looked like saucers, but she couldn't help it. That was the absolute last thing she'd expected to come out of his mouth. "I'm sorry, what?"

He turned in his seat to face her. "Think about it. We want a reaction, right? To get her to come forward and show her face."

"Getting married isn't the way to do that. We need a *temporary* solution. Marriage is—not."

"I know."

She blinked twice, glanced out the window, then stared at him for several seconds. "You're willing to hitch yourself to me to out this person? That's a bit extreme."

"Again, I know. But I think we've proved we can tolerate each other." A wicked smile erupted on his face and brought a gleam to his brown eyes.

Edie fought the blush that wanted to stain her cheeks. Instead, she stared him in the eye, her not amused look on her face. "Regardless, marriage is a terrible idea."

His smile disappeared, and he pouted. "You don't want to marry me?"

"Not yet!" She groaned and covered her face. Did she really say that out loud? She wasn't ready to admit to him how she felt. She hadn't even really admitted it to herself. With a sigh, she lowered her hands.

Jordan threaded her fingers with his. "I know it's an insane idea. But put your knee-jerk reaction aside. It could work."

"It could, but the complications outweigh the benefits."

"They're only complications if we let them be."

"Divorce isn't uncomplicated for anyone."

"Who says we have to get divorced?"

She lifted an eyebrow. "Because to get an annulment, you can't consummate a marriage. I don't know about you, but after last night's experience, I don't want to remain celibate."

"No, I meant, who says we have to split up at all?"

Her eyes bugged out again. "What? You can't be serious. Two weeks ago, we couldn't stand each other."

"You couldn't stand me." He pointed at her, then himself as he talked. "I liked you from the moment I met you."

A quick thrill went through her at his admission. Secretly, she'd liked him from the beginning too. It had just taken her longer to admit it. "Okay, well, it still doesn't change the fact that getting married is a terrible plan. Our lives are thousands of miles apart, we don't love each other—"

"That will probably change," he interrupted.

"Even if it does, there are other factors for why we shouldn't."

Jordan leaned closer. "All of that can be dealt with later. I never said it would be easy, but it is feasible."

Edie huffed and reached for her door handle. "You're insane, Jordie. I can't believe you want to get married. Especially to me." She pushed the door open.

He snagged her wrist, stopping her from getting out. "You're doing it again. Don't."

She looked at him with a frown. "Don't what?"

"You called me Jordie. You're deflecting. And why are you running away? I thought you were done running."

She pursed her lips and stared at a point past his shoulder, angry that he would remind her of that.

"There isn't anyone else I can imagine being married to, Edie."

She rolled her eyes. "Yeah, right. All those women you've dated, and *I'm* the one?" She scoffed. "Get real."

A quick flash of hurt went through his eyes before the brown orbs darkened. "I am. There's never been anyone I can imagine spending my life with until now. Maybe it's because I'm older and I'm ready to settle down. But it's probably just you. Look, I know the timing is awful. Things are still up in the air with us, and our relationship is very new, but I already can't imagine you going back to Costa Rica. At least, not without me." He narrowed his eyes, a wicked gleam lighting his face as one corner of his mouth kicked up. "You know Brooke offered me a job down there, right? That takes care of one part of your argument."

She huffed an exasperated laugh. "You're tenacious, I'll give you that." She hadn't known Brooke offered him a job. But she'd avoided all talk of Jordan with Dean, so she wasn't surprised she was in the dark.

"Does that mean you'll marry me?"

"It means I'll think about it."

His eyes rounded, and he stared at her for a long moment. "Wait. Seriously?"

She chuckled. "Why do you sound surprised? Isn't that what you wanted? To change my mind?"

"Well, yeah. I just figured you'd continue to say no and change the subject."

"Are you having second thoughts?" To her surprise, it upset her a bit to think that he'd changed his mind.

"No. In fact, I'm going to recruit others to my way of thinking. Convince you it's a solid plan."

Edie laughed. She pulled her door closed and settled back into her seat. "Good luck with that. Most people would agree with me that you're nuts."

TWENTY-NINE

It took everything Jordan had to force his heart to slow down. Those two words had flown from his lips and sent his heart rate into overdrive. Not because he regretted it—he didn't. But because he wanted her to say yes. Badly. She'd captivated him. Utterly and completely. Did he love her? The jury was still out on that, but he did know he wanted to see what kind of life they could build together. He knew getting married at this stage was crazy, but the benefits far outweighed the risks. Sure, it would step up their game against his stalker, but mostly, it would tie Edie to him. He'd meant what he said; he couldn't imagine being married to anyone else.

Movement in the junkyard caught his eye. "Mike's coming back." He nodded toward the fence.

Edie sat up. "I wonder what he found."

"Let's go find out." Jordan opened his door and got out. They met Mike and Rex at the gate.

"Did you find anything?" Edie asked.

Mike looked at her for a long moment, then turned to Jordan, not answering. "Before I call the crime scene unit down here to get the car, is there any possibility I'm going to find hair, DNA, or fingerprints belonging to you in it?"

Jordan pressed his lips together and glanced away, thinking. "Maybe on the outside driver's door handle. We drove separately to our one date. When we left, I opened her door for her. They might be on the roof near the door frame too. I leaned against the vehicle a little when we said goodbye." A pit settled in his stomach. He probably needed to contact a lawyer.

"That's it? You never got in?"

"No."

"Okay."

He started to walk toward his car, but Jordan shot a hand out to touch his arm. "You never answered Edie's question."

Mike let out a quick breath. "Her purse is on the floorboard of the passenger side. I haven't opened any of the doors yet because I want to get my gear. You two need to go home. Contact an attorney. Not because I think you did anything wrong, but because I want you to have legal advice going forward. I'll probably have to bring you in for formal questioning if I find your prints on the car. Especially if I still can't get a hold of Justine."

Jordan frowned, but didn't argue. "I understand."

Mike's expression softened. "I'll do my best to find out what really happened to her."

"She was murdered, wasn't she?" Jordan's heart ached to think that someone deliberately snuffed out Justine's life. She was a nice woman with an infectious smile.

"It's looking that way. I don't know any woman who would leave her car parked in a salvage yard with her purse and phone still inside. Nor do I think she walked to the park and committed suicide—assuming the body is hers, of course. I'm going to send another crew to the desert to widen our search range and see if we can find any more remains." His gaze bounced between Jordan and Edie. "You two stay away from there. I will charge you both with obstruction. Got it?"

They both nodded, their expressions solemn.

"Good. Now what else was it you wanted to talk to me about?"

"Oh, right." Edie walked over to the Bronco and opened the passenger door. She leaned in, stepping back a moment later with the note they found earlier in her hand. "This was under the wiper on my car this morning." She held it out as she walked back.

Mike took another pair of latex gloves from his pocket and put them on, then took the note. He read it and let out a low whistle. "You pissed her off." He glanced up. "What did you two do?"

Edie rolled her lips in, color staining her cheeks, and glanced at Jordan. A smile tipped his lips, remembering exactly what they did. A moment later, his smile died and his eyes widened. "Wait." He caught Edie's gaze. Her eyes grew round too. Jordan turned to Mike. "I think she's been watching my house. There's no other way she'd know—"

Mike let out a soft groan. "Please tell me you didn't have sex in front of an open window?"

"No. But—" Jordan stopped and looked at Edie. This wasn't his story to tell.

Edie crossed her arms and frowned, then inhaled a deep breath. "I had a nightmare last night. About my time in the military. I freaked out and ran out of the house in nothing but a blanket. Jordan chased me down and dragged me back inside."

"Whoa." Mike blinked in surprise. "I'm sorry you went through something that would cause you to react like that. Are you okay?"

Her expression softened. "Yes. Thank you for asking."

"Of course. So, the theory is that whoever put this on your

car saw you leave the house practically naked?" He waved the note.

"Yeah," Jordan said. "I don't know where she could have hidden, though. It's pretty open out there."

"True. But you have all those yard lights. In the dark, past the glow of those, you can't see anything. She could have sat on the ground with binoculars and watched. Have you considered putting in some security cameras?"

"I ordered some," Edie said. "They haven't come in yet. Back order."

Jordan grimaced. He was tempted to tell her to cancel the order now, so they could get the system elsewhere.

"Okay. In the meantime, you might want to set up some trail cameras, at the very least."

"I have some of those." He kept a few in his camping gear just so he could see what lurked while he slept. More than once he'd moved because a cougar wandered by.

"Good. Now go home and set them up. And remember what I said. Stay away from the park. I'll call you later." Mike gave them one last stern look, then headed for his car.

"Dammit," Jordan muttered. He looked at Edie. "I don't like this." Things felt like they were coming to a head from multiple directions.

"Me, either. Come on. Let's do what he says. I also want to call Asher again. Find you a good lawyer." Edie touched his arm, then turned to walk to the car.

"Yeah." Jordan followed, running a hand through his hair. And while she did that, he'd set up those trail cams.

THIRTY

"Jordan."

At the sound of Edie's voice, Jordan glanced up from the engine he was busy putting back together. His gaze traveled past her to Mike, who stood in the lobby. And he didn't look happy.

"Mike needs to talk to you."

"Tell him I'll be there in a minute." He worked the ratchet, reattaching a bolt as quickly as he could.

She went back inside without a word. Jordan finished attaching the part he'd been working on and set his tools down. Grabbing a rag, he went inside. "Hey, Mike. What's up? Do you have news?" He prayed it was good news. Like they'd found Justine—alive—and who his stalker was.

"Not good news, I'm afraid. I need you to come down to the station for a formal interview."

Jordan's shoulders slumped.

"What?" Edie stormed forward. "That's dumb. He didn't do anything to anyone."

Mike's face pinched. "I'm just doing my job."

Jordan laid a hand on Edie's arm. "It's okay, honey." He

looked at Mike. "Do you mind if we do this later this afternoon? I want to call my attorney and have her present."

"Of course. How about four o'clock? Then you can get in a mostly full workday."

"That should be fine. Let me talk to my lawyer to make sure, though. If you don't hear from me, we'll be there at four."

"Sounds good." Mike hesitated. "I really am sorry to have to do this, Jordan. You know I don't think you had anything to do with Justine's disappearance or with the body in the desert. But I—"

Jordan waved a hand. "I understand."

"Okay. Good." Mike backed toward the door. "I'll see you this afternoon."

"Yep."

Once the detective was gone, Jordan heaved a sigh, ending on a groan. "He must have found something in her car that points to me."

"Maybe. He did say if he found your prints, he'd have to formally interview you. He might also have cause of death on the body in the desert. Didn't he send another team out there?"

"Yeah." His shoulders sagged. Weariness weighed him down like hundred-pound weights on his shoulders.

Edie touched his arm. "Go back to work. I'll call the lawyer."

"You're sure."

She nodded.

Jordan leaned down and placed a soft kiss on her lips. "Thanks, babe. Let me know if the plan changes."

"I will." She spun away and walked back to the counter.

The rest of the morning and the afternoon dragged by. Jordan got a lot accomplished, but felt like he'd been at work for twice the amount of time he normally was. When it was time to go, he washed up and drove over to the police station, leaving Edie at the garage to answer phones and check out customers who came to get their cars after work. She hadn't been happy about staying behind, but she understood. He was glad he had her. He would have been forced to close early if she wasn't there.

The officer at the front desk logged him in, then led him into the back to a small room with a table and chairs on either side. The bare walls were painted a light gray. From one corner near the ceiling, the red light on a camera blinked. He glared at it as he sat down. It didn't surprise him that Mike wanted to record their conversation, but it irked him that he was a suspect. He hadn't done anything.

A few minutes later, the door opened, and the same officer showed in Jordan's lawyer, Alyssa Webber. When Edie called Asher to have him find the best local defense attorney, Alyssa's name had been at the top of that list. Much to Jordan's chagrin. He didn't want to retain her as his lawyer, but he didn't want to go to jail for no reason, either. So far, though, she'd been wholly professional.

"Hi, Jordan." She flashed him a smile as she walked into the room.

"Alyssa." He tipped his head in greeting. "How are you?"

"Oh, I'm fine." She sat down and opened her briefcase. "Did Detective Deyo give you any indication what this is about?"

Jordan glanced at the camera again. "Are you sure we should be talking in here?" He tipped his head toward the device.

She looked up. "Those don't have any sound. The detective will bring in a separate recorder."

"Oh."

"So, did he? Tell you why he asked you to come in?"

"Not really. I think it has something to do with Justine's

car. Something in there must point to me. I never did more than touch the door and its frame, which Mike knows. If there's something else, I don't know what it is."

"All right. We'll see what he has to say. He should be in soon."

A minute later, her prediction proved true. Mike walked in, carrying a file folder, a notepad, a pen, and a small hand-held recorder.

"Good afternoon. Thank you for coming in." Mike sat down across from them. He turned the recorder on, stated his name and who he was meeting with, then the case number before pausing to stare at Jordan.

Determined not to let his friend make him feel intimidated, Jordan offered him a wide smile. A corner of Mike's mouth lifted, and he clicked his pen.

"Tell me about Justine."

"What about her?"

Mike tipped his hand. "What was she like?"

"Nice. Funny. Pretty. Why does this matter?"

"Tell me how you met."

Jordan frowned. "At a bar. You know this."

"What was the name of the bar?"

"Rafters."

Mike jotted that down. "What was your evening like?"

"The night I met Justine?"

"Yes."

Jordan glanced at Alyssa. She leaned over to whisper in his ear.

"Stick to the details. Leave emotions out of it. He's fishing." She sat up.

Jordan looked at Mike. "It was like any other night when I went out. I wanted to have some fun, blow off a little steam."

"Did you?"

"Yes."

"How?"

"I drank a beer and danced."

"With Justine?"

"Yes, among others."

Mike nodded as he wrote a few notes. "Did you go with anyone or see anyone there who you knew?"

"I frequent the place enough that the bartenders know me. There are probably a few other regulars who would recognize me too."

"Why Justine? Why did you ask her out and not one of the other women you danced with?"

"She was nice. And she wasn't trying so hard to get my attention."

Mike gave him a pseudo-smile. "You like the thrill of the chase, huh?"

"No. I don't like to *be* chased." He gave Mike a hard stare. He knew what his friend was trying to do. It wouldn't work. He refused to admit to any type of stalker behavior. Mostly because he hadn't stalked her. She'd caught his eye because she was pretty. She'd intrigued him because she hadn't tried to fawn all over him. It was as simple as that.

"Tell me how the evening ended."

"We exchanged numbers and made plans to talk in a day or two. She walked out with her friends. I stayed a little longer to make sure my beer wore off, then went home."

Mike hummed, writing. "Okay. Now your date. Tell me about that."

"Not much to tell. We went to dinner. We talked and had a nice time. I walked her to her car, told her I'd call her soon, and we went our separate ways."

"Did you get a goodnight kiss?"

"Seriously?"

"Detective, I hardly think that's relevant," Alyssa said.

"Of course it's relevant. Maybe she spurned him when he tried, and he got angry."

The low-key frown that had settled on Jordan's face turned fierce. "That is total crap, and you know it."

Alyssa laid a hand on Jordan's arm. Jaw working, Jordan crossed his arms and seethed.

"Detective, why don't you offer us some information? It might make my client feel less attacked and more cooperative."

Mike's dark gaze bounced between Alyssa and Jordan. "Fine. The second search we did of Saguaro National Park yielded more body parts. We found a skull. Part of the spine was still attached. The medical examiner said it's a female. Dental records confirm it's Justine Lammers. The M.E. found knife marks on one of the vertebrae. It looks like someone slit her throat."

Jordan winced at the thought of what must have happened to her. "Damn." He blew out a breath and uncrossed his arms. "I didn't kill her. After our date, I tried to call her, but she never called me back. I figured the same thing happened with her that happened with Nicole. Mercy got a hold of her and scared her off." He narrowed his eyes. "Did you talk to Mercy?"

"She's on my list. Explain what happened with Nicole."

"Nothing happened. We went out once, just like I did with Justine. When I called her to ask her out again, she told me she didn't want to get in the middle of what I had with Mercy. I didn't have anything with Mercy by that point. The woman was, and still is, obsessed with me."

"I can confirm that," Alyssa said. "I saw her at a fundraiser dinner last week. We were in a group of people who were talking about the state of the local economy. Someone said something about how a lot of local businesses are feeling the crunch, but she mentioned that Jordan's was doing great. She talked about how she'd been in to get her oil changed and that you looked exhausted. We got a blow-by-blow account of how she thought you were working too hard, so she tried to get you to take a break, but your awful girlfriend, who was working the front desk, wouldn't let you."

Jordan chuckled. "I've worked less since Edie came to work for me than I have in months. But Mercy is correct that my business is going strong."

Mike scribbled another note. "We found your prints on Justine's car. Can you explain that? For the record."

"I touched the door and the frame when I said goodnight to her after our date. I did not get inside."

"Okay. Last question. Do you own any knives?"

"Jordan, don't answer that," Alyssa said. She turned a droll look on Mike. "Nice try, detective. We're done here." Her chair scraped on the floor as she pushed away from the table. "Let's go, Jordan."

Gladly, Jordan thought. He stood.

"Hang on." Mike held up a hand. "I have another question."

Alyssa frowned and opened her mouth to speak, but he cut her off.

"Not one that asks him to implicate himself."

"All right. What?"

"Did you notice anyone watching the two of you when you went out? Did you see anyone you recognized? Anyone at all?"

Alyssa held up a hand. "That's bordering on implication, detective. He's already given you his account. It's up to you to check his alibi."

"I'm just trying to find out if anyone was watching her."

Jordan looked at Alyssa. She nodded, and he turned back to Mike. "No. We went to a place in downtown Tucson." He named the restaurant. "It's not very big. I didn't see anyone there I knew, and no one seemed to be watching us. I wasn't exactly looking for a stalker, though."

Mike blew out a breath. "Okay. Thank you for coming in. I'll walk you out." He reached for the recorder and shut it off, then ushered them out of the room. In the hallway, he touched Jordan's shoulder. "I'm sorry about that."

"Look, I know you're just doing your job, but I don't appreciate the trickery. I didn't do anything, and turning me into a false suspect will only distract the D.A. from going after the real killer."

"I agree, but I can't show you favoritism. When I do find the killer, their defense attorney could use that against us. I refuse to leave any loopholes for this jerk to walk through."

Jordan's brows knit together. That made sense. "Fine. But I'm still pissed."

"I know, and I'm sorry."

"Do you have any leads?" Alyssa asked.

"No. The car was clean. Only her prints were inside. There are a few random ones on the outside of the car that we haven't matched yet. In our climate, that's not unusual. They don't wash away because we never get any rain."

"You know what I don't understand?" Jordan propped his hands on his hips. "Why haven't her friends reported her missing? We met when she was out with friends. But no one has called the police to say, 'Hey, I haven't heard from my friend in a while, and I'm worried.' It doesn't make any sense."

Mike's expression turned thoughtful. "You're right, it doesn't. Do you remember the names of the people she was with that night?"

"Oh, man." Jordan glanced up as he thought. "Leah, maybe? There was one other woman with her." What was that woman's name? He'd talked to both of them. It started with a D. Darcy? Danica? "Daniella. That's it. Her name was Daniella. I don't know their last names."

"That's fine. That's something for me to work with. The techs are trying to access her phone. Hopefully, they'll be in her contact list. I don't suppose that friend of Edie's can find them?" Mike asked, then waved his hands. "No. Never mind. That's a bad idea." He looked at Alyssa. "You didn't hear any of that."

She grinned. "I only heard it when I need a favor."

Mike groaned. "I need some sleep. This case is going to kill me. Or kill my career." He shook his head. "Jordan, thanks for the info. Did you do what I said and put up some trail cameras?"

"Yes. No new activity. She either watched us put them up and is keeping her distance, or she just hasn't been back. Either way, I'm frustrated. I don't like looking over my shoulder all the time."

"Some stalkers are never caught."

Jordan groaned. "Costa Rica is looking better and better."

Mike frowned. "You can't leave town."

"Not now, no. But I got offered a job there. And Edie's there. We were talking about getting married."

"What?" Mike glanced at Alyssa, then grabbed Jordan's arm, pushing him down the hall. "Thanks for coming, Ms. Webber. This is a friendly conversation now."

"Wait. Jordan, are you sure?"

"It's fine, Alyssa. Thanks." He glanced back and tried to smile as Mike continued to shove him down the corridor. "Where are we going?"

"My office," Mike muttered.

A moment later, they reached his door. He opened it and motioned Jordan inside.

"Okay, what is going on?" Mike planted his hands on his hips and frowned once they were inside with the door closed. "First, she was just pretending to be your girlfriend. Then you two slept together. Now you're getting married? What the hell?"

"She hasn't said yes, but I did ask her. I think it's a good idea. We get along now—mostly—and I like her. It might draw my stalker out of hiding too."

"You can't get married to bait your stalker. That's insane."

"Edie said the same thing."

"Smart woman."

"But it's not just about that. I really do like her."

"You should love her if you're going to marry her. That's not a commitment to take lightly."

"I know. And I wouldn't. I have no intention of ever divorcing her."

Mike sighed and brushed a hand over his short hair. "Just tell me if you decide to do it. It really could send your stalker into a rage. I want to be ready."

"You'll be the first one I call. Well, maybe after my mom."

"Does she know about Edie?"

"No. Well, she knows about her in the sense that I met her and several others when I went down to Costa Rica, but not that we're together."

"She's been here, what? Two weeks? And you haven't told your mom?"

"We're not that close; you know that."

Mike gave him a half smile. "My mom would have kicked my ass if I proposed to Carmen and didn't tell her about her first."

Jordan shrugged, not knowing what to say. He'd never been particularly close to either of his parents. His dad was a dirtbag. And while his mom was nice, she'd been so busy working to support them, they never spent much time together when he was growing up. He respected her, but they still didn't see each other often. Holidays, mostly. He called or texted her about once a month just to check in. That was it, though.

"Well, I wish you luck, man. Edie's a fireball. You're going to need it."

"Yeah," Jordan chuckled. "That's part of what makes her so appealing. I'm never bored."

"I can see that being the case. All right, well, go home. I've got work to do." He shooed him toward the door.

"You'll keep me posted, right? Especially if this has anything to do with my stalker?"

"Yes. I hope the cases aren't tied together, but I can't rule out the possibility. Just watch your back, okay? And Edie's."

"You got it. Thanks, Mike."

THIRTY-ONE

By the time Jordan returned, Edie had swept the lobby floor and the shop floor, put all the dirty rags in the laundry bin, cleaned the customer bathroom, refilled the coffee station, checked out four people, and booked another appointment. She hadn't been able to sit still. When the door chime went off at his arrival, she had a small bag of trash from the bathroom in her hand and was on her way into the back to dump it in the larger can. They would take it out to the dumpster when they left.

"Hey." She paused in the doorway to the back room. "How did it go?"

"Fine. Nothing I wasn't expecting. At least on what he found on the car. He did say they found a skull with several vertebrae attached and confirmed it was Justine. It looks like her throat was sliced."

Edie inhaled a sharp breath. "So it was murder, then? Damn. I was hoping she just went hiking and got lost."

"Me too." He sighed and glanced through the bay of windows into the shop. "Did everyone who was supposed to pick up their car already do so?"

"Yes."

"Good." He backtracked to the front door. "We're closed. Let's go get some dinner and go home. I'm beat."

Edie turned, and, after locking up, he followed her into the back room. She tossed the trash into the can, then pulled the bag away.

"I'll do that." Jordan batted her hands away. "Go shut the computer down. Is there any other cleaning left to do?"

"No. I did it all while you were gone."

"Awesome." He lifted the bag free of the can.

Edie retreated to the lobby. She ran the daily report, took out the cash drawer, and shut the computer down before returning to the back. Jordan was at his locker, removing his things. "Do you want to do the drawer before we leave?" He usually took the cash profits from the day to the bank each night.

"No. Just lock it all in the safe. We can do it in the morning."

With a short nod, Edie headed into the office. She opened the wall safe and put the drawer inside, then closed the door. The digital lock beeped as it secured the safe.

"Okay, all set," she said, coming back out. She took her coat that Jordan held out and put it on, then grabbed her purse.

He picked up the trash bag. "Let's go. What sounds good for dinner?"

"That diner we went to. I need more of their fries in my life."

A smile tugged at his mouth as he pushed the back door open. "Sounds good to me."

Edie crossed to the Bronco, waiting a moment while Jordan tossed the trash into the dumpster, then got in when he unlocked the car. The engine roared to life with a flick of his wrist, and they made the short trek to the Cactus Blossom Diner.

The scent of fries hit Edie again as they walked in. She smiled.

"Well, hello again."

Edie turned to see Lori smiling as she headed their way. "Hi."

"He's got you hooked, now, doesn't he? You'll never have a better burger."

"True. I'm craving fries, though, more than the burger. I mean, I won't turn one down, but I *need* the fries."

Lori laughed. "Go grab a seat. I'll be over in just a few minutes to get your order. Do you guys know what you want to drink?"

"Root beer is fine for me," Jordan said.

"Same." Edie smiled at Lori.

"Okay. I'll be over soon."

"Thanks." Jordan put a hand on Edie's back and ushered her toward a booth by the front windows. They paused to let a group of women pass. One of them waved at Jordan and offered him a small smile.

Edie squinted. She looked familiar.

"Hi, Chelsea." Jordan smiled at the woman.

The name clicked in Edie's mind. She was one of Jordan's customers.

"Is your car running well now?"

She nodded. "Yes. Thank you." Her gaze darted to Edie, then back to Jordan. "I heard about the trouble you've been having. I hope everything is okay."

"It's fine. Nothing we can't handle. Thank you, though."

The woman offered him a shy smile. "You're welcome." She glanced past him at her friends, who were nearing the door. "I should go. Have a nice evening."

"You too."

Chelsea walked around them, and they continued to a vacant booth. Sitting down, Edie looked out the window. Chelsea and her friends got into a car parked just down from theirs.

"It's supposed to snow this weekend."

Edie turned back to Jordan. "Oh yeah?"

He nodded. "We should go skiing."

Her eyes widened. She didn't know how to ski.

Jordan laughed. "What's the matter? Don't tell me the fearless Edith Campbell is scared of a snow-covered mountain."

She schooled her features into a blank mask. "Of course not." *Yes.* "I've never been, but I imagine it's a lot like surfing."

"Snowboarding is, yeah."

"Good. I'll take one of those, then." Some of her anxiety eased. She could handle snow surfing. "So, what all did Mike say?"

Jordan's smiled died. "They found my prints on the car, right where I said they would."

"Wait." Edie held up a hand. "How do they know they were yours? I don't remember you submitting prints." Her eyes widened. "Mike didn't take them off a glass from dinner at his house, did he?" That would be a rotten, un-friendlike thing to do.

"No. My prints are in the system."

Her eyebrows winged upward. "Really? For what?"

"I might have gotten into a bar fight when I was younger."

Edie laughed. "Might have?"

His mouth tilted in a half smile. "Yes. I was young and dumb. Luckily, it was minor. We were outside and too drunk to do much damage to each other. I got charged with disorderly conduct. The judge gave me community service and a fine."

"Who did you fight?"

"Some guy I went to school with. He kept hitting on my girlfriend. The funny thing is, she dumped me right after that. Apparently, defending your girlfriend is 'icky.'" He air-quoted.

Edie hummed. "Maybe she thought you were being juvenile."

"Honey, there is nothing juvenile about me." He sent her a heated look.

Fire lit her face as memories of just this morning hit her. No, there was definitely nothing juvenile about Jordan MacDowell. At least, not physically. She cleared her throat. "You can act like a kid sometimes."

"What man doesn't?"

Edie snorted. That was the truth. Even Mr. Serious, Ford, could act like a little boy sometimes. Especially if it involved fishing or one of his boats.

"Okay, two root beers." Lori sidled up to their table. She set the glasses down, then took out her order pad. "What do you two want to eat?"

"I'll just have a burger and fries," Jordan said. He looked at Edie.

"Same here," she said.

"Well, that's easy enough." Lori jotted down their orders. "Okey-doke. It'll be out shortly." She spun around and hurried away.

Edie unwrapped her straw and dunked it in her drink. "What else did Mike say?" She took a sip.

"Not much. Mostly, he asked me about my relationship with Justine. How we met, where we went on our date—that sort of thing. He did get a little... deceptive? He tried to get me to implicate myself. Some of his word choices and tone—they implied that I had a dark side." His mouth flattened, and he shook his head, looking out the window. "Afterward, he apologized. Told me he didn't want to show any favoritism. I get it, but it still makes me feel dirty."

Edie covered his hand. "I'm sorry."

He turned his hand over and threaded their fingers together. "I'll get over it." He flashed her a wicked smile. "You can beat me up later, then ease my pain by showering with me."

A laugh bubbled out of her throat. "Deal."

THIRTY-TWO

A yawn cracked Edie's jaw as Jordan turned into the drive Friday afternoon.

"Tired?"

She glanced at him and nodded. "It's been a long week. And *someone* woke me up early this morning." She narrowed her eyes at him in mock anger. She would never be truly upset with him when he woke her up like that. Not only was it immensely pleasurable, it also banished the vestiges of her nightmares. Piece by piece, she was rebuilding the vault to put those emotions back inside. This time, though, the walls were glass and had air holes so she could deal with things.

He chuckled. "Don't act like you're mad. You enjoyed it."

She grinned. Jordan's hands caressing her body was her new favorite way to greet the day. But they needed to start going to bed earlier if he was going to keep waking her up half an hour or more before her alarm went off. He might be able to run on less sleep, but she couldn't. It was one of the hardest things for her to deal with when she was in the military. Her body loved sleep. "Maybe so, but I'm still tired."

"Is this you telling me you want to sleep in tomorrow?"

"A little, yes. Especially if you're going to make me brave the cold all day." They planned to go snowboarding after lunch. She wouldn't mind the actual snowboarding part, but she wasn't looking forward to the cold. She missed the beach.

He sighed, but grinned. "Fine."

They crested the hill, and the house came into view. The Bronco's headlights washed over Edie's rental in the driveway. She didn't know why she kept the car. It wasn't like she used it much. Jordan had another vehicle she could drive. At this point, it was just costing her money. But finding time to return it was an issue. The garage kept them both hopping during the week.

They rolled closer to the house and her car. The lights bounced off of something glittering in the driveway. Edie leaned forward. "What is that?"

He slowed. "I don't—" A frown creased his forehead. "It looks like glass." Stopping, he put the car in park, and they got out.

Edie gasped. "Dammit!" All her side windows were smashed. She knew she should have returned the car. Groaning, she scrubbed her hands over her face. "Wonderful."

"I'll call Mike." Jordan took out his phone.

Giving the car a wide berth, Edie circled it. She shined the flashlight from her phone on the vehicle and the ground around it, looking for anything that could give them a clue as to who was responsible. Ideally, she'd love to find a scrap of fabric or blood. But she knew better. There was probably nothing.

"He's on his way. He told us to stay in the Bronco."

Edie looked at him over the hood of her car. "Why can't we go in the house?"

"He wants to check it before we go in. Make sure no one broke in and that it's safe."

"Oh." She shuddered. It hadn't occurred to her that someone or something could be in the house.

They piled back into the Bronco and waited for Mike to arrive. Edie peered out the window at the yard. "I hope the cameras caught her face."

"Yeah. Or her car. Anything we can use to identify her. I'm so over this."

"Me too."

After an agonizing twenty-minute wait, Mike pulled up. He got out of his car and grabbed an evidence kit from his back seat.

"You guys didn't touch anything, did you?"

"No." Jordan shut his door and walked over, Edie on his heels.

"Okay. Stay here. I'm going to check the house first. Let me have your keys." He set the kit on the hood of his car and held out a hand.

"They're in the Bronco." Jordan gestured to the truck, then walked over. He shut off the engine, then gave Mike the keys.

"I'll be right back." Mike headed for the front door.

Edie crossed her arms and leaned against the front of the Bronco. "Do you think he'll find anything?"

"I have no idea. I'm done trying to guess what Mercy will do next. I didn't think she was capable of this, so..." He gestured to Edie's car, then shrugged.

"Maybe it's not her."

"Who else would it be?" He leaned on the car next to her.

That was a good question. Stalkers weren't always rational about their reasonings. It could have been something minor that set the person off. In that case, it could be anyone.

Mike reappeared several minutes later. A dark frown sat on his face, but he didn't look any more concerned than he had when he went in.

"Anything?" Jordan asked.

"Not that I can tell. It was locked up tight."

"Well, that's a relief." Edie rolled her shoulders, trying to dispel a little of the tension making them stiff. At least she didn't have to worry about someone having invaded their private space.

"Can you go collect the trail cameras while I process the car?" Mike lifted the evidence collection kit off the hood of his car.

"Yep." Jordan straightened.

Edie pushed away from the Bronco. Together, they walked across the yard to the closest camera, using the flashlights on their phones to guide them out of the area illuminated by the pole lights.

"Oh, hell." Jordan's soft curse made Edie frown.

"What?"

He pointed his light at the camera.

She aimed her phone at it and squinted. "Crap." It was coated in black spray paint.

Growling with frustration, Jordan loosened the strap holding it in place and yanked it off the pole. "Let's go find the others. What do you want to bet they all look the same?"

Edie's lips flattened. "Probably."

They were right. The other two cameras were also coated in black spray paint. With their loot in hand, they went back to the driveway to show Mike.

"You get them?" he asked as they approached.

"Yeah." Jordan held them up. "Don't know how much good they'll be. They're covered in paint."

Mike paused. "For real?" He sighed. "Wonderful. Set them on the hood of my car. We'll pull the cards and look at them in a minute. I'm almost done here."

Doing as he said, Jordan set the cameras down, then they stood back and waited for Mike to finish processing Edie's car and the area around it. When he was done, he stowed the evidence kit and a few bags of evidence he'd collected in the back of his car, then grabbed a laptop from the front seat.

"Let's go inside. It's cold out here." Mike tipped his chin toward the house.

Edie didn't have to be told twice. She booked it into the house, savoring the warmth. Without the sun, the temperature had plummeted rapidly. The forecasted weather change was well on its way.

Flipping on lights, they stripped out of their coats and wandered into the kitchen. Mike set his laptop down, and Jordan opened the door to the memory card on the first camera.

"No way." He let out a soft groan.

"What?" Mike asked.

Jordan turned the camera around. "The memory card is gone."

"Hell. Are the others like that?"

Quickly checking them, they found they were both empty. Jordan gave them a disgusted shove. "I'm done with this chick. We need a new plan."

"She must have eyes on you somehow. I think I'll bring a team out in the morning and check your property and that around it."

"Sounds good. What can we do to draw her out?" Jordan crossed his arms and stared at Mike.

Edie had heard enough. She was done playing nice with this woman—whoever she was. It was time to get her to back off. And for Edie to claim her man. "We can get married."

Two sets of eyes turned on her. Surprise rounded them.

"What?" Jordan dropped his arms. "Are you sure?"

"You two are nuts." Mike shook his head.

Edie ignored him. "Yes." Conviction warmed her and pushed away the last of the chill from outside. She didn't know what her future would bring, but she was sure she wanted Jordan to be part of it. She was falling for him. God help her. She never thought she'd fall for any guy, especially not Jordan MacDowell. But his infectious smile and kind heart had wormed past all her defenses.

A slow, sexy smile spread over his face. His brown eyes lit with a glimmer she hadn't seen before. It took her a second to realize it was joy. He was thrilled she'd said yes.

An answering smile bloomed on her face. He stepped closer, pushing her hair back to cup the side of her jaw.

"Can we be strategic about this, at least?" Mike asked.

Jordan waved a hand, not breaking eye contact with Edie. "Yeah, sure. Whatever." He leaned closer. She stood on her toes, closing the distance.

"You realize this means you have to tell your mom about her now, right?" Mike's voice cut through their moment.

A bark of laughter escaped Edie's throat as his words registered. She pulled back and grinned up at Jordan. "It means I have to tell my family too."

THIRTY-THREE

"Are you ready? I've got them all on the line." Edie poked her head into Jordan's home office later that night.

He glanced up from the pile of receipts on the desk. "Yes." Time to let everyone in on their plan. Pushing back, he got up and followed her into the living room. He paused as they entered. "Whoa." The television screen was divided into four squares, a different view in each one. "I thought we were talking on the laptop."

"We are." She gestured to the device on the coffee table. A long cord trailed from it to the television. "It was easier to see everyone if I hooked it to the TV."

"I guess that's true." He glanced at the laptop. They did look rather squished there.

Edie sat down on the couch and patted the cushion next to her. Jordan sat and waved at everyone. "Hello."

A chorus of hellos came back.

"You weren't kidding when you said you were going to get everyone on the line." Jordan studied the faces. It really was everyone. Dean and Annabeth were in one section. Ford and Brooke were in another. Asher, Sam, and Max were in one together at Max's house, and Edie's friend Ezra and a woman Jordan didn't recognize were in the fourth one.

"What's going on?" Ford asked. "Edie, what's your news?"

"So, things have reached a bit of a boiling point here."

"With the stalker?" Dean asked.

She nodded. "We came home this evening to all the windows on my rental car smashed."

"Didn't you say you put up some cameras?" Ezra cut in.

"We did," Jordan said. "But she spray painted over all of them, removed the memory cards, and put them back up so we wouldn't know."

"What's the status on the security system you ordered?" Asher asked. "I can probably cancel that order and find you something that can get installed quicker."

"I already did that," Edie said.

Jordan looked at her. "You did?"

She nodded. "While you worked on the garage's books. I called the company and canceled the order. It hasn't even shipped yet. I found a different one, but haven't bought anything yet. I was thinking of going into Tucson and looking."

"What were you thinking of getting?" Asher asked.

Edie told him.

"Do you think you can install that by yourself? I can come up and help."

"Actually, that's sort of why we called this meeting," she hedged. "Not to get help with the security system installation, but to invite you all out here." She glanced at Jordan, a tremulous smile forming on her pretty face.

He smiled back at her and took her hand. A low grumble came through the TV speakers as the others noticed their actions. A feeling of rightness settled over him. Having this woman in his life was what he'd wanted from the moment he met her, even if it had taken him a little while to realize that fact. But now that he knew and now that he had her, he didn't intend to ever let her go. With his smile growing, he looked at the TV. "We're getting married."

"What?" Dean said. Several others said the same thing.

"Excuse me?" Ezra's voice rose above everyone else's. "Edie, are you sure about this?"

Her bright blue eyes met Jordan's again. He ran his thumb over her knuckles.

She looked at Ezra. "I am."

"Okay, not to be a party pooper, but why?" Max asked. "You two about strangled each other when he was down here." His mouth pulled. "I mean, I guess that could have been a sign you were attracted to each other and fighting it, but what changed?"

"You're right; it was a sign," Edie said. "We—I—just quit fighting it."

Ezra snorted. "You don't ever just quit at anything."

Jordan chuckled. "He knows you well." He glanced at Ezra. "I wore her down. What can I say?"

Edie smacked his chest. "Put your ego away, Jordie." She turned to the TV. "It's a long story, but suffice it to say my opinion of him has changed. We're also"—she paused and raised a finger—"and this is the part you guys won't like—hoping that our marriage will draw his stalker out into the open."

"Edie, no," Ezra scooted closer to the screen. "That is not a good reason to get married." Jordan was glad the man was on the other side of the country. He looked a bit scary right now. Protective. And while it made Jordan happy that Edie had someone willing to go to bat for her in her life, he didn't want to tangle with him.

"Hang on." Ford held up a hand. "Why do you think this will work?"

"Ford—" Ezra started.

Ford waved him off. "They have reasons. Let's hear them out."

Ezra growled, but stayed silent.

"So far, every time we've escalated things in our relationship, the stalker's message has changed." Edie reached for the stack of papers next to the computer. "These are copies of all the poems she's left. They start out all lovey-dovey. By the time I got here, she was starting to get a little miffed that he hadn't noticed her. Since I've been here, they've become increasingly angrier and more possessive. Except the last one. It was angry, but not possessive. She's pissed."

"Why?" Max asked.

Edie looked down. Jordan squeezed her hand and leaned in. "Hey. There's nothing to be ashamed of," he whispered in her ear. "I bet they've all had a breakdown or two as well."

She looked at him, studying his eyes for a long moment. Silently, he arched an eyebrow, asking her if she was ready to continue. When she nodded, he gave her a quick peck on the lips and pulled back.

Drawing in a deep breath, she turned back to their friends on the TV. "I had a breakdown last weekend. Things between us turned—intimate; and well, the grip I had on my emotions slipped. I had a nightmare."

Solemn silence met her confession. Jordan could see in the eyes of every man on the screen that they knew what kind of nightmare she'd had. Brooke, Annabeth, and the woman with Ezra all looked at their men and offered some reassurance through a touch or a hand squeeze.

"Anyway, I freaked out. I wanted to crawl out of my own skin. Since that's not possible, I did the next logical thing, and I ran. Out the door in nothing but a small blanket I pulled off the back of the couch. Jordan came after me and took me inside." She pulled in a breath and glanced at Jordan. "We think she was outside, watching the house, and saw him chasing me down. The note showed up the next morning.”

“This was right after I called you about Justine's car?” Asher said.

Edie nodded. “That's when we found it, when we went to meet Mike at the junkyard.”

“Read the poem,” Ford said. “The last one.”

Lifting the page, Edie read the short missive by Percy Bysshe Shelley. A fragment called *Omens*. Jordan shuddered as she finished. It was only four lines, but its ominous tone put a pit in his stomach.

“Damn,” Sam said. “I think it's pretty clear what this woman plans to do now.”

“I agree,” Ford said. “Ezra, I hate to say it, but I think their plan is a good one. We need to gain control of this situation. Forcing her hand will help us accomplish that.”

“We still can't be certain of where or when she'll make a move, though,” Ezra argued.

Jordan sat back, listening to them bicker. He caught Dean's eye. Dean shrugged, as if to say he knew this wasn't his decision. It was all the encouragement Jordan needed. He let out a sharp whistle. The call quieted.

“Thank you all for your input. But we didn't call you to ask for your opinions. We called to invite you out here for the wedding. We're going to Las Vegas tomorrow and getting married. You can either come support us, or you can kindly shut up.”

Silence reigned for several long moments. Then Ezra's low chuckle broke the quiet.

“I rescind all my misgivings. Edie, I hope you know what you're getting into. He won't be a doormat.”

“I don't want a doormat. And so you guys don't worry, I didn't say yes just because of the stalker.” She looked at

Jordan. "It had more to do with the effect he's had on me, and how I feel about myself and my past."

Jordan squeezed her hand, feeling tendrils of something foreign creeping through his heart.

"I know we have a lot of growing to do as a couple, but I have faith we'll get there."

"Me too." He leaned in and pecked another kiss on her cheek.

"So, I guess the next thing on the agenda is who can go and how we're all getting there." Ford's voice broke them apart. Jordan turned to look at the screen.

"I can ask Mariana to cover the bar," Sam said. "That frees me up. And Dean."

"Brooke made me hire more help." Ford looked at his fiancée. "My deckhands are great fishermen, so I can do some schedule rearranging and give one of them some experience on one of the smaller charters and one of my other captains experience on a bigger one. I doubt any of them will object to earning some extra money."

"My tours are the same. I have some people who can help out," Max said.

"My computer can go anywhere," Asher replied, smiling. "I'm in."

That left Ezra. He didn't get a chance to reply before the woman next to him spoke. "We're in." She smiled and waved. "Hi, Jordan. I'm Amy, Ezra's wife. We'll be there."

"What about Gretchen?" Ezra asked.

"We'll bring her with us. It's not like we're going to Vegas to drink and have some wild party."

Sam covered a chuckle with a cough.

Ford grinned. "Speak for yourself." Brooke elbowed him, and he laughed. "I'm kidding. We'll behave. Bring the baby."

"What time are you guys planning to get married?" Brooke asked.

"Probably not until the evening. We have a flight out mid-morning, but we have to get our license and book a chapel."

"Can you push the wedding to Sunday?" she asked.

"What are you thinking, babe?" Ford looked at Brooke with a curious frown.

"I'm wondering if Ezra can fly down here and pick us all up, then take us all to Vegas. It would be faster than a commercial flight, because there won't be any connections. More comfortable too, especially for Gretchen. But coming here, then going there is a lot for one day. Especially with a baby in tow."

"I agree," Ezra said. "Gretchen's pretty mellow, but I think that would be a lot for her. Splitting it up would be okay, though. And much better than flying commercial. There will be more room. What do you think, Amy?"

She nodded. "I think that would be fine. We could come down tomorrow morning, then fly out early in the morning on Sunday. How far do you think it is, honey?"

"From Costa Rica to Vegas? Seven or eight hours. It's maybe four-and-a-half down there from here."

"Let's do that, then," Brooke said. "Take the family plane, not the business one. It's bigger."

Ezra nodded.

"Does that work for you, Edie? Jordan?" Ford looked into the camera.

They looked at each other. Jordan lifted a shoulder. "It's fine by me. So long as we're back here Sunday night. I can't close the garage. My appointment book is full."

"I think that's doable." Ezra nodded once.

"It's settled, then." Ford smiled. "We'll see you in Vegas on Sunday."

Thirty-Four

"If we run into the girls while we're out here, Brooke will kill me." Ford glanced over his shoulder.

"Relax. It'll be fine," Jordan said. "It's not like Edie and I didn't spend all morning together already." They'd arrived yesterday, done some sight-seeing, then gone this morning to get their license. Other than the coffee run Jordan went on shortly after they woke up, they hadn't been apart until Brooke separated them.

"It doesn't matter. You heard her. She's reset the clock. No contact until the wedding."

"You'll be fine," Ezra said. "She won't hurt you. Much."

Ford let out a snort.

Jordan ignored them as he walked down the Vegas strip, looking for a jewelry store that wouldn't max out his credit card. He didn't want to be cheap—Edie deserved a nice ring— but he couldn't afford to go high end.

"What about that place?" Dean pointed to a storefront ahead of them and to the right.

Jordan lifted a shoulder. "Let's look." He crossed the street and led their group inside. Soft music played, but the store still felt hushed, like it held some secret. Probably that it was really expensive and didn't need to be. The markup he'd seen on jewelry so far was staggering.

"Hello. What can I help you gentlemen with today?" A man around Jordan's age came around the display case to greet them with a polite smile.

"I'm looking for wedding rings. And I need them today," Jordan said.

"Of course. We keep a selection in stock for just that purpose. It is Vegas, after all." The man's smile turned more affable. "They're over here." He led Jordan to a case in the middle. "Anything in there, we usually have in stock in every size. Usually."

Jordan glanced down. Rings of every color and variety met his gaze. He didn't even know where to start. He looked at Dean. "Help."

Laughing, his best friend stepped forward. "Do you want to start with yourself or with Edie?"

"Edie."

"Okay. Think about what she likes."

"Not flashy," Ezra said.

"But not boring, either," Ford added.

Jordan's head bobbed. "It needs to be simple, but definitely not boring." He looked down at the case. "Should I get an engagement ring and a wedding band?"

Dean shrugged. "She'd probably wear both, but only so long as the engagement ring didn't get in her way."

A platinum band with diamonds embedded in it caught Jordan's eye. "There. That one." He pointed.

The salesman circled the counter and opened the display case. He removed the ring and set it on top of the glass.

Jordan picked it up, trying to envision it on her hand. It was a simple design—just a ring of small diamonds with a thin platinum border. But it was clean and elegant. No-nonsense, but with some depth. It felt like Edie. And the price was right. He glanced up and nodded at the salesman. "This would work."

"You're sure? There aren't any others you want to look at?"

Dipping his head, Jordan looked at the array of jewelry in the case. Nothing else really caught his eye. It was all either too plain or too flashy. "No."

"Okay, then. How about for yourself?"

"Something that compliments this." He gestured with the ring he held.

"Do you want diamonds in it?"

"Hell no. Mister, I'm a mechanic. I'll pop a diamond out in two seconds flat the first time I reach into an engine block."

With a chuckle and a wide smile, the man reached into the case. "Then I suggest this." He brought out a gleaming silver ring. "It's titanium. Almost impossible to destroy. You'd lose your finger before you'd hurt that ring."

"I need that." Dean leaned forward. "I wonder if Annabeth would go for it?"

"It's a popular choice nowadays," the salesman said. "Especially among the working class."

Jordan paused and glanced up at the man's phrasing. "Excuse me?"

The salesman's cheeks reddened. "That didn't come out right. I meant it's popular with people who work with their hands daily. Because it's hard to destroy. Not because it's cheap. I mean, it's inexpensive because it isn't a precious metal, but it's not poorly crafted."

"Makes sense." Jordan decided to give the man the benefit of the doubt. He looked truly apologetic. "Okay. I'll take it. I don't suppose you have the titanium band in a women's ring? Set with diamonds?"

"Not with diamonds, no. At least, not that many. And I

wouldn't recommend buying your bride a titanium ring without her present to try it on. They can't be resized because of the metal's properties."

"Okay. I'll go with the platinum one, then."

"Great. Let me get your ring sizes, then I'll grab the rings and you can be on your way." He reached for an order pad. "What size do you need for your bride?"

Jordan sent a side look at Dean. He hadn't thought to ask Edie what ring size she wore.

Dean held up his hands. "Don't look at me."

"Well, what size did you buy Annabeth?"

"A six. But she's bigger than Edie."

"Amy wears a five and a quarter," Ezra said.

"I bought Brooke a five and three-quarters," Ford said.

"Hell." Jordan sighed, then looked at the salesman. "What would you recommend? I didn't ask."

The man tipped his head. "Do you have a picture of her?"

Jordan's face colored. He didn't.

Thankfully, Dean pulled out his phone. "I do. And it's of her hand, actually."

"Why do you have a picture of Edie's hand?" Jordan asked.

"From when she cut it. Annabeth sewed her up, and I jokingly took a picture of her handiwork." He swiped through his phone, then turned the device around. "Here."

Jordan laughed as he got a look at the picture. Edie held her hand up and glared at Dean. It was a wonder she wasn't flipping him off.

"Pretty lady." The salesman tipped his head. "You could probably get away with a five and a half. I think a six would be too big and a five too small."

"Works for me."

"All right." The man made a note, then grabbed a set of rings on a chain. He chose one and held it out. "Try that on."

Jordan slipped it over his finger, but it got stuck on his

knuckle. The man took the chain back and picked a different one. This time, it fit perfectly.

"Okay. Let me go grab these from the vault. I'll be back in a few minutes."

"Okay, thank you." Jordan backed away from the counter as the man walked away. Turning, he looked at his friends. Dean and Ford looked relaxed. So did Ezra. But Max and Sam stood toward the back, arms crossed. Jordan nudged Dean's shoulder with his. "What's wrong with them?" He tipped his chin toward Max and Sam.

Dean looked over, then grinned. "I imagine Max is having flashbacks. And Sam gets hives at the word commitment."

"What?" Sam glared at him. "I do not. This is all just too —" He swirled a hand, frowning as the word escaped him. "You know what I mean." He folded his arms again and glared. "It's too frilly. I don't do frilly."

Max laughed. "I don't think any of us do."

Sam rolled his eyes. "Oh, whatever. I caught you wearing a tiara and nail polish last week when you watched Margot's twins."

"That's different. They're kids. I'll do frilly for kids."

"For *those* kids, you will."

"What's that supposed to mean?"

Sam turned to face him. "It means—" He stopped, his gaze going to the street outside. A deep frown marred his face. "What the—" He stepped closer to the window.

"What is it?" Ford walked closer, shoulders tense as he looked outside.

Jordan took a step toward them, his own radar going up. What had Sam seen?

"I thought I saw—" Sam shook his head. "But that's not possible."

"Saw what?" Ford asked.

"Nothing." Sam continued to stare down the street.

Suddenly, he turned toward the door. "I'll meet you guys back at the hotel later."

"What?" Ford took two steps after him. "Sam?"

Sam waved and hurried out the door.

Ford turned around. "Anybody see what he saw?"

A chorus of, "No," met his question.

"Should one of us follow him?" Jordan asked. Considering the background of this group, it could be dangerous.

Ford shook his head. "Sam can take care of himself. Let him go."

"Sir? I have your rings if you'd like to take a look."

As a group, Jordan and the others spun around. The salesman stood behind the counter holding two ring boxes. He smiled and gave them a wiggle.

Jordan smiled back and stepped forward, putting his worry about Sam on the back burner. Ford was right. He could handle himself. He'd seen that firsthand when Annabeth was kidnapped. And honestly, he had enough going on today to keep his mind plenty occupied.

He took Edie's ring from the salesman and opened the box. A gleaming wedding band sparkled in the overhead lights. It would look beautiful gracing Edie's hand. He couldn't wait to put it there.

Thirty-Five

Edie stared at herself in the mirror, barely recognizing the woman staring back at her. Brooke had come at her with a makeup brush and a curling iron, refusing to let her walk down the aisle with just powder on her face and her hair in a braid. She'd also made sure they all had the proper attire. Edie had put her foot down, though, when Brooke wanted to buy her a five-thousand-dollar wedding dress. She didn't care how much money the woman had; that was ridiculous. With Brooke's, Annabeth's, and Amy's help, she'd found a dress that didn't break the bank—and paid for it with her own money.

She leaned closer to her reflection, trying to find herself. "If my sister saw me like this, she'd think I'd gone off the deep end."

Brooke chuckled. "What have you told your family, anyway?"

"Nothing. They know I'm in the U.S. working on a favor for Dean, but that's it."

"You haven't told them about Jordan? At all?" Brooke stared at her reflection with wide eyes.

"No. I figured I'd give this some time. Make sure it's actually going to work, then tell them. Maybe do a vow renewal or something and invite them to that."

"You should have invited them today."

Edie lifted a shoulder. "They'd just freak out. They're going to freak out no matter when I tell them, but at least it won't add to my stress level today." It bothered her a bit not to have her family present, but she didn't want them second-guessing her decision. She also didn't want to put them in the line of fire. They were safe in Oregon. She intended for them to stay that way.

"Are you sure you want to do this?" Annabeth asked from her spot on the couch. "It's not too late to back out. Jordan will understand."

"I know he would, but I don't want to back out. I still think this is the right thing to do."

"You're sure?"

"Yes." And she was. She knew it was fast, but it felt right. She should probably think more on why that was, but the L-word was scary. Edie choked back a laugh. She wasn't sure why, since she was getting married anyway.

"Okay. I can't argue. I was ready to marry Ford even before the dummy figured out he loved me."

Laughing, Edie got up and gave Brooke a hug. "Thank you for making me beautiful."

"You were already beautiful. I just brought out the best bits." She looped her arm through Edie's. "Come on. Let's go get you married."

They left the hotel suite and walked down to the lobby. When the others had arrived today, Brooke had taken one look at the accommodations Jordan and Edie had secured, declared them unacceptable for a couple about to get married, and asked the front desk to move them into a suite. Edie had tried to argue that it was pointless—they weren't staying another night—but Brooke hadn't cared. She'd worked her magic and had the room transferred to her name, calling it her wedding present to them. Then she'd booted Jordan out of the suite, telling him it was bad luck to see his bride before the ceremony. It didn't matter to her that they'd already spent the day together; Brooke was determined to see tradition upheld. Ford, ever-indulgent of his fiancée's eccentricities, had just laughed and pulled Jordan from the room, taking him to the second suite they'd booked.

Noise from the casino floor enveloped them as they stepped off the elevator.

"Where are we supposed to meet the guys?" Edie glanced around, looking for them.

"At the chapel. You still don't get to see your groom yet." A wide grin split Brooke's face as she led them toward the exit.

"We need one of those van taxis," Amy said as they walked through the glass doors at the front of the hotel.

"Taxi? Oh no. No bride should ride to her wedding in a taxi." Brooke shuddered. "We're taking that." She pointed to a slick black limousine parked at the curb.

Edie groaned. "Remind me when you and Ford get married to do things to embarrass you." She was already planning a speech in her head for the reception.

Brooke laughed and sauntered toward the limo. "FYI, I'm *really* hard to embarrass, so good luck."

The chauffeur came around and opened the door. Brooke waved Edie and the others forward. Reluctantly, Edie got in. She hated being the center of attention. At least, not for something like this. She just wanted a low-key wedding. To say her vows, get her first kiss as a wife, then to go have a quiet dinner and retreat to bed with her new husband—after flying home, of course. She could only imagine what Brooke had up her sleeve for the reception.

Sliding onto the leather seat, she looked at Brooke. "Please don't make a huge fuss at the reception. I appreciate that you want to make the day special for me and Jordan, but even if we'd planned this out and done it the proper way, I still wouldn't have anything fancy or big. I'm just not that kind of person."

Brooke's smile took on a serious and genuine note. She nodded. "Don't worry. I did book a restaurant for dinner, but I promise there will be no grand announcement to the entire establishment or a band serenading you as you eat. Just dinner. And cake."

"Now, that I agree with," Amy said. "You can't have a wedding without a wedding cake."

"I can handle cake." Edie relaxed a bit. "Thank you for all you've done, Brooke. I truly appreciate it. You didn't have to do any of this. We were content to just say our vows and maybe even get cake from the vending machine."

Brooke wrinkled her nose. "As good as that cake is, we can do better. And you're welcome. I love to plan parties and to spoil my friends. But I promise I'll rein it in." She grinned. "I'll let it all out for my own wedding."

They all laughed.

"Poor Ford." Amy shook her head.

"Hey. He asked your husband to fake a chopper malfunction to propose to me. He'll do whatever I ask of him for our wedding."

"I'm still amazed you said yes after that." Edie chuckled. "I'd have kicked his ass."

"It's a testament to how much I love him that he's still alive."

Conversation turned to Brooke's wedding plans as they made their way to the chapel. Her wedding was still months away, but Brooke, being Brooke, had already made some major headway on the event. Edie had no doubt it would be a tasteful but lavish affair.

The limo slowed to a stop out front of a small white chapel. When the chauffeur opened the door, Edie's heart went into overdrive. This was really happening.

Getting out, Edie adjusted her skirt, then followed her friends inside. Soft music played, and she could hear the sound of the minister's voice coming over the speakers on the other side of the double doors in front of her. Another couple sat on the benches in the corner, holding hands. The woman clutched a small bouquet of pink roses.

"Hello. Welcome to the Love Chapel. Do you have an appointment?"

Edie looked over at the sound of a woman's voice. A smiling middle-aged woman sat behind a dark wood desk.

"Um, yes. Edie Campbell and Jordan MacDowell?"

"Ah. Yes. If you want to have a seat, the minister will be with you shortly."

"Thank you." Edie gave her a polite smile, then turned away. She glanced around again, but the occupants of the room hadn't changed. "Where are the others?" she asked Brooke.

"There's a small anteroom here. Ford brought Jordan here first, and they're all waiting in there. He'll be at the altar when the doors open."

"Oh. Okay." It still amused her how determined Brooke was to adhere to tradition. If it had been up to Edie, she and Jordan would be like the couple in the corner—sitting together waiting their turn.

She looked over at them again. The man had a small black box in his hands and spun it slowly as he stared at the doors. It clicked in Edie's brain what it was, and her eyes widened. "Crap!" she whispered.

"What?" Brooke glanced over, a concerned frown knitting her brows together.

"Rings. We didn't buy rings."

Brooke waved a hand. "Don't worry about that."

It was Edie's turn to frown. "Why? Does this place provide them?" She wrinkled her nose. There wasn't much about a traditional wedding that Edie wanted, but she did want a legitimate wedding ring. Not some overpriced silver thing that felt as cheap as it looked.

"They do, but Ford texted me while we were out dress shopping. Jordan insisted they go to a jewelry store. He's not going to let you wear a cheap ring."

Warmth spread through Edie's belly. Tendrils of it touched her heart, making it thump as an intense feeling of— something—shot through her.

Whoa.

The doors opened, music swelling from inside, interrupting her thoughts. A couple emerged, holding hands. Wide smiles lit their faces. The woman gave the bouquet to the receptionist, and her groom handed the older woman a sheet of paper. She made a copy of it, handing that to them and keeping the original, and then they left.

"So"—the minister clapped his hands from the doorway —"where's my next bride? Edie?"

"Oh." She turned to look at him. In his sixties, the man had a head full of silver hair, perfectly coiffed, and a tan so dark, Edie wondered how he didn't look like a shriveled prune. His gray suit emphasized his slim, elegant frame, and he smiled at her with kind blue eyes.

Her gaze darted to the couple in the corner. "They're not next?"

The groom shook his head. "We're early. I think we're after you."

Edie turned to the minister. "I guess you're looking for me, then."

"Wonderful." His smile widened. "Let me tell your groom

you're ready. Listen for the music. When it changes, that's go time."

Edie swiped her palms on her thighs. "All right. Thank you."

With a nod, he backed into the sanctuary and pulled the doors closed.

"Okay, this is it." Brooke walked over to the receptionist, who handed her a bouquet of deep red silk roses. She crossed to Edie and held them out. "Here. She has other colors if you don't like these, but this color feels like you."

Barely giving the flowers a glance, Edie took them. "They're fine." Honestly, she was just glad to have something in her hands. The urge to fidget crawled through her like ants at a picnic.

Brooke cracked the door open and peeked inside. "They guys are coming in." She glanced back at Annabeth and Amy. "Let's go take a seat."

With well wishes and words of encouragement, the three women slipped through the door, leaving Edie alone in the vestibule. She pulled a shaky breath in through her nose and pressed her lips together.

You can do this. You want *to marry him.*

She rolled her neck and paced a few feet. Spinning on her heel, she marched back to the door.

"You know—"

Edie yelped and spun around, laying a hand on her heart. "You scared me."

The receptionist smiled. She'd come up behind Edie like a stealth bomber.

"Sorry, dear. I just wanted to say that I met your young man when he came in with his friends. He's very enamored with you. I get the feeling your wedding is rushed. I won't ask why." Her gaze darted to Edie's belly, then back to her face, which heated with embarrassment. "But he very much wants to marry you."

"I'm not pregnant."

"Even if you were, that's okay."

"Right. But I'm not. We just have—reasons—for wanting to get married."

"Everyone does." She patted Edie's arm. "Anyway, I thought you should know he's eager to marry you. I think he loves you very much. So take heart in that and use it to banish some of those nerves. He'll treat you right."

Of that, Edie had no doubt. Over the last few months, and especially in the last few weeks, she'd learned Jordan lived by a firm set of principles that included respecting people, even if they didn't deserve it. Sure, he was boyish at times, but he was kind and compassionate. Caring. When she'd flipped out from her nightmare, he'd been gentle with her and listened without judgement. He could have easily backed away and told her he didn't want to be involved with a woman who carried her baggage. But he hadn't. He'd embraced her and told her it was okay to be not okay.

That warmth spread through her belly again. This time, when she felt it touch her heart, she recognized it for what it was. She was in love with Jordan MacDowell.

Thirty-Six

Why was this taking so long? Jordan clasped his hands more tightly in front of his waist and forced his feet not to tap. He glanced at the speaker mounted in the corner, willing it to start playing the wedding march so they could get on with it. He was ready.

"You know, if you clench your teeth any harder, you won't have any left to eat your wedding cake later." Dean leaned forward from his position just behind Jordan to whisper over his shoulder.

Jordan sucked in a breath and forced his muscles to relax.

"You don't have to do this. We can come up with a different way to draw your stalker out."

"For the millionth time, I'm not marrying her just because of that." He glared at Dean over his shoulder. "Stop trying to dissuade me."

"I'm not. I just want you to be sure. It's marriage."

"I am sure, so shut up."

Dean held up his hands. "Fine. But if you break her heart, I don't care that you're my best friend. I'll beat the snot out of you."

"I'll beat it out of myself." He never wanted to hurt Edie. She meant the world to him, and he wanted her to be happy. Always.

"Good."

The music changed and swelled.

Finally.

The doors opened and Edie stood there in a long, satin, ivory dress that hugged her curves. Her flaming hair hung in loose waves around her shoulders, set off by the light color of her dress. Clutched in her hands was a small bouquet of red roses. She looked like a fiery angel.

And she was his.

He cleared his throat. "Damn," he whispered.

"Double damn. She looks great," Dean said.

With agonizingly slow steps, Edie proceeded down the aisle until she faced him.

"Hi." She offered him a tremulous smile.

"Hi." He smiled back. "You look fantastic." He touched her hair, fascinated by the way it moved about her like this. She rarely wore it down.

"Thank you. So do you."

He spared a quick glance at himself. He'd packed the one suit he owned. A charcoal number he'd bought several years ago. He'd left his tie at home, though. It felt too formal for what they wanted. He was glad he did. While her dress was elegant, it held an air of casualness. It suited her well.

"Are we ready to proceed?" the minister asked.

"Yes," Jordan said.

Edie nodded and handed her bouquet to Brooke, who acted as her maid-of-honor. Jordan took her hands in his, and they faced the minister.

Words floated around them, but Jordan hardly registered what was said. He repeated his vows, listened to Edie say hers, then felt the cool metal band settle around his finger to signify their commitment. It was over in minutes, but the change that settled over him was profound. His life wasn't just about him anymore. He had a wife.

A wife. Edie was his wife.

When the minister pronounced them husband and wife, he gathered her into his arms. Holding her gaze for a moment, hoping she could see how happy he was, he closed the gap and kissed her. It was a kiss like no other they'd ever shared. Poignant and full of fire, it was a promise to each other that they were in this together now.

Clapping and a sharp whistle from Max pulled them apart. Grinning, Jordan took Edie's hand and turned to face their friends. With a tug and a broad smile, he pulled her back down the aisle. They made it through the doors, and he swept her into his arms to kiss her again.

"We did it," she whispered, awe in her voice.

"We did. Are you happy?"

She framed his face. A bright smile spread over hers. "Yes."

He kissed her again as the doors opened behind them, spilling their friends into the room.

"Who's ready to party?" Max's voice raised over the din.

"After they sign their license." The minister stepped around the group with a smile. "You two hustled out of there before you made it official." He held up the paper they'd gotten from the marriage license bureau earlier in the day.

The receptionist walked up with a clipboard and a pen. The minister thanked her, then handed both to Jordan. He scrawled his name on the document, then passed it to Edie. She put her signature next to his.

"Perfect." The minister took the clipboard and pen and signed his name below theirs. He passed the items to the receptionist. "Samantha will make you a copy quickly, and you can be on your way. Congratulations."

"Thank you." Jordan shook his hand.

"You're welcome. I hope you have a happy life together." Smiling, he turned toward the couple in the corner. "It's your turn."

Jordan looked at Edie. "You ready to go eat some cake, Mrs. MacDowell?"

She laughed. "Yes."

"Come on." Brooke motioned them to the door. "The limo is waiting for us."

With their newly minted marriage certificate in hand, they headed outside. Somehow, the eleven of them fit themselves into the limo, and they set off for the restaurant Brooke had booked.

Jordan tucked Edie into his side and held her hand. He touched the platinum and diamond band he'd slipped onto her finger. "Do you like it? I tried to pick out something that still had some personality, but that you could wear without it getting in the way. We can get you a proper engagement ring if you want."

"I do like it. It's perfect. And don't waste your money. It would just sit in a jewelry box. You were right to get this." She touched the ring with one finger. "Thank you. It's lovely."

He pressed a quick kiss to her lips, then left her mouth to trail kisses along her jaw to her ear. "I like your dress. It'll look even better on the floor of our bedroom later."

She smacked his chest and chuckled softly. "You better stop. We're in public."

He hummed and kissed her neck, then sat up. It would be a long evening. They still had their flight home before he could ravish her.

The limo pulled up outside of the restaurant, and they got out. Inside, the host led them to a small room. The staff had pushed several tables together to make one large square table. To the side against the wall, a two-tiered wedding cake sat. Covered in white frosting, red roses cascaded down the side.

Jordan's phone buzzed in his pocket. He pulled it out to see a text from Mike, asking how things were going. He showed it to Edie.

"You can call him, if you want. Just tell me what you want to drink. I'll order it while you're gone."

"Water and a glass of white wine."

She nodded, then stood on her toes to peck him on the cheek. "Hurry back."

"I will." He stepped from the room, dialing Mike.

"Hey, man. You didn't have to call. I didn't mean to take you away from things," Mike said when he answered.

"It's fine. We just got to the restaurant for the reception."

"So, you really did it, then, huh?"

"We really did."

"Good. Now I don't look like a liar." Mike chuckled. "I deliberately ran into Mercy and mentioned what you were up to. We'll see what happens next."

"Ah, so that's what you meant by being strategic about this."

"Yep. I spread the word about your marriage. Mercy wasn't the only one I told. I mentioned it to Lori at the diner too. Within earshot of several others."

"Just out of the blue? Don't people think you're nuts?"

"I worked it into conversation. I didn't just announce you were off getting married. Don't worry. I'm not dumb, Jordan."

Jordan scoffed. "You tried to pin a murder on me. That's pretty stupid."

Mike sighed. "Are you still on that? I told you I was just doing my job."

He did, but he liked giving Mike a hard time. With a chuckle, Jordan leaned against the wall and crossed his ankles. The door beside him opened and Sam walked out, a pensive look on his face. He held a champagne glass. Seeing Jordan, he nodded, then walked toward the main doors. Jordan still didn't know why he'd run out of the jewelers earlier. Whatever it was had left him in a dark mood. The man was usually reserved, but he'd been even more so this evening.

"Anyway, I've got eyes on your house and your garage." Mike's voice pulled Jordan from his thoughts. "Hopefully, we'll catch some action."

"You going to keep those eyes there when we get home?"

"Yes. At least for tonight. We're more likely to get a knee-jerk reaction today than another day. I can't promise anything after tonight, though."

"That's fine. I think Asher's coming back with us to set up a security system. We should be good."

"Okay. Go enjoy your reception, now. And congratulations."

"Thanks, Mike." After saying goodbye, they hung up. Jordan pocketed his phone and went back to his bride, pushing the conversation to the dark recesses of his mind. He refused to think about his stalker. She may have prompted his quick marriage, but she wasn't the reason.

He stepped into the private room. Edie looked up. Seeing him, a happy smile lit her pretty face.

Jordan's heart thumped.

She was.

THIRTY-SEVEN

"Are you sure you'll survive without me?" Edie clutched handfuls of her husband's work shirt, holding him in place. "Asher and I can go buy cameras later."

Jordan rolled his eyes. "I survived without you for months. It's one day. I'd rather you guys get the security system up and running than have you answer my phone. I'll just change the voicemail message, so people know I'm too busy to answer."

She frowned. "Fine. But if things get hairy, call me, please? I can come help out for a little while and get you caught up."

"I'll be fine." He pecked a quick kiss on her lips, then covered her hands with his and stepped back. "I need to go. Car maintenance waits for no one."

She chuckled. "Okay. I'll see you this evening. Have a good day."

"I will." He kissed her again, this time with more passion.

Edie's blood heated, remembering last night. It was a wedding night to remember, that was for sure. They'd barely made it in the door before he'd pressed her against the wall and sealed their lips together. She'd never had sex standing up before. It wouldn't be the last time they did that.

She pushed away before she decided to make him late. "Get out of here."

He grinned. "Yes, ma'am." With a quick kiss, he left.

Wandering to the dresser, she grabbed some clothes to go take a shower. She was being lazy today. Normally, she was up and dressed before Jordan. But he'd worn her out last night. And since she knew she didn't have to go in with him, she'd taken advantage of that and stayed in bed while he got up. She could do with a little more sleep, but that wasn't going to happen. Asher would be here in less than an hour to pick her up.

Hurrying through her shower, she dressed, then went downstairs and made herself some breakfast. Asher arrived a few minutes after she finished and had washed her dishes.

"Hey." She smiled, opening the door for him.

He stepped inside. "Hey. You ready to go?"

"Yes. I just need my jacket." She retreated to the kitchen and grabbed her coat from the hook by the door and shrugged into it. Stepping into her shoes, she picked up her purse and house keys and followed him outside.

She took one look at his rental car and laughed. "Why did you rent a sports car?" The gleaming black Mustang shone in the morning sunshine.

He shrugged. "Why not?"

"Will it fit everything we need to get? We can take Jordan's truck if we need to. He fixed it."

"It's just some camera boxes and some insulated cables. It'll be fine." He opened the driver's door and nodded to the passenger side. "Get in."

Edie sighed and got in. She hoped the car had good brakes. Asher liked to speed.

The engine roared to life, and he grinned. "I love this car."

Chuckling, Edie put on her seatbelt. "I'd like to not make

Jordan a widower the day after we get married, so please keep the craziness to a minimum."

Asher laughed and put the car in gear. They shot forward. "You're a spoilsport."

"No. I just want to live." She clutched the door.

"Relax. I'll behave." He let off the gas, but still took the turn onto the road faster than she would have liked. The car stayed glued to the pavement, though.

"So, are you happy about being a married woman?"

"Yeah. Surprising, I know." She gave him a droll look, then turned to watch the scenery pass. "It's funny; I never really thought about getting married. Like, in the back of my mind, I knew it would probably happen. One day. It was always 'one day.' I just never imagined when that one day would be. Or who it would be with. Jordan's made me realize I was more or less just going through the motions of life. I was existing on the surface and not really living it because I didn't want to chance letting my emotions have any control."

"I can see that. You were a hard woman to get to know. And even now, I feel like there are parts of yourself you don't share."

A pang of misgiving went through her. "I'm sorry."

"Don't be. We all deserve to have things we keep to ourselves. I just hope you share more of yourself with Jordan than you do with the rest of us."

"I do." Her voice was quiet. "He saw me at my worst and didn't run. In fact, he helped me banish it. No one else has ever done that. He also suggested I go talk to someone again."

"Are you going to?"

"Probably, yeah." She looked at him. "I talk to him, but he's just a vent for my fears. I need someone who can help me process them." Her glass-walled prison was holding for now.

"Do you need help finding a therapist? I can do some digging. See who's around here who's good."

"No. I'm not even sure we're staying here. Did you know Brooke offered him a job at the new resort?"

"I'd heard that, yes. He's considering it?"

"Yeah. Once I know where we'll end up, I'll find someone to talk to. I'm good for now, though."

"Good. I'm glad things seem to be working out for you two, Edie. He's a good guy."

He was. She just hoped they could make it work. They still hadn't talked about how they felt. She knew she loved him. But she didn't know where he stood. And she was too scared to ask, afraid if she did, he wouldn't feel the same. Then where would she be? She didn't want to find out, so for now, she was keeping her feelings to herself. She'd show him in other ways.

Edie dipped her head to hide her smile.

Many, many other ways.

Thirty-Eight

"Okay, you little bugger. Where are you leaking from?" Jordan shined his light into the engine compartment of Mr. Dardino's car and traced the washer fluid hose from the reservoir. He'd noticed when he topped it off that a puddle formed under the car. He knew he didn't spill any, so that meant there was a leak somewhere.

Wetness gleamed in the light from the hose about half an inch from the bottom of the reservoir. Right where it bent to turn back up toward the windshield. He wiped the fluid away and waited. It welled from the bend. Mr. Dardino needed a new hose.

Removing the line, Jordan drained the washer fluid into a pan. He'd give the client a quick call and see if he wanted it replaced today. If not, he'd reattach the hose, but leave the reservoir empty. It would all just leak out anyway.

With the tank drained, he grabbed the handheld phone from his workbench and dialed the number on the work order.

"Hello?"

"Hi, Mr. Dardino. It's Jordan at MacDowell's Garage.

You have a leak in your washer fluid hose line. A pretty decent one. I've drained the fluid, so it doesn't just end up all over the ground. Would you like me to replace the line today?"

"Um, sure. I guess. How much extra is that going to run me?"

"Not too much." He named a figure. "I can get you a more exact estimate, but it'll take me a few minutes."

"No, that's fine. That's reasonable. Thank you, Jordan."

"You're welcome. It should be done in a couple of hours. I don't think I have any of that hose type on hand, so I'll have to get it sent over from the parts store."

"That's fine. I wasn't planning to pick it up until later this afternoon, anyway."

"Okay. It'll be ready for you."

"Thank you. See you then."

"Yep, bye."

"Bye."

Jordan hung up and went to where he kept his hose supplies. He was ninety-nine percent sure he didn't have any of that type of hose; he didn't do many washer fluid hose repairs. But there was a chance he was wrong. Rifling through his supplies, he didn't see what he wanted. He'd have to get some.

Moving over, he checked his drawers for a fitting to connect the new piece to the old, but didn't see that either. He picked up the phone again to call the parts store.

"Meyer's Auto Parts, this is Brian."

"Hey, Brian. It's Jordan. I need a couple things." He listed the parts.

"You'll have to come get it if you want it today. Neal's out sick," he said, mentioning his delivery guy.

Jordan wrinkled his nose. He hated leaving the garage with no one here. It meant he had to close. But he wouldn't be gone long. The store was just down the road. "Okay. I'll be there in about ten minutes. Thanks."

"Yep."

He hung up and put the phone down, then hurried into the lobby. He'd stick a sign on the door.

After scribbling a note on a piece of printer paper and taping it to the door, he climbed into his Bronco and took off for Meyer's. The bell on the door dinged as he entered.

Brian emerged from the stacks behind the counter. "Hey. I just gathered your stuff. Let me grab it. It's on the order shelf." He disappeared into the stacks again.

"Hi, Jordan."

He turned at the female voice behind him. "Oh, hello." He offered Andrea Harris a polite smile. "Everything okay with your vehicle?"

She nodded. "I needed some new car mats and some upholstery cleaner." She waved the can in her hand. "My dog found a large mud puddle on our walk the other day. I've only made a dent in the mess on the back seat. And I decided it's easier to clean rubber mats, so I tossed the carpeted ones."

"That makes sense. They are definitely easier to clean." He had rubber mats in all his cars for that very reason. Oil and grease didn't come out of carpet very easily.

"Okey-dokey." Brian returned.

Jordan turned around. He reached into his pocket for his wallet.

"What is that?"

Andrea's shocked tone made him pause. He glanced at her. "What is what?"

She pointed at his hand. "That."

He lifted his left hand. She'd seen his ring. "My wedding ring. I got married."

"What?" Her screech could have cured the deaf. "To whom?"

"My girlfriend, Edie."

She blinked rapidly. "Oh." She offered him a watery smile that didn't meet her eyes. "I guess we can't all be lucky." Looking away, she stepped around him and set the can on the counter. "Excuse me." Spinning on her heel, she left.

"What do you want to bet hers isn't the only heart you broke by getting hitched?"

Jordan stared after her. It wasn't like he hadn't noticed the way she—and other women—looked at him. But he'd never imagined taking himself off the market would cause such a visceral reaction. It made him wonder who else might react like that. "Yeah." Shaking his head, he turned back to Brian. "I never led anyone on, so I don't understand it. I've always tried to be nice to people. If some women took that the wrong way, I'm sorry. I was just being kind."

"Oh, I know. But some women see a good-looking man and their brains lay claim without them giving permission. They'll get over it. There's always someone else for them to chase." He shook his head, exasperated, as he picked up the scanner and rang up Jordan's items.

Jordan gave a short, noncommittal hum. Andrea's reaction had given him something to think about. Just because Mercy was his most vocal admirer didn't mean she was the craziest.

"Okay, anything else for you?"

"No, that's all."

Brian gave him his total. Jordan handed over his business credit card, signed the screen when prompted, and picked up his stuff. "Thanks, Brian. Have a good day."

"You too. And congratulations."

"Thanks." Smiling, he lifted a hand in farewell and left.

Thirty-Nine

Jordan's cellphone buzzed in his pocket as he unlocked the door to the garage. Fishing it out, he shoved his way into the building as he answered. "Yeah?"

"Hey, it's Mike. Have you heard from Mercy today?"

"What?" Jordan paused just inside the door. Nerves skittered through his body, leaving him feeling prickly. "I haven't found any notes, if that's what you mean. And she hasn't come into the shop. Why?"

Mike sighed, then hesitated.

"Mike, tell me what's going on."

"Can you give me an account of everywhere you've been in the last twenty-four hours?"

"Not without my lawyer present." His voice hardened. "Why are you back to treating me like a suspect?"

Mike sighed. "Mercy's dad called this morning. They were supposed to have breakfast together, but she never showed up. When he went to her house, her car was there, but she wasn't."

Alarm bells rang in Jordan's head. "Did you try calling her?"

"Straight to voicemail, which means either she's out of range or her phone's off."

"What if I could make it come back on? Could you get a warrant to get her location from it?"

Mike groaned. "Do I want to know how you can do that? It's that friend of Edie's, isn't it? Wait. No. Don't tell me."

Jordan chuckled. "My lips are sealed. But let me be clear; my ability to make her phone turn on is not because I have it in my possession."

"I never thought you did."

"Give me a few minutes. I'll call you back."

"Okay. I'll need a few to get the warrant." He hung up.

Jordan let out a soft growl. This was ridiculous. He called Edie.

"Hey, hon."

He could hear the smile in her voice when she picked up. It slightly improved his mood. Only slightly.

"We just got back to the house with all the equipment. What's up?"

"Is Asher with you?"

"He's unpacking the car. I'm in the shop, getting a ladder. Why?"

"I need to talk to him."

"Okay."

He could hear her moving now. The shop door opened with a quiet squeal, then shut. Wind made the line crackle as she crossed the yard.

"What's this about?"

"Put him on speaker and I'll explain."

"Okay, hang on."

A moment later, he heard her call Asher's name. The other man's voice sounded in the distance.

"You're on speaker now," Edie said.

"So, Mike just called. Mercy's missing and her phone's off,

they think. Asher, can you do what you did with Justine's and turn it back on?"

"Yeah. But I have to say, if another anonymous tip comes through you guys, the D.A.'s office is going to start getting pretty suspicious."

"I know. I just want you to turn it on. Mike's going to get a warrant for her phone. He just needs to be able to find it."

"Oh. Well, that I can do."

"And if you want to track it, just so we know where it is, I won't argue."

Asher chuckled. "Noted. Give me a few minutes. I'll let you know when it's done."

"Great. Thanks."

"No problem."

Jordan blew out a breath.

"He's heading inside," Edie said. "You okay?"

"Yeah. Just frustrated. What does it mean that she's missing? Did she go dark because she heard about us and doesn't want to be disturbed? Is she planning something? Did something happen to her? I mean, we don't know for certain that she's the one sending me the notes. I just assumed it was her because she's been the most vocal about putting a claim on me. It could be someone else." He gave her a brief rundown of his encounter with Andrea Harris.

Edie let out a low whistle. "Okay, I see your point. Do you think she's capable of sending the notes? Or of murdering Justine?"

"Maybe? I don't know her that well, but I do know she's not the brightest bulb in the box. I'm not sure poetry would be her style. As for the murder part? Possibly. She was a little unhinged at the auto parts store. Not crazy, just—holding on by a thread, you know?"

"Yeah. Well, mention it to Mike. He might want to look into her too."

"I will." Jordan blew out a breath. "I better get back to work."

"Okay. I'll text you when Asher's done, so you can call Mike back."

"Sounds good. Thanks, babe."

"Yep. Love you."

Jordan froze. What did she just say?

"Shit. Did I say that out loud?"

He cleared his throat. "You did. Did you mean it?"

She let out a little groan. "I did. But that is not how I intended to tell you. It just slipped out." He heard her draw in a shaky breath. "Do—do you feel that way too?"

A slow smile tipped up his mouth. His heart thumped in his chest as love smacked him in the face. It had been brewing, but hearing her say the words set it free. "I do."

"You do?" Her voice had turned to nearly a whisper.

"Yes." It was his turn to groan, but not in exasperation. His was a groan of frustration. "You have terrible timing. I want nothing more than to show you how much, but I'm stuck here until I get all this work done."

She chuckled. "Well, there's always this evening. I'll put my wedding dress on so you can take it off of me."

Jordan's body stirred. "I like the sound of that." Despite his desire to do so yesterday, he hadn't gotten the chance. They'd returned to the hotel after dinner with just enough time to change before they had to leave for their flight home. There'd been no consummating their marriage until they got back to Arizona. He'd thoroughly enjoyed peeling her jeans and sweater off of her, but it wasn't that dress.

"Me too. Don't dawdle." She hung up.

Staring at the phone, he let out another groan. How was he supposed to work now?

FORTY

Despite fearing the day would drag, it was late afternoon before Jordan knew it. He stepped back from his last car and picked up a rag to wipe his hands. All he needed to do was rotate the tires, and his day was done. All his customers who had cars to pick up had already done so. The mechanic gods were smiling on him.

The lobby door chimed. He glanced over and saw Chelsea Bridges walk in. A frown knit his brows. Maybe not.

Weaving through the garage, he opened the door. "Hi, Chelsea. What brings you in? It's not that sensor again, is it?"

"No. It's—" She stopped and wrung her hands together. "I feel silly, but I didn't know where else to go."

His frown deepened. "What's wrong?"

"I put the rear seat down to tote some boxes and now I can't get it back up. I've never done that before, so I don't know if I'm just missing something, or if the lever I think brings it up is broken—" She took a breath to stop the flow of words. "Can you take a look?"

"Sure."

Relief slackened the pinch to her features. "Great, thank

you." She turned around and went back out the door. Jordan followed.

"Did it make any sort of noise when you lowered it?"

"Not that I remember. Honestly, there's probably just a lever I'm missing."

"Could be."

They reached her car, and he opened the rear driver's side door. "Is it both sides that are stuck?" She had a split bench in the back.

"I don't know. I only tried the long side."

That was the side he was on. He reached for the lever and pulled. The back flipped up, and he glanced back, a smile forming. "There you—" His words died in his throat, and his eyes widened. Fear made his heart skip a beat. Chelsea stared back at him, fury in her blue eyes. Her expression matched the menace of the matte black gun in her hands. "What are you doing?"

"Get in the car."

"Why? I don't understand. Why are you pointing a gun at me?" He wasn't dumb; he knew why. She was his stalker, not Mercy. But he needed to stall. To think.

"Don't play dumb. It doesn't suit you. Get in." She pushed the gun closer.

Jordan's gaze darted around the parking lot and to the road beyond. His business sat down in a bit of a hole and had a shrub line bordering the front. It was hard to see into the lot from the street. No one could see them. And the cameras outside wouldn't help him in this situation, even though they were in full view of the lens. They weren't a live feed with anyone watching on the other end.

He assessed her posture. She meant business, but her stiff shoulders and the way her fingers kept readjusting on the grip of the gun told him she was way out of her comfort zone. He could get the gun away from her rather easily, but the car door was in the way. He shifted his feet.

"No!"

The gun moved closer to his chest. Jordan held up his hands. "Whoa. Calm down."

"Stop moving. Get in the car. I know what you're thinking, and I won't let you disarm me. I know what you can do. I've watched you practice. I'm not dumb."

Pulling a gun on someone wasn't exactly smart, but he kept his mouth shut.

"Get in."

He weighed his options. If he got in, there was no telling where she would take him. But it would give him an opportunity to get away safely when they arrived. If he tried to disarm her now, there was a decent chance he'd get shot. She was too close.

Resigned to escaping later, he slid onto the seat.

"Get the handcuffs out of the seat pocket and put them on." Chelsea gestured to the back of the driver's seat.

Jordan groaned. "Come on."

"Just do it."

Shoulders slumping, he reached inside and took out a pair of handcuffs. They were good ones too. Not the kind you could just pick up at a novelty store. He clicked one around his wrist, leaving it a little loose, then did the same with the other.

"One more click on each wrist."

He looked at her through his lashes.

"Do it!" She waved the gun.

"You don't want to shoot me, Chelsea."

"But I will. Not to kill, but you won't be going anywhere." Her aim dropped, and the tip of the gun pointed at his leg.

Deciding not to chance it, he did as she asked.

She slammed the door shut.

Jordan waited until she was getting in the driver's seat, then grabbed the door handle and yanked.

The door stayed closed.

She looked back as she got in. "The child lock is on. I told you; I'm not dumb." She started the car.

"Where are we going? And you know Edie will come looking for me soon, right? She's expecting me home for dinner."

"She won't find you. I've made sure of that."

Jordan's heart stopped for a second, then started up at three times the pace. He didn't like her tone. "What did you do?"

"Don't worry about it. Your *wife* won't be a problem." She sneered at him in the rearview mirror.

He pressed his lips together and glared back. She might not think so, but Edie would be an issue. So would he.

Forty-One

Darkness met Edie's gaze as she peeked out the front curtains at the drive. Jordan was late. She checked her watch for the hundredth time in the last ten minutes. Now, at forty-five minutes past when she expected him home, it was time to call.

She marched into the kitchen and picked up her phone from the counter. Before she could dial, it rang. Her heart skipped, hoping it was Jordan, but the local number that appeared wasn't one she recognized. Frowning, she answered. "Hello?"

"Edie, it's Mike. Tell your friend thank you for turning Mercy's phone back on. We found her." The grim note in his voice told her it wasn't a nice find.

"Crap. She's dead, isn't she?"

"Yeah. She was stuffed into a dumpster behind a vet clinic in town."

Something niggled in the back of Edie's mind.

"Anyway, I just wanted to let you know what we found. If she's Jordan's stalker, that's over."

Edie grimaced. "I don't think she is. I think both deaths and the stalker are connected. Do you have any leads?"

"No. There aren't any cameras on the backside of the building that show the dumpster. Just the door. We dusted for prints, but those have to process."

"What about other businesses nearby? Do any of them have cameras pointed that way?"

"No. It's mostly residential right there. We walked the street behind the clinic, but no one saw anything unusual, and no one has a doorbell camera."

She let out a soft growl, frustrated. "Why is this person a ghost? And why kill Justine and Mercy?"

"I don't know. Jordan's the only one who connects them both. Speaking of, is he there? I tried to call him, but he didn't answer."

"No. I was getting ready to call him myself. He said he'd be home on time tonight, but he's not back yet. I thought maybe he stopped at the store or something on his way, but it's been longer than it should have been if he did that."

"I'll swing by the garage and see if he's still there. Keep trying to call him. And let me know if you reach him or if he comes home."

"I will. Thanks, Mike."

"Yep." He hung up.

Edie brought up her contacts and called Jordan. It rang and rang, then rolled to voicemail. She hung up without leaving a message.

She stared at the phone for a long moment, debating what to do. She didn't want to leave the house and retrace his route from town, just in case he came home. But she couldn't sit here and do nothing.

Scrolling through her contacts, she found Asher's number.

"Horn."

"Asher, have you heard from Jordan in the last hour?"

"Jordan? No. Why?"

"He's late. And Mike just called and said they found Mercy Dixon dead in a dumpster in town."

"What? Damn. I take it you've already tried calling him?"

"Of course. It goes straight to voicemail. Mike tried, too, before he called me. I'm worried."

"Let me see if I can find his phone. Hang on."

She heard rustling on the line, then the sound of him typing.

"What's his number?"

Edie told him.

The soft tap of the keyboard resumed.

She was so focused on the call, the beeping coming from the garage took a moment to register. When it did, she turned, frowning.

"Something's beeping."

"What?"

"In the garage. I hear beeping." She walked toward the door.

"What kind of beeping?"

"Like a watch or a timer."

"It's probably just one of Jordan's tools or something."

"Maybe." She continued to frown at the door. He had a bunch of things in the garage, but it was mostly household and garden stuff. Most of his mechanical tools were in his shop.

She reached the door and opened it. The beeping grew louder.

"That's loud."

"Yeah." She stepped into the garage. The noise was coming from the workbench. Nearing it, she zeroed in on a white rectangle and extended a hand to pick it up. "It's just a timer."

She pushed the stop button. "It must have fallen over and set itself."

"How did it fall over?"

"I'm not sure. Maybe one of us knocked it over when we were working?" A tingle of awareness skittered up her spine. She spun around, peering into the dim garage. Nothing looked amiss, but the creeped out feeling she had wouldn't go away. "Something doesn't feel right."

"You think someone's there?"

"No. We've been crawling all over the house most of the day. If someone's inside, they're damn good at hide-and-seek. It's more a feeling that someone *was* here."

"Do a walk through. See if you notice anything else." There was a short pause. "Huh. That's weird."

"What is?" Edie turned to go back inside.

"Jordan's phone isn't at the garage. It's moving down the highway."

"Okay? So, he's on his way home?"

"Away from town and the house."

"What? Where's it going?"

"South. It's on I-10 going through Tucson. He just passed Sentinel Peak Park."

She paused on the step leading into the house. "His mother lives in Tucson. Is he going there?" She couldn't imagine why he wouldn't call to tell her, though, if there was an emergency.

"Um, let me find her address and check it. Do you know her name?"

"Cara MacDowell." When they'd filled out their marriage license, parents' names had been one of the questions. She'd made note of the woman's name, as well as Jordan's father's.

Soft clicking came over the line and several long moments passed before Asher spoke again. "No. She lives on the north-east side of the city. He'd have gotten off the interstate before that if he was going there."

That tingle came back. Something wasn't right.

Her phone beeped in her ear. She pulled it away to look at it. Mike was calling her. "Asher, Mike's calling me. I'll call you back."

"Put him on conference."

"Oh. Okay. Hang on." She pressed and held the accept button on her phone, then added Mike to the call. "Mike, you're on conference with Asher."

A brief pause came over the line. "Your computer guy?"

"That's me. Hi," Asher said.

"Hi. Let me guess. He's looking for Jordan too?"

"Yes. His phone is going down I-10 in Tucson right now. What did you find at the garage?" Edie braced a hand on the door frame, hoping he just dropped it in someone's car and didn't know it and was still at the garage.

"His Bronco's there, but he's not. The door was still unlocked, but the building is empty."

Edie muttered a curse. "Go back inside and check the security cameras." She gave him the passcode. "I'm on my way."

She grabbed the knob and turned it, but never got any further. A wave of pressure and a blast so loud it drowned out even the beating of her heart in her ears struck her and sent her flying across the garage. She smacked into the far wall. The last thing that registered before the world went black was the flash of pain and the air whooshing from her lungs.

FORTY-TWO

Jordan's phone buzzed in his pocket for the fourth time. He didn't dare answer it. If Chelsea hadn't noticed he still had it, he didn't plan to cue her in. Eventually, she'd leave him alone. He'd use it then. Instead, he kept his eyes glued to the road, watching for signs and keeping track of where they were going. They'd made it through Tucson and were now well south of the city, headed for the Mexican border. He didn't know if she planned to take him across. If so, well, good luck to her. He didn't plan to go quietly. He also didn't have his passport, and he was still handcuffed. The guards would take one look at his cuffed hands and lack of ID and detain them both.

Ten minutes later, she slowed and took an exit toward Arivaca Junction. But instead of driving into town, she went east, away from everything and deeper into the desert.

"Where are we going?" He glanced around, hoping to signal someone, as she stopped at the stop sign.

His phone chose that moment to buzz again.

Chelsea's gaze flicked to his in the mirror, then she turned around. "What was that?"

"What was what?" He wanted to shift and muffle his phone, but didn't want to draw attention to it.

Her gaze went to his leg. "What's in your pocket? Do you have your phone?"

He stayed silent, not about to confirm anything.

With a curse, she turned around and stepped on the gas, driving through the intersection and straight to a gas station. Pulling up behind it, she slammed the gearshift into park and swung around. "Give me your phone."

Jordan didn't move. He met her gaze, defiant.

A muscle in her jaw ticked. "Jordan."

"Come get it."

She let out a soft scoff and picked up her pistol. "How about no? Give it to me."

He continued to stare at her.

She pulled the hammer back.

"You're really going to shoot me? Here in a busy parking lot? Where there are cameras?"

"Do you really want to find out? Give. Me. The. Phone."

Banking on the assumption she wouldn't be so bold to shoot him in public, he folded his bound hands and stared her down.

She ground her teeth together and growled. "Fine. I won't shoot you here, but in about five minutes? Different story." She put the gun down and put the car in gear. They rocketed out of the lot and onto the main road, going through the small town.

Jordan's apprehension grew as they reached the edge of town. She drove for another minute, then pulled to the side of the road. In a flash, she faced him with the gun again.

"No witnesses now. Give me the damn phone."

Something in her eyes told him he couldn't bargain his way out this time. Glaring at her, he reached into his pocket and handed it over.

"Thank you." She snatched it, then opened her door and dropped it on the ground.

Jordan ground his molars together. "Where are we going?"

Chelsea met his glare in the mirror with one of her own, then looked at the road. Turning the car around, she headed back to town.

His anger simmered hotter. She didn't want to talk? Fine. He hoped she thought she'd managed to control him. He didn't need his hands free to defend himself. Once they stopped, he wouldn't be at her mercy anymore.

For another twenty minutes, she drove deeper into the desert on the other side of the interstate toward Mount Hopkins. The road forked, and she went south again onto a dirt track. Jordan braced his feet against the base of the seat in front of him as they bounced along. Finally, a small white house came into view. She pulled up to it and stopped by the porch.

"Stay put." She glanced at him over her shoulder, then opened her door, gun in hand.

"No problem," he muttered as he watched her get out.

She yanked his door open, then stepped back, aiming her pistol at him. "Get out."

He unfolded his tall frame from the backseat and stood in front of her, glaring. She backed up several paces, out of his reach.

"Inside." She tipped her gun toward the house.

Jordan pivoted on the balls of his feet and walked toward the porch. She'd have to look away to unlock the door. That could be his chance.

"It's unlocked. Go inside."

Dammit. The muscles in his jaw worked. He turned the doorknob and pushed. The old steel door creaked on its hinges as it swung inward. Warm, stale air washed over him as he stepped inside.

"Sit down over there and cuff yourself to the chair." She pointed at a large wooden chair in the center of the room. It wasn't bolted down, but looked like it was made of oak or some other heavy hardwood.

Jordan crossed to it and sat down. At least it was padded.

"Handcuff." She tipped her head to the silver cuff dangling from one of the chair's arms.

"Really?"

She stalked closer. "I don't think you're taking me seriously. I'm done playing games, Jordan. You're meant to be mine. With your wife out of the way, you can be."

He slid forward on the seat, muscles vibrating. "What did you do? Where's Edie?"

"Probably under a pile of rubble in your house, dead."

The breath left his lungs and his heart stopped. "What?" The word came out barely a whisper.

A slow, dark smile spread over her face. "Growing up around here with my dad, well, he was good for one thing. I learned how to be invisible in the desert. You see, Dad didn't have much respect for the law, especially when it came to when and how he could hunt. He thought he should be able to take whatever he needed whenever he wanted. I didn't eat store-bought meat until I was a teenager. And that was only because I had a job and could buy my own food then. I grew up learning how to track and ambush game."

She lifted a shoulder. "People aren't much different. Though I have to give Edie credit. She was a little harder to hide from than most. I had to be more careful once she showed up. But you two still never saw me. I hid in plain sight. So, when she and that friend of hers left this morning after you went to work, I knew it was a now or never kind of situation. I snuck in and planted some explosives in your bedroom. It went off, oh, about"—she looked at her watch—"thirty minutes ago."

Her smile turned frighteningly maniacal. "You see, I wanted to give her enough time to get worried about you, but not enough time for her to actually come after you. An hour sounded good. You could have stopped at the store, right? So, she probably waited what would be an acceptable amount of time for that. Then she probably started calling you and your friends. I'm sure Mike Deyo was on that list. He probably checked your garage. And I'm sure she called that friend you came back from Las Vegas with."

Rage tinted her cheeks red. She stomped closer, raising the gun to point at his face. "How could you marry her?" Her voice came out as a choked whisper full of hate. "It's me you're supposed to love. Not her. Me. Someone you've known for years, who brings you treats at Christmas and on your birthday. Not some woman from out of town I've never even seen before." She readjusted her grip on the pistol. "Now put the damn handcuff on, or I swear I will make you bleed."

Harsh determination glittered in her eyes. Jordan picked up the handcuff and awkwardly wrapped it around one wrist. "Happy?"

She let out a mirthless laugh. "Not in the least." She lowered the gun. "But one day, we will be."

Never. He glared at her back as she walked away. Grinding his molars together again, he wrenched his gaze away and studied his surroundings. The main room wasn't much to look at. A couch and recliner took up most of the space. To his right was a cramped kitchen separated from the living room by a small peninsula. In front of him was a wall, with an opening to a hallway that led to the bedrooms and probably at least one bathroom. A backdoor sat opposite the front door at the end of a run of cabinets. If he could get free, he could be out either door in just a few strides.

He glanced at his hands. He just needed to figure out how to do that.

FORTY-THREE

"Edie!"

Sound came at Edie from far away. Pain ricocheted through her brain like a ping-pong ball. Every breath she took sent fire raging through her torso. Wetness bathed her arm and one of her legs.

"Edie!"

The acrid smell of smoke reached her nostrils. Fear punched her in the stomach, stealing her breath. She gagged and tried to roll, but something held her down. Panic clawed at her throat. *No. No!* This wasn't happening. Not again. A harsh, terrified scream tore from her throat.

"Edie, hang on! We're coming."

She writhed, trying to break free of her prison, barely registering the voices. She had to get out. Had to move.

Light pierced her eyes. She scrunched them closed.

"Edie! Oh, thank God."

Through a squint, she peered up. Dark hair and a face dusted with a short beard filled her vision. "Asher. I'm trapped."

"I know. We're working on it." Wood clacked together.

Edie couldn't see the others, but she could hear them working. Some of the fog of panic lifted from her brain. This wasn't like last time. Help was here.

"Can you tell me where you hurt?"

"Um." Her voice cracked. She swallowed and wet her lips, then tried again. "My chest. And my head."

"Okay. Can you move your limbs?"

"Yes."

"Good. Just lie still for now, okay? Wait until we get you free and the paramedics check you out. They're probably going to want to immobilize you and take you to the hospital."

"No. They can't. We have to find Jordan."

"We need to get you free first and make sure you're okay. You can't do much if you're all broken."

A frustrated sob tore from her throat and a tear leaked from her eyes. "Dammit. Why is this happening?"

"Because this woman is sick."

Someone called Asher's name, and he turned. After a short pause, he nodded, then looked at her. "I need to help them move debris. You hang tight and *don't move.*"

A short laugh that was more of a sob escaped her. "Couldn't if I tried. Get me out of here, Asher."

"Working on it." He stood up and disappeared from view.

Shouts, sirens, and the sound of building materials banging together created a bubble of noise that drowned out everything else, even her thoughts. She didn't mind that. She didn't want to think about her situation. Every ounce of self-preservation and willpower she had was going into keeping her from descending into a full-blown panic attack. So, while the people she couldn't see moved the house off of her, she focused on her breathing. In. And out. In. And out. Slowly, the urge to scream and the need to run ebbed. When the beam holding down the drywall that pinned her finally lifted, she felt more in control.

A face she didn't recognize appeared above her. His turnout coat marked him as a firefighter.

"Hi, there. My name's Jason. I don't want you to move yet, okay?"

"Okay."

More debris was lifted off her body until she laid there, exposed.

"I'm going to feel along your limbs and torso. You tell me if it hurts, all right?"

"Yep." She clenched her teeth, steeling herself against any pain. When he made it to her ribs, she winced.

"The ribs hurt?"

"Yes."

"All over, or just in a few spots?"

"My chest aches, but the worst of the pain is on the left toward the bottom."

He moved his hand and lightly pressed. "Here?"

"Ow! Yeah." She pushed his hand away.

"Okay." He moved down, checking her pelvis and her legs. Nothing else hurt.

"How about your back? Does that hurt anywhere?"

"No."

"Neck pain?"

"No. My head hurts, but not my neck."

"I'm not surprised. You have quite the goose egg there." He pointed at her head.

Edie brought a hand up and touched her forehead near her hairline. A lump the size of a tangerine met her fingers. "Damn." She grimaced. That would take some time to heal.

"All right. You have some cuts on your arms and legs, but it doesn't feel like anything's broken. I'm going to put a collar on you as a precaution, and we're going to pull you out on a backboard."

She groaned. "Do you have to? I'm fine."

"Ma'am, your house exploded and buried you."

Edie groaned again, knowing he was right. "Fine."

Several of his colleagues joined him, and they worked in tandem to immobilize her and bring her out of the rubble. They set her on a gurney, where a paramedic wrapped a blood pressure cuff around her arm.

Asher appeared in her field of vision. "Hey. You look like crap, but not as bad as I feared."

One corner of her mouth tilted. "Gee, thanks. What's going on? Do you know what happened? Have you heard from Jordan?"

"No, on both counts. But I'm working on it. You worry about yourself. Let me worry about Jordan."

She snorted. "Yeah, right."

His mouth twisted into some semblance of a smile. "I know it's hard, but try." He backed up a step, glancing over his shoulder. "I just came to check on you. I'll meet you at the hospital later. Hopefully, I'll know more."

Edie grabbed his hand before he could walk away. "Find him, Asher. Please."

He squeezed her fingers. "I will do my damnedest, Edie. I promise." With another quick squeeze, he let go and jogged away.

She choked back another sob and took a shaky breath. Closing her eyes, a tear squeezed out. *Please, God. Let him be okay.*

FORTY-FOUR

The monitor blared at Edie as she took the pulse-ox clip off her finger. She glared at it and yanked a sticker off her chest.

Metal on metal screeched as the curtain whipped back, and a nurse appeared. "Ma'am, what are you doing?" She walked forward. "You need to leave that stuff on. The doctor—"

"Told me I'm fine, except for some broken ribs and a concussion. I'm leaving."

"Ma'am—"

Edie rolled her eyes and stood up. She swayed slightly and her vision turned gray at the edges, but that soon faded. She yanked the rest of the leads off her chest. "I have a husband to find. Has Detective Deyo arrived? Or my friend, Asher Horn?"

The nurse clamped her lips together, fine lines fanning out from the corners. "I'm not sure."

"Okay. I'll check on my way out. Is there a payphone I can use in the lobby?"

With a sigh, the nurse propped her hands on her hips. "Ma'am—"

"Don't." Edie held up a hand. "My husband is missing and probably in the hands of the same psycho that blew up the house. I am fine, I promise you. Nothing some pain killers and time won't cure."

The woman blew out a breath. "Okay. No, there is no payphone in the lobby. But here." She reached into her scrub pocket and took out her cellphone. "You can use my phone to call your friend, if you want."

"Oh." Edie smiled and took the device. "Thank you."

Before she could dial, the doors at the end of the hall opened, admitting Mike and Asher. "Never mind. That's them." She gave the nurse her phone back and walked around her.

"Geez, Edie. You look—"

Edie waved a hand, cutting off Mike's words. "I'm fine. What have you found out?"

Asher and Mike shared a look, then Mike spoke. "The fire crew found evidence of explosives. From what the arson investigator can tell so far, it looks like it originated on the far side of the house from where we found you. It was a damn good thing you were in the garage."

She shuddered. If Jordan had been home, they would have been on that side. Probably in the shower, washing away the day's grime.

"What about Jordan? Any leads?"

"His phone is stationary just off I-19. Outside of Arivaca Junction. I'm getting ready to head down there. It's still in Pima County," Mike said.

She nodded once. "Let's go."

"Whoa." Asher grabbed her wrist. "You're not going anywhere. Mike and his deputies are going."

Edie arched an eyebrow. "I will break every single one of

your fingers if you don't let me go right now."

He frowned at her, but let her go. "You're in no shape to go traipsing through the desert. Not to mention, you aren't dressed for it." He motioned to her outfit.

Glancing down, Edie grimaced. The thin scrubs and flip-flops the hospital gave her were only slightly better than the torn, dirty, and blood-stained wedding dress she'd begged the staff not to cut off of her. It hadn't worked and was now in the trash. "I guess I do need to change."

"It's better than what you had on when they pulled you out of the wreckage. Why were you even wearing—" Asher stopped and held up a hand. "Never mind. I can imagine what you two had planned this evening, and I'm sure it was something that would fry my eyeballs and rupture my eardrums." His face pulled, and he shuddered. "Don't want to think about any of that. Come on. I'll take you to get some clothes, and we'll wait together to hear what Mike discovers."

"No. You can take me to get clothes and then we can follow him."

"Edie, I can't let you—" Mike started.

"I'm not asking, Mike. I can't sit around idle. And you might need me to get to whoever this is. Speaking of, did you look at the footage from the garage cameras?"

"I did."

She waited for him to continue. When he didn't, she raised her eyebrows and rolled a hand. "And?"

He sighed and took his phone out of his pocket. "The footage isn't very good, but this is what it caught."

Eager for information, Edie took the phone and pressed play. A woman approached the front door, head down. "She knows the camera is there."

"Yep."

"Do we ever see her face?"

"Sort of. I don't recognize her, though. Keep watching."

A moment later, the woman exited with Jordan and they walked to her car. Edie gasped.

"What?" Mike asked.

"I know who that is. I recognize the car."

"You do? How?"

"I've been working the desk, remember? Her name is Chelsea. I can't remember her last name. But she brought her car in a couple weeks ago. I remember her specifically because when she made the appointment, she asked if Jordan could give her a ride to... work." Edie frowned and bit her lip as she remembered the conversation and what Jordan said. Her eyes widened, and her gaze shot to Mike. "You said you found Mercy Dixon in a dumpster behind a vet's office?"

"Yes."

"That's where Chelsea works. I don't know if it's that one, but she works at a vet's office. Jordan mentioned it when I asked him about the ride."

Mike's expression darkened. "You're sure?"

"Yes."

"Okay. You're getting your wish. Let's go." He tipped his head toward the exit, turning. "I'll call Carmen and have her bring you some clothes to the garage. I need you to look up her file."

Edie squinted up at him as she hurried to keep up. "Why does it matter? We need to go south to where his phone is."

"Because they might not be there," Asher said. "We need to know more about her. If your brain wasn't addled like a smoothie, you'd recognize that."

"I'm fine."

"That's BS, and you know it. But I'm not going to stand in your way. Just please don't do anything dumb."

"No promises." She would do whatever it took to bring Jordan home alive.

FORTY-FIVE

Steam wafted into the air as Chelsea moved about the kitchen. Jordan watched her work, amazed that she could act so... normal. After all she'd done, with him sitting here handcuffed to a chair, she made dinner like it was a regular evening at home.

"What's your plan, Chelsea? You gonna keep me locked up here and we play house until I give in and accept you as the woman in my life?"

She looked at him, then went back to stirring the stuff in the pot on the stove.

"Oh, I get the silent treatment? Not a good way to endear yourself to the man you claim to love."

"Maybe I feel like you don't respect me."

"Damn straight." Jordan knew it wasn't wise to poke the bear, but he couldn't help himself. If what she said was true, if Edie died when his house blew up, he didn't care what happened now. He'd go down swinging and take this bitch with him. "You pushed me into your car at gunpoint and claim to have murdered my wife. Why would I respect you?"

"Because I love you!" She slammed the spoon down and

came around the counter to hover in front of him like an angry wasp. "Everything I've done has been for you. To save you from yourself. You make some dumb choices, Jordan. I got tired of watching you flounder."

"I wasn't floundering."

"Really? Meeting women at bars—sleeping with Mercy Dixon, of all people—isn't floundering?"

He swallowed, realizing she'd basically just admitted to killing Justine. "No. I admit, Mercy was a mistake, but Justine was nice. So was Nicole."

"Justine was little more than a hermit. The weekend I followed her, she went to a bar for a few hours and sat in a corner by herself, then went home. People tried to talk to her, but she waved them away. You'd have been miserable with her. And Nicole just wanted to play the field. She wasn't interested in anything serious."

"Why did you kill Justine? And why spare Nicole?"

"I never intended to kill anyone. I just wanted them to back off. Nicole was easy. Mercy got to her first. But she didn't do anything about Justine, so I took matters into my own hands. It was unfortunate that she saw me put the note on her car, warning her to leave you alone. I couldn't take the chance she'd call the police. So, we went for a ride. It was just dumb luck that you two found her. Like, for real? Of all the places you could go hiking, you go there?"

"Karma's a bitch."

"Maybe, but she's lost this time." A cold smile spread over her face. "I got what I wanted."

"Hardly. I might be here, but I'll never be yours."

"Yeah? Well, you'll never be Edie's either, because she's dead." She whirled around and went back to the kitchen.

Jordan's heart thumped. God, how he hoped that wasn't true. He swallowed back the lump in his throat. "You didn't answer my question."

"What question was that?"

"What happens now? Are we playing house?"

"We're waiting."

"For?"

"Our ride."

His breath froze in his lungs. "Ride? To where?"

"You'll see. I think you'll like where we're going. Well, maybe not the first place. But the second, you will. We'll hang out there for a while. Until the heat dies down."

"Then what?"

"Then we start over somewhere safe."

"Start over?"

"Yep. You and me."

He shook his head. Did she not hear anything he said?

"I know it seems far-fetched now, but one day, we'll be happy. You'll see." Her blue eyes shone with determination as she glanced at him from the kitchen.

This time, Jordan kept his mouth shut. The woman he thought she was—the one he thought he'd gotten to know over the years she'd been bringing her car to him—was nowhere to be found. A crazy person had taken over. And there was no point in arguing with a crazy person.

Forty-Six

A chill went through Edie as she stepped out of Asher's car and walked toward Jordan's garage. She hugged herself, trying to hold in some warmth. Now that most of her adrenaline was gone, she was feeling the winter weather in her thin scrubs.

"Crap, Edie. I didn't even think about how you're dressed. Here." Asher shrugged one arm out of his jacket.

She waved a hand at him. "Keep it. We'll be inside in a moment, and Carmen's bringing me better clothes."

"You're sure?"

"Yes." She hustled toward the door and pulled the handle, letting them all inside. Making a beeline for the computer, she woke it up, then logged in. It only took her a moment to pull up the schedule. "Chelsea Bridges."

"I'll call it in." Mike took out his phone and stepped away several paces.

Asher moved closer to Edie. "You mind if I borrow that for a minute?" He tipped his head toward the computer.

A knowing smile spread over Edie's face. "Have at it." She moved aside and let him have the keyboard.

His fingers flew as he pulled up the internet browser. She barely saw the screen he logged into before a search engine popped up and he typed a query into it.

"What are you on?"

"My private server. It's untraceable." He kept his eyes on the screen, his fingers still flying over the keyboard.

"What are you looking for?"

"I'm starting with her identity, then moving to her family history."

"Family history?"

"It can tell us a lot about her mindset. How we're raised shapes how we think as adults. It can also tell us if she has access to any property."

Windows opened and disappeared as he looked for info.

"What are you doing?" Mike walked over, off the phone now.

"Nothing. Staying occupied while we wait."

Mike let out a snort. "Yeah, right. What did you find out?"

"She's lived in Tucson for ten years. But before that, she lived with her dad near Amado."

"What?" Mike blinked, surprise in his eyes. "That's near where Jordan's phone is."

"Yep." Asher nodded to a map on the screen. "Did you know her dad still lives there? And that there's a record of property in her grandmother's name that's in the desert, not far away from his house?"

"How do you find all this stuff so fast?" Mike looked more closely at the screen.

"Fast typer. And I can speed read. How about we head south with this information? By the time your office can confirm it, we'll already be there, ready to act."

With a groan, Mike swiped a hand over his face. "You guys are going to get me fired."

"Nah. Everything I found was public record."

The front door opened. The three of them looked up to see Carmen walk in with a bag, a bright smile on her face that died a swift death as she took in their serious expressions. "What?"

"Nothing." Mike walked forward, hand outstretched to take the bag from her. "Thank you, honey."

"You're welcome. What's going on? Edie, are you all right? Mike told me about the house."

"I'm fine. Thank you for bringing me some clothes."

"Of course." Carmen continued to study them with a deep frown. "Something else is going on. Where's Jordan?"

Mike tipped his head back and looked at the ceiling. Edie and Asher shared a look.

"He's missing, babe," Mike said. "We have a lead, so hopefully, all this will be over with soon."

Her frown darkened. "Michael Deyo, are you planning to go rogue?"

"Why would you think that?"

"Because you're here with them, and I don't see a single other cop."

"I called it in. My team is working on it."

"Uh-huh. Sure. But you're not going to wait for them, are you?"

Mike's mouth worked, and he stayed silent.

Carmen sighed. "Just be careful."

"I will."

Edie took that as her cue to go change. "I'm going to get out of these scrubs." She backed toward the door behind her, then turned and hurried through. In the employee bathroom, she stripped out of her outfit and slipped into the t-shirt and leggings Carmen brought. She shrugged into the oversize zip-up hoodie and slid her feet back into the hospital-issued flip-flops, then exited the bathroom, leaving her scrubs where they fell.

"Okay, I'm ready. But just one thing."

"What?" Asher asked.

"Can we stop at a store quick on the way down south? I need better shoes." She lifted one foot and pointed at the flip-flop.

Mike chuckled. "I'm not sure. Those shoes might help me keep you under control."

"Doubtful." Edie walked past them, heading for the front door. "Let's go." She had a husband to save.

FORTY-SEVEN

Edie squinted through the darkness. The desert was a black void at night, especially when the moon had yet to make an appearance. It didn't help that her head pounded in a steady rhythm, rattling her skull. Her vision was slightly fuzzy too. She could use some sleep and some pain meds, but both would have to wait.

"We need to wait for backup before we go down that road," Mike said, bringing the car to a halt at a T-junction.

"I just want to do some recon," Asher said. "Turn the interior lights off so I can open my door."

"No. You're staying put."

"The hell I am. I will go through the damn window."

Edie rolled her eyes as she listened to Mike and Asher bicker. She pushed the button to roll down the rear passenger window, then hopped up onto the sill, liking Asher's idea.

"Edie, what are you doing?" Mike swiveled in his seat.

"Getting out."

Mike cursed, reached for his door handle, then cursed again before punching a button on the dash beside the steering column. As he opened his door, Edie lowered her feet to the ground.

"What is it with your little group? Do none of you ever listen to directions? I thought you were former military."

"I am. Doesn't mean I've ever liked blindly obeying orders." Edie turned in a circle, assessing what she could see of her surroundings. "Asher, which way is the house?" He'd done more digging as they drove south and found some aerial shots of the property in Chelsea's grandmother's name. The pictures showed a small white house just off a dirt road.

"That way." Asher pointed into the distance toward a pinprick of light.

"Got it." Edie stepped off the road into the desert brush in her brand-new sneakers.

"Hold up a minute, dammit. Back up is coming. We can wait a little longer."

"You can." Edie kept walking. "Bring them along when they get here. Though they might not be needed then." She was perfectly capable of bringing down Chelsea Bridges. Her rage alone at the woman's gall would give her all the strength she needed, concussed or not.

Footsteps sounded behind her, then Asher came up on her left. "You know, we should at least come up with a plan."

"We can once we see what we're dealing with. It's hard to plan for what we don't know."

"Right, but we're unarmed."

She scoffed and held up her hands. "No, we're not."

"You know what I mean. Jordan's just as good at martial arts as you are, but she still captured him. And he didn't have a concussion and broken ribs."

"Yeah, well, he didn't have rage on his side. She tried to blow me up. And she kidnapped my husband. I won't even feel my ribs, trust me."

Asher sighed, but said nothing. Just traipsed along beside

her as they carefully picked their way over the uneven ground. Edie was glad. She didn't want to argue. Nothing would stop her from doing this. He'd have to tie her down and lock her up.

"You really love him, don't you?"

Asher's quiet observation brought tears to her eyes. "I do. God knows he's annoying enough I should hate him, but he's also kind and smart. He listens and doesn't judge. And he makes me feel safe. Not from external threats—though, I suppose he does do that—but more from my inner demons. He helps me banish them when they try to take over. And not just bury them like I've been doing. The demons go back in their box when we talk, slightly more cowed than the last time I locked them away. I can't let anything happen to him, Asher."

"We'll get him back, Edie." He laid a hand on her shoulder.

Edie sniffed and nodded. "We will." Failing wasn't an option.

When they were within fifty yards of the house, they slowed, staying in the shadows as they moved closer. Finally, they reached the house. Edie eased toward the window and peered inside. The gauzy curtains blocked most of her view, but she could see shapes. None that looked like people, though.

Gritting her teeth, she glanced at Asher and shook her head. He tipped his, motioning for her to follow. They rounded the corner of the house, testing windows as they went. On the front, they found one on the corner that was open.

Carefully, Asher eased the sash open. It stuck momentarily, then gave way to slide up with a soft swish. He nudged the curtain aside and peeked in. Edie kept watch outside. "Anything?" she whispered.

He backed out. "No. It's clear." He crouched and made a cradle with his hands. "You go first."

Edie put her foot in Asher's hands and let him help her through the window. She climbed in, wincing as the movement put strain on her ribcage. It hurt like the dickens, but she didn't care. She glanced around, noting that she was in a bedroom.

Asher's torso appeared. She grabbed his hand and held him steady as he brought his legs inside. Together, they crept toward the door. He grasped the knob and turned it, slowly easing the door open. Edie prayed it wouldn't squeal.

Someone must take good care of the house, because the door opened without a whisper. They edged into the hallway, keeping to the wall as they moved toward the living room. Part of the room appeared, as well as part of the kitchen. Edie didn't see anyone. With slow, deliberate steps, she walked closer. Taking a deep breath, she said a prayer and rolled her body to take a quick peek into the room.

She frowned and did it again. What the hell? She looked at Asher. "It's empty."

FORTY-EIGHT

It took everything Jordan had not to slide forward and wrap his bound hands around the neck of the man driving the car. He was over being a prisoner, but he didn't want to die in a car crash. Plus, Chelsea still had her gun. Her father was armed too.

Jordan clenched his jaw. He still couldn't believe her dad showed up, ready to help her squirrel him away. What kind of parent condoned her actions?

The crazy kind, his subconscious mind argued.

Jordan bit back a snort. True. Very true. At least he knew where they were going. Well, sort of. After they left the house, they'd stopped in the middle of the desert and gotten into her dad's truck. Once her car was covered with some brush, Steve had headed south. Jordan figured they were going to cross into Mexico. It would be easier to evade the authorities there. How they would get across, though, he didn't know. There weren't many gaps in the fence anymore, and the cartel in this area watched those.

After another twenty minutes of bumping through the desert, the car slowed. Jordan eased a hand toward the door, then stopped, remembering the child locks. *Dammit.* He wasn't opposed to jumping out and making a run for it. Especially if he caught sight of border patrol. But it didn't do him any good if he couldn't get out of the car. He'd have to come up with another way to signal them if he saw them. He couldn't count on Mike realizing he was missing and putting all the local, state, and federal agencies on alert to save him. He might think Jordan blew up with his house.

The car's headlights illuminated a gap in the fence. Jordan shook his head. Of course, this asshole knew where the breaks were. They drove through unimpeded.

Wonderful. Things just got more complicated. He was on foreign soil, without a passport. At least he had his ID. Chelsea hadn't taken his wallet, which was something. What he wanted to know, though, was why the cartel didn't stop them.

Ten minutes later, they pulled up to a house. Jordan peered at it in the car's headlights. Calling it a house was being generous. The sides were corrugated tin, nailed to four-by-fours. Single-pane windows broke up the façade; lights glowed through the layer of dust coating them.

"Get out." Chelsea's dad, Steve, looked at him over his shoulder as he opened his door.

"Can't. Kid locks, remember?" Jordan pointed at the door.

Chelsea got out and yanked open his door. Steve rounded the rear of the vehicle, pointing a gun at him as Jordan emerged.

"Don't try anything stupid."

"Wouldn't dream of it." Jordan followed Chelsea toward the door. It opened before she could reach for the knob. A tiny woman of Mexican heritage stood in the doorway.

Steve offered her a wide smile. "*Holá, mi amor.*"

She didn't return his smile. Her gaze wandered past him. "*¿Quién es eso?*"

"*Él es de Chelsea.*"

Jordan lifted his cuffed hands, touching a finger to his temple and tipping it toward her. "Ma'am."

She eyed his handcuffs, then looked at Steve. Rapid-fire Spanish burst from her lips, an angry frown on her face.

Steve's relaxed countenance changed. He stalked toward her, backing her into the house. Jordan heard a sharp smack and the woman cry out. A child yelled, then Steve hollered for the kid to be quiet. Jordan clenched his fists. This bastard just kept giving him reasons to want to beat the snot out of him.

"Chelsea! Bring him in," Steve said from inside.

"Go." She motioned Jordan toward the door.

He eyed her. Out here in the open, he could take her easily. One kick is all it would take to knock the gun from her hands. He could scoop it up and run. But what happened to that woman and the kid if he did? He couldn't leave them here to suffer.

So, he walked forward and into the tiny house. The woman sat on an old two-seat sofa under one window, cradling a small boy to her side. Tears ran down the child's face.

Jordan looked at Chelsea. "Who are they? What are we doing here?"

"Juanita is my stepmother. Diego is my brother."

"Oh, that's just grand." Jordan turned a disgusted look on Steve. "You let your wife and son live in squalor? I thought you were scum when you condoned your daughter's actions, but now I realize you're lower than that. Scum is too good for you."

"Shut up and sit down. I know Chelsea wants you to live, but if you cause problems, I'll have no qualms about killing you. She can find a different man to marry."

"I'm already married."

He hesitated and looked at his daughter. "What's he talking about?"

She huffed. "He got married in Vegas over the weekend. But don't worry. I took care of her."

"Oh. You're sure?"

"I blew up his house with her in it."

"But did you verify she died in the explosion?"

"Well, no, but—"

"Dammit, Chelsea. Is it that woman you told me about? The one working for him at his garage?"

"Yes."

He groaned. "Why didn't you just shoot her? Do you have any idea who she is?"

"Some bimbo he met on vacation."

"No, she's not. I looked into them both when you told me what you wanted to do. She's a former Army officer. People like that have connections. If she's not dead, we could have problems." He raised his gun and pointed it at Jordan.

"Whoa." Jordan held up his hands and shifted, making sure Steve's line of fire didn't include Juanita and Diego.

"Dad, what are you doing?" Chelsea held up a hand and stepped between her father and Jordan.

"I know you want to keep this one, but he's not worth it, Chelsea. We need to take him back over the border, shoot him, and let the coyotes dispose of him."

"You mean like Justine?" Jordan raised a brow. "You did a bang-up job of that."

"Shut up!" Chelsea screeched. She paused, closing her eyes for a moment and taking a deep breath, then looked at Steve. "We will verify she died. If she didn't, we'll make that happen. It's not that hard to kill one woman. I've done it twice now."

"Twice?" Jordan frowned. If the second person wasn't Edie, who was it?

Chelsea spared him a glance. "Yes, twice. Mercy got rather

vocal about how she intended to win you back. I didn't need more competition. Edie's enough."

"So you killed her? Why didn't you threaten her and scare her off like you intended to with Justine?"

"Because Mercy's hard to scare. You've met her. She thinks she and her family are gods." A chilling smile crossed her face. "She doesn't think anything now."

"Okay, fine." Steve held up a hand. "You go back to Tucson and make sure his wife is dead. But I swear, Chelsea, if he gives me problems, or you can't take care of her, I don't care how much you love him. I will kill him."

Jordan glared at the man. He could damn well try, but he had no intention of dying. Not now that he had hope Edie could be alive.

Forty-Nine

Clouds scuttled across the sky, darkening the day and matching Edie's mood. She glared out the window of Asher's hotel room. It had been two days since Jordan was taken. Two long days of chasing their tails and coming up with nothing. It was like he and Chelsea walked off the map when they left that house. And the authorities were sure they'd been there. They'd found tire treads consistent with the car Chelsea drove off in from Jordan's garage. They'd also found fresh remnants of a fried chicken and mashed potato dinner in the trash and automotive grease on a chair in the middle of the room. The one with a handcuff attached to it.

It still boiled Edie's blood to think that the bitch had handcuffed him to a chair. She must have had a weapon; one Jordan believed she'd use. Edie couldn't think of another reason why he would let her do that.

A knock on the door drew her attention. She spun around and stood. Finally.

Asher opened the door.

"What do you know? Has anything changed since we

talked?" Ford strode into the room, Sam, Max, Ezra, and Dean on his heels.

"No. Still no sign of them," Asher said.

"Thank you for coming." Edie came forward.

Ezra grabbed her and pulled her into a hug. "Anytime. How are you holding up?"

She clenched her teeth, warding off the press of tears at his gesture. "I'm fine. Pissed."

"Good," Ford said. "Channel that and use it to find them."

She rolled her eyes. "What do you think I've been doing? We don't know where to look, though. Asher traced her background. We found property in some relative's names. That's where we went Monday. They were there, as you know, but we don't know where they went after that. She only has one living relative, her dad. And we haven't been able to track him down. Though that's not surprising. He's not the most law-abiding citizen."

"We think she had help," Asher said. "Detective Deyo found a second set of tire tracks at the house. They were bigger tires. Probably for a larger SUV or a truck."

"Any sign of her car?"

"No. Both sets of tracks merge with the road and turn south. We lost them amidst all the other treads. The authorities are looking for it, but it could be anywhere in the desert."

"What about that road? Did you follow it?" Sam asked.

"Deyo's team did, yes. It forks in several spots. They could have taken any of them. It's a vast area to search. And after two days, they could be anywhere."

"What about a drone?" Ezra asked.

"The sheriff's department sent one up, but not until the next morning. They didn't find anything."

"If she's smart, she went into Mexico," Max said. He crossed his arms. "I mean, think about it. The sheriff's office, even the state and federal authorities, would only focus on U.S. soil. If they got across the border, we don't have any reach over there. It would all be on the Mexican authorities. How willing are they going to be to search for someone who might not even be there?"

"That's a good point," Ford said.

"Yeah, but where would they cross?" Dean asked. "There aren't many gaps in the Arizona fence anymore. And the cartel monitors the area. No one gets across in those spots without the cartel knowing."

"True. But she, or whoever she's working with, could have paid off the cartel." Asher turned and opened his laptop. He brought up a satellite image. "I've been studying the border, thinking the same thing you are. There are a few spots they could have slipped through." He pointed to a couple of areas. "I think we should go down there and take a look. Maybe even take a trip—legally—across the border and investigate from the other side."

"I like that plan," Edie said. "When can we leave? I'm sick of sitting around twiddling my thumbs."

"I'd like to buy a drone," Asher said. "Then we can go."

Ford nodded once. "Let's do it, then."

The group helped Asher pack up his things. Edie had been staying with Mike and Carmen, but spending most of her day with Asher as he did the things only he could do. She'd felt redundant and useless, but it was better than sitting in Mike's living room feeling that way *and* being out of the loop.

With the cars packed up, they headed into Tucson to an electronics store. While Asher browsed their drone selection, Edie flipped through the pictures on her phone from her wedding. As much as she'd protested, it had been the best decision she'd ever made. No matter what happened, she'd always be grateful for the impact he'd had on her life.

Her phone buzzed in her hand, and Mike's name appeared. She glanced at her friends and answered. "Hello?"

"Hey. A patrol car just spotted Chelsea's vehicle cruising past the garage."

Edie gasped. "What? Was Jordan with her?" Six sets of eyes swiveled her direction.

"Don't know. I'm headed over that way. I'll keep you posted."

"Okay, thanks."

"Yep." He hung up.

"What?" Ezra asked.

"That was Mike. A patrol officer spotted Chelsea near the garage."

Ford looked at Asher. "Pick your drone and let's go."

In minutes, they were back in the full-size SUV Ford had rented and were heading north again. Edie kept her gaze glued to the road, studying every car on the opposite side of the interstate. Chelsea wasn't getting away.

Her phone rang again as they entered town.

"Put it on speaker," Ford said from the driver's seat.

She touched the icon. "Mike, you're on speaker."

"I've done several circles around the block at the garage. She's not here."

"Why would she come back?" Ford asked.

There was a brief pause on the line. "Who's that?"

"Ford," Edie said, distracted as she contemplated his question.

"Who the hell is Ford?"

"Oh. He's a friend. The group that came to Vegas for the wedding is here. Well, minus their wives and fiancées."

Mike groaned. "Are these people like your friend, Asher?"

Edie chuckled. "Maybe."

"Forget about who we are," Ford said. "We need to figure out why she's in town. What does she want enough that she'd risk coming back? She has to know the garage cameras caught her kidnapping Jordan."

"I don't know," Mike said. "He doesn't have any medical conditions, so it's not like she came back hunting for medication. Clothing she could buy. Tools? Maybe she needs him to fix something, and it takes a specialized tool."

Edie's mind raced as she ran through possibilities. Only one really had any merit. "Me. It's me." She met Ford's gaze in the rearview mirror, then looked at Sam, who sat next to her. "Think about it. She wants Jordan for herself. But he married me. She tried to kill me. What if she's making sure she succeeded?"

"Oh, that's a good point," Dean said from behind her.

"It is," Mike agreed. "And it's all over town that Edie lived."

"So, let's say she drove past the house and the garage," Ford said. "Edie's not at either place, so if she stopped and casually asked someone about what happened, would people know where Edie was staying?"

Mike sucked in a breath. "Shit. Carmen."

Edie's heart rate kicked up. "Ford, turn around."

He pulled a U-turn without question.

"Mike, we're headed to your house."

"Me too. I'll see you there."

The line went dead. Edie put the phone in her lap and directed Ford to Mike's house. As they turned down his street, a familiar vehicle drove by.

"That's her!"

Again, Ford made a U-turn. Chelsea sped up.

"She knows she's been made." Ezra leaned forward, peering at Chelsea's car from the front passenger seat. "I don't see anyone else in the vehicle."

Edie didn't either. She picked up her phone and called Mike.

"Hey. She's not—"

"We're behind her. Leaving your neighborhood."

"Crap. How did I miss her? I've been here several minutes. Carmen's fine. And no one's come to the door."

"I don't know, but we need a patrol car to help us stop her."

"On it."

Edie heard the crackle of his police radio and the tinny sound of the dispatcher's voice, confirming his request.

"Whoa." Edie gripped the back of the seat as Ford made a hard turn to stay on Chelsea's tail.

"Sorry," he muttered. "Her car's more nimble than this thing." The engine growled as he stomped on the gas and closed the distance.

Maybe. But their vehicle was faster. Edie uncurled her fingers and fed Mike directions. She heard sirens, then saw a patrol car coming up from behind. "Mike, tell them we're the good guys."

"I will, but you need to let them pass."

"No problem," Ford said. "They need to get ahead of her. I'll stay on her tail, so she can't backtrack."

Tires squealed, and Edie gripped the seat again as Ford made another hard turn. The patrol car surged forward, passing them. Ford rode its bumper.

"You're making the deputy nervous," Mike said. "Dispatch is requesting you back off."

"Fat chance," Ford muttered. "Dean?"

"Yeah?"

"Where's she going, do you think?"

Dean studied the area. "The highway, I'd say. That last turn brought her back on a course toward it."

"Is this the road to merge with it? Is there another?"

"There's one more on-ramp nearby, but it's further south, and she'll have to turn again and go through a neighborhood."

Ford was silent for a long moment.

"What are you thinking?" Ezra asked.

"Mike? Can you get your deputies to funnel her toward the southern on-ramp?"

"Yes. I like the way you think."

Ford slowed and turned left. "Dean, direct me to that ramp."

They wove through streets, breaking several traffic laws. As they turned out of the neighborhood they were in and onto the main road, Edie saw lights up ahead.

"It looks like Mike got units into position." She pointed.

"Yeah. She's got nowhere to go now." He pulled up behind the unit blocking the street and put the car in park.

Edie got out, the others right behind her.

A sheriff's deputy waved his arms as they approached. "You can't go through."

They didn't need to. From her right, Edie could see Chelsea coming, several patrol units on her heels. One street down, a state patrol officer stood on the side of the road with a coiled spike strip.

Chelsea saw him too. She slammed on her brakes, but it was too late. He whipped the strip out, and she drove over it, puncturing all of her tires. Her car rolled to a stop, and the police surrounded it. In moments, they had her out of the car and bent over the hood as they placed her in cuffs.

Mike arrived on scene. Edie pushed past the deputy blocking the road and ran toward Chelsea.

"Hey! You can't go over there!"

"Edie!" Ford's voice rose over the deputy's. "Christ."

She didn't stop, though, even though she could hear him and the others behind her. She barreled into the cops holding Chelsea and grabbed her. "Where is he?" She spun the woman around, Chelsea's body making a thud as Edie slammed her into the car. "What did you do with him?"

Chelsea's eyes widened.

A local cop grabbed Edie's arm. She yanked it free and shoved the officer. "Get off!" Another set of hands grabbed her. "No! Let go!"

"Edie." Ezra's voice sounded in her ear as his arms closed around her, and he backed up. "Edie, stop."

"Let me go, Ezra. She needs to talk." She struggled in his arms. Fire raced through her side, but adrenaline allowed her to ignore it. "I don't want to hurt you, but if you don't let me go…"

"You're not hurting anyone." Ford appeared in front of her. He wore his stern, naval commander face that told Edie he meant business. The others came around and flanked him.

She sagged in Ezra's hold. "Dammit," she whispered, her voice harsh. The pain lancing her ribs registered, and she winced.

"Are you calm now? Can I let go and you won't tear her limbs off?" Ezra asked.

"No promises. She better talk."

"Give her the chance, okay?" he said quietly.

"Fine."

He released her. Ford held her gaze for a moment.

She nodded, telling him she had herself under control. And she did. Mostly.

He turned to let her pass, then he fell in beside her. The rest of the team stood a few paces behind.

As she approached, the cops stiffened, some of them putting a hand on the butt of their gun.

"It's okay." Mike held out a hand.

Edie walked up to Chelsea, balling her fists so she didn't grab the woman and shake the tar out of her again. "Where is Jordan?"

"Nowhere you'll find him."

"Really?" Edie cocked her head. "I think we're already

pretty close. Otherwise, why would you come back? I mean, I know you're here for me, right?"

Chelsea's eyes shifted, but she stayed quiet.

"If you're not scared of me—of me finding you—then why come back to kill me? It's not like Jordan would freely marry you, so you can't be worried about any 'marriage'"—she air-quoted—"between the two of you being legit." She took another step closer. "No. You're worried I'll find you. Find where you're hiding. I mean, I already found that little white house that belonged to your grandma. Did you enjoy your dinner? Fried chicken, right? But really? Boxed mashed potatoes?" She tsked. "What kind of woman makes homemade fried chicken and boxed mashed potatoes for her man?"

Chelsea's eyes widened.

"Yeah. We found your trash. And the second set of tire tracks. So, who's your accomplice?"

"You're crazy. I don't have one. It's just me."

Edie hummed, not believing her.

"Answer the question, Chelsea," Mike said. "All your friends are accounted for. So are your co-workers. You don't have any family left except your dad. Is it him?"

The slight widening of her eyes before she schooled her face and glared was the only tell Edie needed. A grin split her face. "Bingo." She rubbed her hands together. "Now we're getting somewhere. Daddy's had a few run-ins with the law, right, Mike?" She glanced at him, and he nodded.

"Has a thing against law enforcement. Rap sheet a mile long." Mike spread his arms wide. "That tells me you probably have Jordan stashed off the grid somewhere." He squinted. "Mexico?"

Chelsea's nostrils flared.

"Bingo, again." Edie pointed at her, then let her hand drop. "Where?"

"You'll never find them. And even if you do, Dad won't let

him live. He'll kill him—kill them all—before he'll let the cops take him down."

Ezra stepped forward. "All? That's an interesting word choice. Who else is with them?"

Chelsea's shoulders dropped. She looked at the ground. "No one."

"That's crap." Edie took another step closer. Her fingers twitched; she wanted to wrap them around Chelsea's throat and make her talk. She stuffed her hands in her pockets. "Who's there? How many men do you need?"

Chelsea rolled her eyes. "Jordan is the only man I want."

"So, who else is there, Chelsea?" Mike asked, keeping his voice low.

She looked at him. It was then that Edie saw the despair and fear in her eyes.

"It's someone you love, isn't it?" Edie asked. "Someone other than Jordan."

A tear trickled down Chelsea's cheek. She turned her face away.

"Chelsea?" Mike's soft plea made the woman's face crumple. She bit her lip, choking back a sob. More tears trailed down her cheeks.

She turned bleak eyes on him. "My little brother."

Edie turned round eyes on Ford. They had a new mission now: rescue the kid.

"You have a sibling? We didn't find one in the records search we did on you." Mike crossed his arms and tipped his head, studying her.

"You wouldn't. He was born in Mexico and lives there with his mother, who's also a Mexican citizen."

"How old is he?"

"Five."

Edie's anger flared. "You kidnapped Jordan and took him to the same house as your five-year-old brother?"

"I didn't. Dad did. It was his idea to hide him there. I just wanted to cross into Mexico with him. Dad decided it would be better if we stayed with Juanita while he procured travel and accommodations for us deeper into the country. I wanted to drive in the dark, but he argued it wasn't safe."

"It's not," Ford said. "The cartels are active at night. Even with Jordan along, you'd be vulnerable. They'd just see you as a young American couple."

Chelsea sniffed and wet her lips, tossing her head to get the hair out of her face. "This has all turned into such a mess. I just wanted Jordan to notice me. He dated everyone else. Why couldn't he look at me?" she cried. "Everything I did was for him. *Everything*."

Mike laid a hand on her shoulder. "Chelsea. If we drive you to the border, can you show us where you crossed and help us find them?"

She shrugged off his hand. "No. No, he'll kill me. Kill them."

"He's going to kill them even if you don't help," Ford said softly.

Her face crumpled again.

Edie opened her mouth to speak, but the look Mike sent her made her shut it again.

"Think about your brother, Chelsea," he said. "You want him to live, yes?"

She nodded, still crying.

"Then you need to help us find your dad. Before he can hurt them."

Edie's breath came in shallow puffs as she waited for Chelsea to make a decision.

"He'll hear you coming. It's in the middle of nowhere. He'll hear."

Asher stepped forward. "Maybe not. I think I have a plan."

FIFTY

The sun beat down on the back of Edie's neck, and she wished for yesterday's cloud cover. She'd slathered sunscreen on all of her exposed skin, but she wouldn't be surprised to still end up with a sunburn. It would be worth it, though, if they ended the day with Jordan and Chelsea's family safe.

She took a swig of her water, then replaced the cap and wandered over to where Asher tinkered with the drone he bought yesterday. One of the Mexican *Federales* looked on. She didn't know how it happened, but Ford had made some calls—so had Ezra—and they'd been granted access to Mexico and received a contingent of the Mexican Federal Police to help them conduct their mission. She was grateful. She'd be more grateful if they'd let her have a gun, but apparently there were some strings even Ford couldn't pull.

"Okay. Everybody, stand back. Time to launch this thing." Asher picked up the controller for the drone and switched it on.

Edie hung back as the rotors spun up. The whining pitch shifted, and the drone lifted off the tailgate of the

Federales' pickup. They were a couple of miles from the coordinates Chelsea gave them. The plan was to use the drone for recon, then hike in on foot once they had the lay of the land.

The desert landscape flew by on the screen attached to Asher's controller. As he neared the coordinates, he slowed. A small, ramshackle house came into view. The rusted tin roof sported several holes. Edie could see the weathered boards holding the structure together. It looked like one stiff wind would blow it all apart.

"Geez." Asher shook his head. "This guy is a piece of work. What kind of man leaves his woman and their child to live in a place like that when he has a comfortable home elsewhere?"

"A scummy one," Ford said. "Pan over and see if there are any vehicles."

Asher turned the camera. A rusted-out white pickup and a late-model gray truck with a king cab sat side-by-side near a lean-to full of old tools and five-gallon buckets.

"Looks like he's still there," Asher said.

"Yeah. Do a perimeter sweep." Ford swirled a finger.

Asher flew the drone in ever-widening circles.

"I don't see any booby-traps or fencing," Sam said. "Do you?"

"No." Asher paused, then turned the drone around. "It looks like he thinks he's safe by being so far out. I wouldn't doubt that he's made some deal with the cartel, too, that keeps him safe."

"Agreed." Ford looked up at the group that had formed around Asher. "Set the drone down and let's head out." He made eye contact with the Mexican federal officer in charge, who nodded. He turned away and gave orders to his men.

Edie got her backpack out of Ford's vehicle and strapped it to her back. There wasn't much in it. Some medical supplies and water. But out here, and on this mission, those were a necessity.

The group set off across the hard-packed desert, the Mexican police in the lead. Two of the *Federales* stayed behind; they would bring vehicles over once their commander gave the all clear.

Edie adjusted her sunglasses and tried not to look at the desert camo covering the federal policemen's bodies. They all wore the same thing, trying to stay as invisible as possible to Steve Bridges while they walked toward his hideout. The last time she wore this garb with Ford and Ezra alongside her, she'd been nursing a broken arm and a broken mind. Her arm had fully healed, but her mind was still mending. It had come a long way—even more so with Jordan in her life—but the demons still clawed at the door, wanting free.

She gave her shoulders a shake and sucked in a deep breath before blowing it out slowly. She needed to focus. Pulling on some techniques her former therapist taught her, she calmed her mind. She'd been using them since her nightmare. At first, they hadn't helped much; she'd been out of practice. Jordan's presence had done more for her. But with him gone the last few days, she'd needed something, so she'd worked on them. It had helped. She felt a little more in control when her thoughts started to spiral or when she woke up from a bad dream. She knew she still had work to do, but she was on the right road, at least.

Her gaze wandered over the landscape, taking it in. It was pretty here. And lusher than she thought it would be. There was enough vegetation to give them some decent cover. It was a mix of oak and pinyon trees as well as cacti. If the circumstances were different, she wouldn't mind the hike.

Their boots ate up the ground at a steady clip, and they were soon within sight of the small tin house. The vegetation thinned as they neared the structure, so they stayed close to the trees. Asher sent the drone back up and aimed the camera at one of the windows. He'd sprung for the fancy version that had a zoom lens. Edie wished it had infrared so they could see through the thin metal walls. Even with the window open, their view inside was limited.

"I see the woman," Asher whispered. "She's at the stove."

"Go to the other side," the *Federales* commander, Luis Hernandez, said. "That window is open too." He pointed at the screen.

Asher circled the house, giving it a wide berth. He aimed the camera at the window and zoomed in.

"Oh, thank God." Edie laid a hand on her chest. Jordan sat in a wooden chair, his hands cuffed to the legs, looking tired and dirty, but unhurt.

"Now, where's Daddy?" Asher shifted the drone, trying to get a different angle.

A woman's voice drifted outside. Edie tipped her head, trying to make out what she said. "It sounds like she's yelling at her son."

Hernandez nodded. "She's warning him to get his toys out of the middle of the floor before his father comes back inside."

Asher cursed. "He's outside? Where?" He moved his thumb on the controller, pulling the drone back. "He wasn't out when I did my recon pass."

"He must have gone out for some reason. Maybe to get something from his truck?" Ford glanced in that direction.

The sound of a vehicle approaching made Edie stand up straight. "Crap. Or he gathered reinforcements. Maybe he's realized Chelsea isn't coming back and needs help to move Jordan."

"Whatever the reason, we need to get into position." Hernandez turned away and radioed his men.

Edie looked at Ford. "What do we do?"

"What we've been trained to do. Rescue the hostage.

Follow the *Federales* lead. We'll sweep in and secure Jordan, Juanita, and Diego. I need you to focus. Can you do that? If not, you stay back and let us handle it."

She glared at him and told him where to shove it.

He grinned. "There's the Edie we know and love. Okay, everyone—"

"Ha! Yes!"

"What?" Ford turned at Asher's whispered shout.

"Jordan spotted the drone." He grinned. "He knows we're here and coming."

"Good. He'll be ready to help us. Fan out. Be ready to go in," Ford said.

"For the record, I want my gun," Sam muttered.

"Me too," Max said.

Dean and Ezra echoed the sentiment. Edie did, too, mentally. She didn't like being unarmed. She understood it, but she didn't like it. At least they were given Kevlar and allowed a knife. She wasn't sure the Mexican authorities realized just how much damage their group could do with a blade. She doubted they would have been permitted to have them if so.

They moved toward the house, each shadowing a federal police officer. Staying hidden, they waited while an ancient blue truck pulled up and parked near the house. Two men hopped out of the bed. Steve Bridges got out of the passenger seat. The driver stayed put while the three men went inside.

Edie listened as Hernandez communicated with his men. She ground her molars when she heard him tell them to hold their positions. To wait for them to come out. She didn't think waiting was an option. She'd seen the guns tucked into their waistbands. They weren't here for dinner. They were here to kill Jordan and bury his body. Bridges was done waiting on his daughter.

The front door opened, and Juanita ran out, clutching her

young son. She glanced back, her eyes wide. The look of terror on her face told Edie all she needed to know. They were out of time. In moments, her husband would be dead.

She glanced at Ford. He was already watching her. His eyes grew round. He shook his head, the fierce look on his face warning her to stay put.

Edie took a deep breath. "I'm sorry," she mouthed. Then she ran.

FIFTY-ONE

Jordan stared out the window, fighting to keep his expression neutral. Was he really seeing what he thought he was? He wanted to scrunch his eyes closed, rub them, then look again, but didn't dare. If his eyes weren't playing tricks on him, there was a matte gray drone hovering near the trees.

The drone tipped side-to-side, effectively waving its wings at him. His heart skipped. The calvary was here. But who was it? He glanced at Juanita. She had her back to him, stirring a pot of beans on the stove. Diego played on the floor on the other side of the couch with some toy cars. Jordan squinted, trying to make out anything else lurking amongst the scrub. Nothing moved.

The low whine of an engine wafted through the window. Bridges was back. Jordan's muscles tensed. His rescue couldn't be at a better time. Steve had been antsy since last night. He hadn't been able to reach Chelsea yesterday. Around ten this morning, a man had shown up—Juanita's brother, and from the looks of his tattoos, a cartel member. Steve left with him.

The snarling smile he'd aimed at Jordan before he walked out the door told him if Steve didn't make contact with Chelsea in the next few hours, he probably wouldn't live to see the sunset.

Scuffling sounded outside the door, then it flew open. Steve entered, flanked by two men. His cold gaze landed on Jordan for a moment, then he looked at Juanita.

"*Lleva a Diego afuera.*"

Juanita flipped off the gas burner and hurried around the counter to scoop Diego off the floor. The boy protested, but she clutched him to her chest and hurried outside like she was told.

"You know, I thought about what you said. And you're right. Juanita and Diego do deserve better accommodations." Steve gave him a calculating smile, malice glittering in his blue eyes, and took the canvas bag from the man on his left. What he pulled out made Jordan's blood run cold.

Steve looked at the bundle of explosives, then at Jordan. "And I figure if I can take care of a problem in the process, even better." His smile faded. "But first, unlike my daughter did, I'm going to make sure no one can escape." He turned to the man on his right. "*Mátalo.*"

The man pulled a pistol from his waistband.

"Bridges!"

Jordan's heart stopped. That sounded like Edie.

A man shouted in Spanish outside. Just seconds later, more voices erupted, shouting commands in Spanish.

Steve looked at his buddies. "What the hell?"

One word from the fracas outside caught his attention. *Federales.* If that was Edie out there, she'd brought the cops with her.

"*Son los Federales,*" one of the men said.

Steve ran around behind Jordan's chair. He told the one with the gun to make sure he didn't move, then unlocked the cuffs from the chair legs. Once he'd cuffed Jordan's hands in front of him, he nudged him to his feet. "Get up."

Barking more orders, Steve pushed him out the front door, his buddies bringing up the rear. Jordan squinted against the bright sunshine. One thing stood out, though. "Edie." She stood behind the dusty blue truck parked out front, a Mexican police officer at her side. He had a weapon trained on them. Huddled near the bumper were Juanita and Diego.

"*¡Suelta el arma! ¡Estás rodeado!*"

Jordan looked away from his wife toward the voice shouting from the edge of the yard that they were surrounded. His eyes widened. Men emerged from the trees, rifles pointed at them. Behind them, another line of men emerged. They were unarmed, but Jordan recognized them. A wide smile covered his face. "Oh, you're screwed, Bridges. My wife brought her little army."

"No!" Bridges growled through clenched teeth. He pulled a gun from the small of his back and pointed it at Jordan's temple. "If I die, you're going with me."

"The hell I am." Jordan edged forward, forcing Bridges to come with him.

"Stop moving."

The cold metal of the gun barrel dug into Jordan's forehead. He ignored it and took another short step. He wanted to give the *Federales* room. They were too bunched up right outside the door.

"Let him go, Bridges," Edie said. "It's over."

"Back off. All of you. I'll shoot him." He pressed the gun harder into Jordan's temple.

Okay. That hurt. It was time to end this. Jordan made eye contact with Edie. "You remember that first time we sparred in my home gym and you kicked my ass?"

Recognition lit in her eyes. "Of course." Casually, she

lifted a hand and touched the police officer's shoulder. Her mouth moved almost imperceptibly. The man adjusted his grip on his gun.

Everything happened over a few quick seconds. The moment Jordan was sure the officer understood her, he dropped to the ground and swept a leg out, spinning. The move knocked Bridges off his feet, and he hit the ground with an oof. Jordan lunged, landing on top of the man. He grabbed Steve's wrist and slammed his hands against the ground, dislodging the weapon.

Chaos erupted around them. The *Federales* descended upon them, barking orders at the other two men to drop their weapons. Steve stared up at Jordan, his blue eyes wide with disbelief.

One corner of Jordan's mouth lifted. "I bet Chelsea told you I was just a mechanic. I'm guessing she didn't mention my hobbies? You only got a small taste of what I can do." His smile disappeared. "Be grateful." He grabbed Steve by the collar and hauled him to his feet.

A cop walked up. "I take him. You okay?" the man asked in broken English.

Jordan nodded. "I'm fine." He turned away as the officer took control of Bridges. "Edie?" Her name barely left his mouth when she barreled into him. He raised his arms and slid them around her shoulders. The handcuffs pinched his wrists, but he didn't care. He kissed the top of her head. "Oh, thank God. You're alive. Chelsea said she blew up the house with you in it."

"She did. But I was in the garage." She looked up at him, moisture streaming down her cheeks. "I wasn't sure I'd ever see you again. I was determined to, but—" She gave him a watery smile. "It's been a rough few days."

"I bet. Are you okay?" He lifted his arms, letting her go, so he could touch her face. "You look all right."

She took his hands. "I'm fine. Concussed and a little broken, but nothing time won't heal."

"Broken?" He frowned. "Where?"

"My ribs."

His frown deepened. "And here I was, squeezing you."

"It's okay. I'm all right." She framed his face. "I love you. Please tell me there aren't any more crazy stalker women in your past?"

Dean walked up, then, a grin on his face. He dangled a handcuff key from his fingers. "Good to see you in one piece, man. You want out of those things?"

"God, yes." Ignoring the fact they'd rubbed parts of his wrists raw, he wanted them off so he could hold his woman the right way. He lifted his hands toward his friend.

Dean deftly unlocked the cuffs, then took them. "There you go. Free."

"Thanks." Jordan put a hand on Edie's hip and the other behind her head and pulled her in for a deep, soul-searing kiss. When he lifted his head long moments later, she blinked up at him with a dazed look.

"No more crazy women, except for you. You're all I need. I'm so glad you're okay. I love you, Edith."

She skimmed his cheekbone with her fingers. "I love you, too, Jordie."

Epilogue

Three months later...

Edie hummed to herself as she cut the tape on a box of surf wax. The shop was empty for the first time in over an hour, and she was eager to restock the shelves. Tourist season had officially started. Which was fine. It kept her occupied and gave her brain less space to think about how much she missed Jordan. After the fiasco with Chelsea and Steve Bridges settled, they'd sat down and talked about their future. Edie had been ready to give up her life in Costa Rica, but Jordan had surprised her and told her he wanted to sell his garage and take Brooke up on her offer. So, he was in Arizona, closing on the sale of his business and residential properties. His visa paperwork had also recently been approved. She couldn't wait for him to come home to her next week.

The front door opened, and she bit back a groan. It had been like this all day. The moment she tried to process her new inventory, someone came in. "I'll be right there," she said over her shoulder, then repeated herself in Spanish. She set her knife down and picked up the box. She might as well put the wax out while her new customer shopped. Pasting a smile on her face, she exited the back room. "Hello—" She froze as the identity of the newcomer registered. When it did, a wide grin split her face. She set the box down with a squeal. "Jordie!" In a few quick strides, she was hurling herself into his arms.

He caught her, his strong hands on the backs of her thighs, holding her in place as she wrapped her legs around his waist. "Hi," he said with a grin.

She framed his face. "What are you doing here? I thought you weren't closing until Monday?"

"Stuff went through quicker than anticipated. We closed yesterday afternoon. I wanted to surprise you. Are you going to kiss me hello?"

With a laugh, she captured his lips.

After a few intense moments, he broke away with a groan. "How about you close up and we go home?" Need made his voice thick.

Edie's body responded. She battled back the wave of heat that made her core clench and her skin tingle. "I wish we could." She frowned and unwrapped her legs from his waist to stand on the floor. "It's been busy, and I gave my help some time off since I thought I'd be free."

He pouted. "Are you sure?" He leaned in and nuzzled her neck. "I'll make it worth it."

Edie's eyes rolled back. She swallowed hard and pushed him away. "Uh-uh." She shook a finger in his face. "Behave. I can't close."

His mouth flattened. "Fine." The heated look in his eyes didn't leave, though. "But later? If you made dinner plans with anyone, cancel them. You're mine."

A delicious shiver ran through her. "No plans. We'll have all night together."

"Perfect." He pulled her in and kissed her once more.

Edie inhaled a deep breath through her nose, getting drunk off his scent. She'd missed him so much.

The door opened again, admitting two chattering women. They paused, catching sight of Edie and Jordan, who pulled apart.

Edie smiled at them. "Hello. Sorry. He's been gone several weeks and just got home."

The shorter of the two women grinned wickedly. "Honey, don't apologize. I'd kiss him like that too. Even if he hadn't been gone." She raked her gaze over Jordan's muscular form.

Edie offered her a polite smile and ignored her innuendo. "How can I help you?"

"The resort manager at our hotel said you offer surfing lessons," the taller woman said. "We were hoping to sign up." Her gaze darted to Jordan briefly.

"Come over to the counter and let's see what's available." Edie motioned them over, glad Jordan was still a novice at surfing and far from helping her teach people how to ride the waves. She couldn't imagine sending him out into the water with these two. They'd probably try to deliberately drown so he could save them.

"Do you have more stock in the back that needs to be put out?" Jordan pointed at the box she'd set down.

"Yes. Have at it. I've been trying all day."

He grinned. "Never fear. Your savior is here."

Edie just shook her head and sighed. "I'm not sure I missed your ego."

He laughed and grabbed the box.

While he put the inventory away, Edie scheduled the women for surfing lessons in the morning. As they were getting ready to leave, more customers came in. Through the rest of the afternoon, Edie and Jordan stole a few quiet moments together in between patrons. By the end of the day, she was ready—more than ready—to close up and go home. After securing the cash from the register, Edie flipped off the lights, and they exited through the back door.

"So, how have you been doing while I've been gone?" Jordan laid a hand on her back between her shoulder blades.

She glanced at him. A concerned frown drew his eyebrows down over his dark eyes. She gave him a happy smile. "Not too bad. There have been a few sleepless nights where I can't keep the demons away, but nothing I can't handle. That therapist I found in Golfito has been a tremendous help."

"Yeah? Good. I'm glad you found someone to talk to."

"Me too. I like having my feelings back out in the open again." Her smile grew. "It's let me love you the way I should."

"That's good, because I love you too." His eyes took on a fiery look. "I intend to show you just how much in about five minutes."

Anticipation heated her blood. They reached her little blue truck, and she dug her keys out of her pocket. Before she could insert the key in the lock, a honk drew their attention. Edie glanced up and saw Dean's black truck pulling into the lot. She didn't bother to hold back her groan. "Seriously? This better be quick. Does he know you're here?"

Jordan huffed. "He's the one who brought me to your shop, so I don't know what he wants. Maybe we should have stayed in Arizona. It would be quieter."

They approached the driver's side as Dean brought the truck to a halt. He rolled down the window. Edie's frustration evaporated as she saw his face. "What? What's wrong?"

"It's Sam. He needs our help."

Thank you for reading *Jordan's Journey!* I hope you loved it! Want to learn why Sam needs help? Check out *Sam's Salvation* on Amazon: *https://books2read.com/u/3y9g7J*

If you'd like to read more about Jordan and Edie (and the

other characters in this series), join my mailing list. Subscribers get a bonus chapter or scene after every book! You'll also get access to exclusive teasers, giveaways, and the occasional book recommendation, as well as sneak peeks into my world as I create my stories. Scan the QR code below to sign up and get your bonus scene!

Keep reading for a sneak peek at *Sam's Salvation...*

Sam's Salvation

Wagner Brigade
Book 4

ONE

People milled on the busy Las Vegas strip just outside the window. Sam Brackley crossed his muscled arms and watched the passersby, waiting for Edie's fiancé, Jordan, to pick out a wedding ring. Vegas was a study of humanity. In one glance, he saw several nationalities and ethnicities, as well as multiple fashion styles—some of them bordering on obscene. He doubted there was another place on the planet where a person could see so much diversity in one location.

"What's wrong with them?"

Jordan's question drew Sam's attention. He turned to see him talking to one of their other friends, Dean, and tip his chin toward Sam, and Max, who stood next to him.

Dean looked over, then grinned. "I imagine Max is having flashbacks. And Sam gets hives at the word commitment."

"What?" Sam glared at him. "I do not. This is all just too —" He swirled a hand, frowning as the word he wanted refused to come out. He clenched his teeth, hating that his mind didn't want to work right. Damn brain injury... "You know what I mean." He folded his arms again and glared. "It's too frilly. I don't do frilly." That still wasn't the word he wanted, but it would have to do. Shopping for women's jewelry was not his thing. Even when he had a woman. He preferred to show his appreciation of her in different, more personal ways. Though, this shopping excursion was necessary. Most women expected a wedding ring when they got married.

Max laughed. "I don't think any of us do."

Sam rolled his eyes. "Oh, whatever. I caught you wearing a tiara and nail polish last week when you watched Margot's twins."

"That's different. They're kids. I'll do frilly for kids."

"For *those* kids, you will." Those two little girls had Max wrapped around their little fingers. Their mother did, too, for that matter.

"What's that supposed to mean?"

Sam turned to face him. "It means—" He stopped as something outside caught his attention. He squinted, frowning. "What the—" He stepped closer to the window. Was that —? No. It couldn't be.

"What is it?" Ford asked. Sam felt him move closer.

"I thought I saw—" Sam shook his head. "But that's not possible." He stared a moment longer at a woman on the other side of the road who had stepped out of a restaurant. She just looked like someone he thought he used to know.

"Saw what?" Ford asked.

"Nothing." Sam continued to stare down the street. The woman looked up from her phone as she stepped into the throng of people. Sam's heart stopped. It *was* her. Ten years older and with darker hair, but he'd never forget that face. He turned toward the door. "I'll meet you guys back at the hotel later."

"What?" Ford took two steps after him. "Sam?"

Sam waved and hurried out the door. He couldn't lose her. Dashing across the street, he wove between people, bumping into a few as he ran after her. Even in four-inch heels, she was moving at a good clip. She'd always been a fast walker.

Ten feet behind her, he called her name. "Audra!"

She didn't react. Muttering a soft curse, he skirted around a group of young women already dressed to party hard, even at four in the afternoon. With another long stride, he reached out and touched Audra's arm. "Audra."

She stiffened beneath his touch, pausing to turn. Coffee-rich brown eyes met his. They widened slightly before her expression blanked.

"I'm sorry. I think you have the wrong person."

Sam frowned. That was her voice—minus her accent. "No. I don't. What happened to your accent?"

Her nostrils flared. "This is how I always sound." She backed up a step, and her gaze darted to the side. "I'm sorry." Turning her back on the direction she'd looked, she kept backing away. "Don't follow me, Sam." Her lilting British accent returned. She stared at him for another long moment, then spun on her heel and hurried away.

Sam's eyes followed her as she briskly walked away from him. When she reached the other side, a man in a dark suit stepped away from an elegant black car. Sam backed up, fading into the crowd, but kept them in sight. The man said something to her. She pinned him with a glare, said something, then slid into the backseat of the vehicle. Closing her door, the man glanced up, scanning the crowd. Sam melded into the shadows behind a potted palm. With a fierce frown, the man rounded the hood of the car and got into the driver's seat. A moment later, the car pulled away from the curb. Sam stepped away from the palm as they drove past, taking note of the license plate.

Audra turned her head, meeting his gaze. Sam frowned, watching her leave.

Audra, what did you get yourself into now?

Two

Standing at his balcony window, Sam gazed down at the bustling street below. Even at eleven p.m. the city was wide awake. He flipped the lock holding the door closed and pulled on the handle, opening it the inch the bar in the track allowed. Wind rushed in. The cool air smacked him in the face, but it did little to calm his racing thoughts. All evening, Audra's wide brown eyes had lurked in his mind. What was she doing here? And sounding like an average midwestern American? It was an act; when she switched to her normal voice proved that. But why? British intelligence didn't operate in the U.S. Not like that. It was possible she was working with a U.S. agency, but which one? And why?

He blew out a breath and crossed his arms, still staring down at the street. The Sphere lit up the sky; the image shifting from an ad for the new Disney movie to a sleeping emoji face. That thing was an eyesore, even if the technology was impressive. But it played into the Vegas experience, so it fit right in.

Sam rolled his neck and stepped away from the window. He needed to move. Crossing to the small duffel he brought for the one-night trip, he dug out some running gear and quickly changed. Maybe pounding the pavement would pound Audra out of his head.

Downstairs, he exited the smoky lobby straight into a cloud of marijuana-scented air. Wrinkling his nose, he took off, hoping he could escape the smell. He knew he'd never find the clean, fresh air of home, but something that resembled a normal city would be nice.

Audra's face kept pace with his footfalls as he ran, refusing to leave his brain. He ran faster. Why couldn't he get her off his mind? It had been ten years since he'd seen her. Ten years since their little interlude in Roda. Sure, their time together had been amazing, but they'd both known it was temporary. When he left to rejoin his unit, he'd had no regrets. Over the years, he'd thought about her, sure. What man wouldn't revisit some of the greatest sex of his life? He'd even inquired about her a time or two, making sure she was doing okay. A month before Sam's convoy was ambushed and his life changed, she'd gone off the grid. After he left the service and joined Ford in Costa Rica, he'd asked Asher to check into her whereabouts. He couldn't find her.

Which brought him back to why the hell was she in Vegas pretending to be an American? She was either deep under-cover, or she'd crossed over to the dark side. He was betting on the former, but she had a reckless streak, so he couldn't rule out the latter.

Turning a corner, he found himself on the same street where he'd been earlier that day when he saw her. He slowed his pace as he came up to the restaurant. Tipping his head, he read the sign. Byrne's. Sounded British. Or Irish. He didn't stop. No need to attract attention in case someone was around who might have seen him earlier.

Instead, he crossed to the kebab shop across the way. He'd get a late-night snack and watch the place for a bit. After placing an order, he sat down at one of the tables tucked behind a pillar and turned his chair to face Byrne's. He knew the odds were slim she'd show up again, but he could probably learn a bit about what she was up to by who came and went. It was none of his business, and he didn't know what he'd do with the information. But he had to know. He had to be sure she was safe.

Twenty minutes later, he had a decent idea what was going on. Several men with mafia tattoos had pulled up and entered the restaurant. He'd bet his pension it was a front for the Irish mob.

Sam scowled. How the hell did she get mixed up with them? And why? The New IRA had been quiet as of late. Even if they weren't, it would make more sense for her to be embedded with them in Ireland or the United Kingdom. Not in the U.S.—with an American accent.

The restaurant's front door opened. Audra emerged, dressed in a short black cocktail dress and a black fur coat. A man out front asked her something, to which she shook her head and walked several yards away. She dug into her small black clutch and pulled out a piece of chewing gum, stuffing it into her mouth. Sam smiled, remembering her habit of chomping on spearmint Extra every time she was annoyed.

He got up from his seat, tossing his trash in a can as he jogged down the sidewalk. There was an alley twenty feet behind where Audra stood. It was a long shot, but he maybe he could get her out of sight and get some answers.

Keeping an eye on her, he went several storefronts down before he crossed the road again. When he reached the alley, he leaned on the corner of the building closest to her, then started whistling the song they'd danced to the night they'd spent together.

She straightened away from the building where she'd been leaning. She stared straight ahead, but Sam knew her eyes were looking everywhere but at the jewelers. He kept whistling. After a few moments and a glance at the restaurant, she stuffed her hands in her coat pockets and wandered his way, looking like a woman just out for a stroll.

Audra passed him without a word, but turned into the alley. She wandered into the shadows. He only knew she stopped because he could no longer hear her heels clacking on the asphalt. With a quick survey to make sure no one was paying them any attention, he followed.

Discover what happens. Get your copy HERE.

About the Author

Ashley started writing in her teens and never stopped. Her first novel, Smoky Mountain Murder, came out in 2016, and she has since published two more series and has plans for more. When not writing, you can find her with her nose stuck in a book or watching some terrible disaster movie on SyFy. An avid baseball fan, she also enjoys crafting and cooking. She lives in Ohio with her husband, two kids, three cats, and one very wild shepherd mix.

Website: https://ashleyaquinn.com
Facebook Reader Group: facebook.com/groups/
349932159616427

goodreads.com/ashleyaquinn

amazon.com/Ashley-A-Quinn/e/B07HCT4QST

facebook.com/ashleyaquinn.writer

instagram.com/ashleyaquinn.writer

Dean's Dilemma

Jordan's Journey

Sam's Salvation